THE STAR HUNTER

By
EDMOND HAMILTON

I0541529

ARMCHAIR FICTION
PO Box 4369, Medford, Oregon 97504

*For more information about Armchair Books and products, visit our
website at…*

www.armchairfiction.com

Or email us at…

armchairfiction@yahoo.com

ONE WEAPON TO RULE THE WHOLE GALAXY...

That's what was at stake. A colossal weapon never-before dreamed of. A weapon so powerful it could send planets crashing into their suns. If it fell into the wrong hands it could mean disaster on a galactic scale. And it was now up to Hugh Mason to insure its destruction. The scientist who had created this monstrous weapon had fled to the space-rubble infected Marches of Outer Space. But Mason faced certain death if he ventured into these outlaw-controlled outer regions of space. Yet, if he didn't go, the galaxy itself would find itself at the mercy of interplanetary outlaws—or worse!

Well known science fiction author Edmond Hamilton has spun an outer space adventure tale that you won't be able to put down.

FOR A COMPLETE SECOND NOVEL, TURN TO PAGE 73

CAST OF CHARACTERS

HUGH MASON aka BROND HOLL

*He was physically altered to look like a known galactic outlaw.
But would he be able to fool the outlaw's accomplices?*

HOXIE

*This crusty old space dog was a lovable rogue. Try to imagine
Gabby Hayes in outer space.*

GARR ATTEN

*More or less the "boss" of the galaxy's outlaws. He had dreams
of an outlaw kingdom—and now he had the weapon to do it.*

LUA

*She was a beautiful woman in peril on a distant outlaw planet.
But was she really as defenseless as she seemed?*

RYLL EMRYS

*The ultimate weapon—that's what he had created. And it made
him the most sought-after man in the galaxy.*

FAYAMAN

*One of the better known outlaw captains of the Marches.
Nothing would please him more than a dead Brond Holl.*

OLIPHANT

*Unconscious and dying—he held information that was vital to the
survival of the Terran Empire. Could he be revived in time?*

CHAPTER ONE

THE WRATH of the King of Orion flamed across the void. Out from the Hyades sped his hunters, and from Mintaka and Saiph and Aldebaran, grim ships of war sped headlong between the stars in vengeful search for the small and secret ship that had dared violate their domain.

The coded messages of anger and alarm flashed far away. And across the galaxy the star-empires heard, and alertly watched their own frontiers. The Kingdom of Cassiopeia, the federated Barons of Hercules who held a thousand suns and worlds, the Kings of Leo and Hydra and Draco, all these and a score of smaller realms clear away to the Marches of Outer Space sent forth their fleets to watch, jealous of the great empire of Orion, and more jealous still of the equally great and far older Terran Empire whose ship it was that the hunters hunted.

The fleeing ship was a Class Five Scout of the Terran Navy, a tiny toy craft compared to the great cruisers and heavies that pursued it. Its guns were popguns, it had hardly any armor, but it could go fast. It was going very fast now, a mote of metal flying toward the Terran frontier. But, Hugh Mason knew with fatal knowledge, it was not fast enough.

"We haven't got a prayer," said Stack. Red-eyed and unshaven, he did not look like the captain of a Scout as he stood with Mason behind the pilot in the little control room. He looked like a tramp.

"Those cruisers behind can't catch us," said Mason.

"No, they can't," said Stack. "But what about the ones ahead? They'll be fanning out from Aldebaran right now."

Mason made no answer but his mouth tightened as he looked out the broad control-room window, the window that was really a complicated scanner translating scrambled-up rays into ordinary light.

The light of a million stars beat upon him from the titanic panorama of stellar glare and cosmic gloom. Amid the abyssal lamps of sapphire blue and diamond white and smoky orange there glowed like a friendly beacon the whitish-green magnificence of Sirius, and beyond it the far yellow spark of Sol, old capital of the Terran Empire and the fountainhead from which man had spread through the galaxy. But closer and almost dead ahead was the blood-colored flare of Aldebaran, whose system was near the limits of the Orionid Empire.

Mason had often wondered how this stupefying vista had looked to the first men who had gone out from Sol to colonize the galaxy, thousands of years ago. Their frail starships had been borne out into the great deeps by their courage and faith, their dream of a peopled galaxy living in peace under universal law. But the dream had crumbled. One center of government could not hold the whole galaxy. The independent kingdoms had sprung up, rejecting the authority of the Terran Empire, yet taking old Terran titles of royalty for their chosen sovereigns. Oldest, biggest, was the Terran Empire that still would have no sovereign except its elected Council. But others were almost as strong, and their kings yearned for greater glory, like Janissar of Orion.

Thinking of that, Mason's hands clenched upon a stanchion. Between his teeth, he said,

"We've *got* to get Oliphant back to Terra before he dies. He's the key to everything."

Stack shrugged hopelessly. "Aldebaran is one of Orion's main fleet-bases. They'll know we're coming. Communic beams are faster than ships."

Mason said harshly, "I know all that. In case you've forgotten, I was a flight officer before I went into Intelligence."

Stack flushed. "No offense."

Mason turned then. He was thirty-two and he felt like a hundred-and-two, a dark man with stubble on his face and a desperation in his eyes. He said,

"We're both beat to pieces. Forget my crack. If we start slanging each other, we're licked. We've got to think fast."

Stack gestured toward the great star ahead that like a bloody eye watched them come.

"Their cruisers will fan out east, west, zenith, and nadir from Aldebaran. We have to go around Aldebaran's planetary system, yet if we swing wide around their cruiserscreens we'll run into ships coming up from Aleph and Channar."

Mason looked at the star-blazing firmament and said, "Once past Aldebaran, the Terran frontier isn't far. But you're right, we can't swing wide around their cruiser-screens."

"So we have to hit their net and try to crash through it," said Stack.

"They'd blow us out of space," said Mason. His jaw tightened. "There's only one hole, one way through them."

"There won't be *any* hole," said Stack. "From Aldebaran system out every direction, they'll be so tight a fly couldn't get through—"

Of a sudden, looking at Mason's drawn face, he was silent. Then in an altered voice he said, "Now I get it. One hole. Right through Aldebaran's planetary system itself."

"That's it," nodded Mason.

Stack mopped his brow, and the pilot turned and flashed a startled glance at them. Stack said,

"You know what our chances will be, at these speeds?"

"I know we haven't any chance at all, any other way," said Mason. "Set it up on the computers. I'm going back to see Oliphant."

He left the crowded control-room and went back along the narrow companionway that was the axis of the SC-1419. A Scout-class starship had barely room for its machinery and its eight men. Its whole metal fabric seemed to vibrate in every atom from the thrust of its massive drive-units, as it bolted at milli-light-speeds toward the frontier.

MASON SQUEEZED between towering ion-drive assemblies that smelled of hot metal and into the tiny cubby where Oliphant lay strapped in a bunk. One of the crew, young Finetti, was sitting beside him and looked up at Mason.

"He's worse," said Finetti. "Pulse, respiration, everything."

"He hasn't come to?"

"Not for a minute, ever since we picked him up," said Finetti. He added, "I wish I could do more for him. I'm not a medic, just a spacer with six-months' first-aid training."

"You're doing fine," said Mason. He bent down over the bunk.

"Oliphant," he said.

The man in the bunk did not answer. His thin face was gray and immobile, the eyes shut. There was only a faint rise and fall of the mass of bandages that swathed his whole torso.

He was a small man. But to Mason, he loomed gigantic. For Oliphant, his friend and superior, had done a thing no man in all the history of Terran Intelligence had done before. He had gone right into the throne-world of the Orionid Empire, deep in the Pleiades, in search of a secret, and he had come away again.

He hadn't had to do it. He was high enough in the service to give the job to Mason or anyone else. But the peace of the galaxy was an uneasy one, with only the weight and power of the Terran Empire keeping the jealous star-kings from each other's throats. And when the rumor had come from Orion, Oliphant himself had gone in to learn the truth.

A rumor, a whisper, filtering by devious channels across the void. The whisper had said that Janissar, King-Sovereign of Orion, was a happy man. That he was reaching toward a power, a weapon, a something that would make Orion supreme. If he got it, if he used it to enlarge his empire, the peace of the galaxy would be torn to shreds. It might be only a baseless rumor. Oliphant had gone in to find out.

It was the SC-1419 that had taken him to a dead, airless globe in the Pleiades, sneaking secretly into Orion space. In his little flitter, Oliphant had gone away from there, heading for the throne-world of the king of Orion. They had waited, and finally the flitter had come back. But it had come back on auto-pilot, with Oliphant inside it mortally wounded and unconscious. And he had remained unconscious ever since, and whatever he had learned was still locked in his brain.

"Oliphant!" said Mason again, close to his ear. "It's Mason. *Mason.*"

The waxen face did not stir. Oliphant was far away in realms of sleep where friends and stars and empires meant nothing.

"I don't think he can last all the way home, sir," said Finetti. And added anxiously, on a questioning note, *"If* we get home."

Mason slowly straightened up. "Do all you can for him. We'll get home. We—"

The annunciator in the wall said, in Stack's voice, "Mason!"

Mason went back to the control-room on the double. The hysterical whirring of the computer was just ceasing, as he entered.

Stack said stolidly, "Their cruisers ahead have radar-ranged us. We're running right onto them now."

Mason glanced through the scanner-window. Aldebaran was now a great red blaze amid the stars, a little to the right. Its smaller companion-sun was almost hidden in its glare.

"To fool them on our intentions, we shouldn't turn toward it till the last moment," said Stack. "That means, when they start shelling us."

Mason nodded. "It's your ship."

"Is it?" said Stack sourly. "It was until I came under Intelligence orders. Now I don't know."

Mason did not answer that. He watched, and waited. Out there in the star-gleaming void ahead of them, the cruisers of Orion were closing toward them, their target-trackers were at work, and—

A beautiful red-gold flare blossomed to their left, blotting out the whole universe in its blinding radiance. An instant later, another flare burst on their right, this one so close that the scout was tossed around like a photon on the crest of a solar prominence. Guns inconceivably far away were loosing missiles whose self-powered ion-drive hurled them at milli-light-speeds faster than any starship.

Stack said to the pilot, "That's close enough. The pattern's set up. Turn off and go on auto."

The pilot moved switches and then sat back, his hands hanging idly, his shoulders quivering.

The scout swung sharply and plunged toward the red blaze of Aldebaran, like a moth bent on suicide in the mighty star.

"I *hope,*" said Stack, "that nobody gets in our way."

The skin between Mason's shoulders crawled, as he watched the great red star and its small companion leap toward them. Already, at this speed, the thronging specks of its eighteen planets were coming into sight.

To run through a planetary system at milli-light-speeds was flatly forbidden by every law in the galaxy. It was also sheer madness. A computer could allow for the position of every planet and moon and minor body in the system. A computer could not allow for the interplanetary shipping that thronged between those worlds. They were taking a calculated risk and if they hit anything they would never know it at all.

No human pilot could make the abrupt compensations and changes of course necessary to avoid all those circling worlds and moons. The auto-pilot clacked smugly to itself as it rushed them on.

Mason glimpsed a fleck of light that came up with heart-stopping speed, growing like a blown-up balloon into a vast, ice-clad planet with a host of little moons, reeling past them and dropping behind.

HE CLUNG to a stanchion as the auto-pilot clacked and the SC-1419 heeled over sharply. They went rushing along the rim of an asteroidal zone that was like a mighty river of stone in the sky, then heeled again and now Aldebaran and its little companion were glaring again in their faces, bigger than ever. The two suns marched away abruptly to the left as the auto shifted their course, and a huge planet of saffron and black swung past.

Stack made a sound that was not quite a laugh. "I'll bet there are some surprised men back in those cruisers." And then he said, "The hell with them. I'm scared."

He had reason to be, Mason thought, for he too was scared, right down to his backbone. They were rushing in among the inner planets where shipping was heaviest and if they hit or even grazed a ship, if—

He wanted to close his eyes, not to look at the red and orange and dun-colored planets and moons racing past them. He thought that the auto-pilot had gone crazy, he thought that they'd never make it, and then the immense, overwhelming limb of Aldebaran was ahead and the SC-1419 was running down on the gap between it and the smaller companion sun.

They shot through that pass between the glaring suns, and on across the planetary orbits. They had made it halfway, and Mason was sweating, and the pilot sat hunched in his chair and closed his eyes.

The auto-pilot had gone crazy indeed, it wanted to kill them, it was hurling them headlong toward a great orange planet that widened out with frightful rapidity. Then the metal mind clacked, and they heeled over, past a far-swinging moon like a copper shield, and heeled again and rushed on.

And something like an eternity later a voice was saying, "We're through. By Heaven, we *made* it."

The SC-1419 was in deep space again, bolting for the far lights of Sirius and Sol and the Terran frontier, and Aldebaran and its worlds were falling behind.

Stack, his face red and glistening, shouted, "It'll take those cruisers a while to swing back around outside their system— they'll never catch us now."

Mason, dazedly, became aware that someone was tugging at his arm. It was Finetti, his face gray with fear and excitement.

"Mr. Mason, he's going. He can't last many minutes!"

Mason crashed back from his pinnacle of new hope. They had dared the citadel of Orion, and run the gauntlet of its starships, and escaped, and all for nothing if Oliphant died.

He plunged back along the companionway, with Finetti at his heels. One glance at Oliphant was enough. His eyes were still closed, his face still unmoving, but his color had become ghastly and his respiration was imperceptible. He was, obviously, dying.

Mason looked at him. He knew what he must do, what Oliphant himself would want done, so that his life was not sacrificed in vain. But it took him moments before he could speak the words.

"Give him electroshock stimulant," he told Finetti.

Finetti stared, startled. "But in his condition, it'll kill him almost instantly."

"Almost," said Mason. "He may be able to talk. He's going to die anyway in a few minutes, nothing can save him. *Give it!*"

His voice lashed Finetti into action. Finetti, his hands trembling affixed the electrodes. The whine of the apparatus filled the cubby.

Oliphant twitched. His body shuddered, writhed. Suddenly his eyes opened, staring blankly upward.

Mason bent over him. "John, it's me—Hugh Mason. What did you find out?"

Oliphant whispered, a dribble of words. "I made it out. I didn't think—they shot me as I was getting into the flitter—"

"What did you find out? What's the new thing that Orion's got?"

Oliphant's eyes focused on his face. He spoke painfully, slurredly.

"What it is exactly, I couldn't find out. It's something that was discovered by Ryll Emrys, one of their greatest scientists. Something of cosmic power. But Ryll Emrys has fled from Orion, taking his secret with him—"

Mason bent closer, for now Oliphant's voice was failing fast.

"Ryll Emrys fled to the Marches of Outer Space. Orion has sent one of their top agents, V'rann, after him. They'll risk anything to get him back, they—"

The voice stopped suddenly, and an incredulous look came into Oliphant's eyes. "Why, I'm dying, I—" Then understanding came into his eyes, and he whispered, "Thanks, Hugh."

Finetti bent over him, and after a moment he straightened up. "He's gone."

Mason was silent, looking down at the still face. Then he said,

"He did his job. And now there's a bigger job for someone else to do. In the Marches of Outer Space."

CHAPTER TWO

THE TWO EARTHMEN were like giants walking through the galaxy. They strode between the shining constellations, and the great streams of stars washed against their breasts, and their shoulders and heads towered up colossal above the million tiny suns.

This was not the real galaxy but an infinitely smaller simulacrum of it, a planetarium on a grand scale that filled this whole hundred-foot circular room deep beneath Terran Intelligence Building, on Sirius Four. Complexes of lenses projected accurate images of every important star in the galaxy. It was all here—the star-clusters and lone suns and dark rogues, the magnificence of the great constellations, the whole sweep of the galaxy.

One of the two men was Hugh Mason. The other was Valdez, chief of Terran Intelligence, a deeply worried man. His thin face twitched slightly, and his deep eyes roved alertly as they walked through the great swarm of light-flecks. He pointed to the soft lines of green light that delineated the snaking frontiers of the Terran Empire, and Orion Empire, and all the kingdoms beyond.

Valdez stopped, and his hand stretched out like the hand of a god as he pointed over the tiny stars to a region at the galaxy edge that had no lines of delineation.

"The Marches of Outer Space," he said. "No kingdom out there owns them. None of the star-kings there will *let* a rival conquer them. So they remain a jungle of independent worlds."

Mason nodded, a trifle bitterly. "And because Cassiopeia and Draco and Lyra have kings jealous of each other, the Marches remain a haven for every outlaw, criminal and ambitious adventurer in the galaxy."

Valdez went farther, and stood with the shining stars of Ursa Major floating around his chest, looking at that nameless region of stars out on the Rim.

"Yes," he said. "Quroon—that's the big green star beyond the Dumbbell Nebula—is the center of all the activity in the Marches. Someone will try setting up as king someday, at Quroon."

Mason stared at the far-flung fringe of stars, and he heard again the dying voice of Oliphant saying, *Ryll Emrys fled to the Marches of Outer Space. Orion will risk anything to get him back—*"

"That fugitive scientist is the key to everything," Valdez was saying. "Why did he run away to the Marches? What was it he'd discovered—what power or weapon? It must be something plenty big, if he's so important to Orion."

"It's big," muttered Mason. "Oliphant said they were sending a top agent after him. One of their aces, named V'rann."

V'rann—a name that rang like an ominous bell. Whoever V'rann was, he must be good to be sent on such a mission.

"It figures," Valdez said tensely. "Orion wouldn't send a fleet into the Marches after the man, except as a last resort. The star-kings near the Marches would be up in arms if they did. But if their secret agent can get Ryll Emrys out of there and fetch him back—"

Mason nodded grimly. "Just so. And *we* can't let Orion get hold of this man and his secret again, no matter what. It's up to us to get hold of Ryll Emrys first."

Valdez looked at him. "You know how risky it'll be, Mason. Do you still want the job?"

Mason said flatly, "Oliphant was my friend. I'm going to pick up where he left off. Yes, I want it."

They went on out of the little simulated galaxy, out of the big hall and to Valdez' office.

"You know," said Valdez, "that any Intelligence man or lawman who goes into the Marches is liable to get short shrift."

"I know," Mason said. "I plan to go in as a no-world man, an outlaw seeking refuge."

"No good," said his chief. "It's been tried, and never works. A new man, a man they don't know, is watched so closely he can't do anything."

He drew a small photo from his desk and tossed it across to Mason. "Look at this man."

The man in the photo was about his own age and size, Mason thought. But his close-cropped hair was bleached colorless, his rawboned, powerful face was deeply reddened, and his blue eyes were cold and insolent. It was a strong face, tough and reckless.

"His name is Brond Holl," said Valdez. "He was an officer in the service of one of the Hercules Barons. He killed the Baron's brother in a quarrel, and had to flee to the Marches. He was one of the toughest of their outlaw captains out there."

"Was?"

Valdez nodded. "A year ago, the Cassiopeian Navy got a tip that Brond Holl was on his way to plunder one of their small new star-world colonies. They tried to grab him but he got away—but they had forced him into Terran space and our own cruisers scooped him up. He's doing a sentence out in Sirius Sixteen prison, right now."

Instantly, Mason understood what was in his chief's mind. He looked at the photo with a sharper interest. He said,

"Hair and eye color wouldn't be a problem, these days. But his face isn't much like mine."

VALDEZ SHRUGGED. "It'd take a few days, even with modern ultra-fast healing techniques. But a few muscle-grafts, some plastic pads inserted into your facial tissues—and we'd make you Brond Holl's double."

Mason looked up from the photograph, frowning. "For me to break for the Marches as Brond Holl, the real Holl would have to 'escape'. How many people would be in on it?"

"Three—four—including us," said Valdez. "It's too risky to let more know. We'd get Holl out and while we're taking him secretly to a new hidden cell, you can be stealing a fast flitter and taking off."

"With the Terran Navy after me?" Mason said.

Valdez shook his head. "We can get around that, by timing it properly. If you high-jump it to the Marches, you'll be all right."

"It has to be a high-jump," Mason said decisively. "I wouldn't have a chance of getting through three kingdoms. I can use the time—I'll need a lot of tape-studying to *be* Brond Holl as well as look like him."

Four nights later, Mason crouched shivering in the shadow of tumbled rocks on Sirius Sixteen, peering down at the small official spaceport of Naval Prison. There was only one of the two moons in the sky, enough to shed an eerie glow over the dark, stony world.

The prison itself bulked massive in the background, gleaming with many lights. Down here on the small spaceport were two big supply-freighters, a few small interplanetary flitters, and one flitter that was considerably bigger than the little planet-hoppers.

"I'm timing it for a visit of the Deputy Inspector from Sol," Valdez had said. "His long-range flitter can take you where you want to go. It's a four-man job, but you can handle it alone on auto."

Mason, watching and waiting, thought grimly that there would be considerable confusion if some roving guard stumbled on him here. He wore a regulation prison coverall. He also wore the face of Brond Holl. Chemicals had quickly bleached his hair and altered his eyes from brown to blue, and the super-surgery and ultra-fast healing skills of modern medicine had given him a replica of the Herculean's face.

Mason glanced at his chrono, then picked up the square metal case beside him by its strap. He started stealing down through the rocks toward the spaceport.

The case was heavy. It was going to be an awkward nuisance, but he had to have it for it contained the tapes that would teach him to *be* Brond Holl.

The spaceport was not guarded strongly. The guards were concentrated in the prison itself, on the sound, old principle of locking up the thief instead of locking against him. And Sirius Sixteen Prison contained some of the most noted thieves in all the galaxy.

"The devil!" said Mason to himself in a furious whisper, as he crept closer to the long-range flitter.

Someone was in the flitter. Its airlock door was open and sounds came from inside.

Probably, Mason thought, a crewman had stayed to check over something. He damned such conscientiousness. This could mean a delay, and even a few minutes delay could be fatal. Presently the prison guards would discover that Brond Holl had got out of his cell—not knowing, of course, that Valdez and his men had taken him out secretly. Then the alarm would sound, and he'd have to move fast if he, impersonating Brond Holl, were to escape.

Mason grasped at an idea. There was no time to weigh its chances. Time was running out on him. He crept to the shadow of the flitter, and crouched down by its metal flank, close to the open airlock.

He waited, a fine sweat coming onto his forehead despite the chill of the night. The pale moon peered down at him in silence.

Like the bursting of a bomb, the screeching alarms cut loose at the prison. Mason tensed. He heard the crewman inside the flitter running toward the airlock. The man jumped out, peering excitedly.

"What in the—" he was saying under his breath.

Mason rose up from the shadows behind the crewman and hit him, not hard but quite scientifically. The man went down without a sound.

The diabolical raving of the alarms kept going, and lights sprang on to sweep the whole area outside the prison. The guard-batteries would be springing to attention, Mason knew.

Moving with frantic speed, he hauled the unconscious crewman to a safe distance. He snatched the man's side-arm off him, then bounded back, tossed his metal case inside the flitter, jumped in after it and spun the airlock-door shut.

He got a slight break, now. The mini pile, the power-source of the flitter, was running, the technician he had slugged must have been making a routine test. One glance at its indicators, and Mason ran forward to the cockpit, strapped into the pilot-chair, and then punched buttons fast.

The flitter went up out of there like a freed genie, standing on its tail for a moment with the searchlight beams swinging to catch it. Then the ion-drive hurled it away from Sirius Sixteen in a dizzying rush.

Even as Mason's fingers reached frantically toward other buttons, the missiles began exploding nearby.

HE PUNCHED the switch marked EVASIVE PATTERN. The auto-pilot took over and the flitter began a series of crazy gyrations, changing direction every two seconds in an unpredictable pattern. But despite the random divergencies, it held its main course.

Mason gripped his hands tightly together and waited.

Flares like the lightning of a cosmic thunderstorm exploded all across the sky. The flitter was out in clear space, weaving and reeling this way and that, the guard-batteries unable to get a clean fix on it. It was up out of the shadow of the planet now, and bursting into the overpowering white glare of Sirius itself.

"Now!" thought Mason, and snapped off the EVASIVE switch.

The flitter, on full ion-drive, went away on a straight line, building light-speeds.

The flares continued to dance behind him for a moment, and then abruptly stopped. At this speed, he was out of the batteries' range.

Mason mopped his brow. "That ought to be realistic enough to deceive anybody!"

At this moment, word would be flashing out that Brond Holl had somehow got out of the prison, had stolen an inspector's long-range flitter, and was breaking for deep space.

So far, so good. That was the word that he wanted to go out, to pave the way for his coming to the Marches. But the cruisers of the Terran Navy would be getting the word, too.

Valdez had timed this fake "escape" for a time when there would be no formations of Terran warships close to Sirius. Otherwise, the whole "escape" would be impossible.

"Let's just hope," Mason told himself grimly, "that Naval Intelligence hasn't overlooked any cruisers."

The flitter was running at mounting speeds, and the enormous glare of Sirius was well behind him. But long-range radar would still be probing for him.

He and Valdez had planned carefully. He sent the flitter angling toward the Dog-star Shoals, a great sweep of interstellar debris with a few small and uninhabited stars and worlds in it.

As soon as he had the Dog-star Shoals between him and Sirius, he was masked from radar and free to take his true direction. It was roughly zenith by zenith-west—a course that would slant him up out of the main swarm of the galaxy, heading westward.

After a time, Mason put the flitter on auto-pilot again and slept. When he had slept and awakened several times, he woke finally to find that the flitter, now at full-milli-light-speed velocity, was above the main lens-shaped swarm of the galaxy.

This was the "high jump" crossing above the galaxy instead of through it. There were only a few faint scattered stars up here. And the laws and navies of the star-kingdoms did not run here.

Mason looked down through the scanner-windows at the vast, burning cloud, each spark of which was a sun. The flitter, moving many thousands of times faster than light, seemed barely to be crawling.

"And now the tapes," he told himself. "I've got to be Brond Holl to the life before I hit the Marches."

Yet Mason delayed breaking out the tape-machine and tapes. He had never made the high jump before. Now, caught in a strange fascination, he looked down at the mighty continent of suns above which he was moving.

His mission, his hopes, the plans and fate and future of the Terran Empire itself, all shrank to insignificance in his mind. What were the yearning and fears of men, compared to the titanic majesty of this slow-wheeling island-universe that moved through the greater deeps on the path of its own cosmic fate, forever separated from the other giant swarms of stars whose lonely light flickered from far away. The immensity of the spectacle rebuked the pettiness of men.

And yet, Mason thought, the hardy sons of Adam had with insolent courage ignored that rebuke. They had pressed out from Earth in their first star-ships, so long ago now that the memory was only legend, to star after star, world after world. Those planets that bore intelligent life, whether humanoid or alien, they either had let alone or had landed upon by agreement. They had kept on and on, until finally the vast and growing star-realm broke down of its own weight into all the independent stellar empires and kingdoms that marched back beneath him now.

Back there behind him already stretched the far-flung suns of the Terran Empire, still the biggest of all, stretching from Arcturus to far Centaurus, with its historical center at little Sol but with its real capital at Sirius. And south and west from it loomed the fierce bright suns of the Empire of Orion, and beyond that the faraway kingdom of Argo whose rulers boasted great Canopus itself as the sun of their throne-world. And east from it, far away too, shone the blazing magnificence of Hercules Cluster, that awesome hive of suns held in fee by the federated Barons who ranked themselves equal to any of the kings of stars.

MASON'S GAZE swept ahead, over the shining stellar nations he was crossing in this high jump. Cepheus and

Cassiopeia, the two allied kingdoms of the north, and the huddle of smaller star-kingdoms that had banded themselves together in the League of the Polar Suns, and beyond that the Kingdom of Lyra from which Vega watched like a fierce blue eye, and farther still the no-man's-land of fringe stars that was the Marches of Outer Space.

Mason came out of his dream, then. The Marches were his destination, and unless he played his part well there, he would not live long.

He got out the tapes. It was time that he quit being Hugh Mason, Terran agent, and became Brond Holl, outlaw from Hercules.

"I wonder," he thought, as he adjusted the encephalograph, "if V'rann, the Orion agent, will use the same kind of trick. Probably."

No use to worry about that yet. He relaxed, and switched on the little machine, and let the recordings pour into his mind.

All the memories of Brond Holl had been caught on these tapes by the electro-encephalographic recordings Valdez had made of the outlaw in Sirius Prison. The whole past life of the man unrolled in Mason's mind, as he lay in the rushing flitter, day after day.

With the recorded memories of Brond Holl's earlier life, Mason was not so deeply concerned. But the Herculean outlaw's life at Quroon concerned him much indeed, and he ran those tapes again and again. He learned all that the man remembered about Quroon City, and about the outlaw captains of the Marches. Garr Atten, the big Hydran who was unofficial leader of the captains; and Fayaman of Draco who was no friend to Brond Holl at all, and Hoxie, the old Terran, and others like Shaa of Rigel and Kikuri of Polaris who were humanoid, not human.

But then Mason learned an upsetting thing. Brond Holl's mind had held a fierce conviction that it was someone at Quroon who had secretly sent out the tip that had got him captured.

"The devil!" thought Mason. "If that's so, I've got Brond Holl's enemies, as well as that agent from Orion, to guard against while I look for Ryll Emrys."

He dismissed the disturbing possibility from mind for the present, and began the task of learning how to impersonate Brond Holl.

Mason put on the visi-audio tapes that had been made of the outlaw. He watched them over and over, studying every mannerism, tone of voice and gesture of Brond Holl. He practiced being the Herculean, striding back and forth in the flitter, swearing at the confinement, frowning blackly.

When he thought he had finally absorbed all that he could from the tapes, he carefully destroyed them all.

The flitter sped on and on. Even at its milli-light-speeds, the voyage seemed endless. But finally, its auto-pilot changed course. The flitter was coming down from the high jump, angling down over the frontier between the Kingdom of Lyra and the Marches of Outer Space.

Mason did not relax his tension when he was down over the frontier. Lyra cruisers prowled into the Marches at times, and would have heard the flash about Brond Holl's escape in a Terran flitter.

He breathed a little more easily when he saw looming up ahead a gigantic, glowing cloud. It was the Dumbbell Nebula— a vast cloud of cosmic dust illumined by the light of the stars deep inside it. The dust made radar unreliable, and he would be safer to cut through the nebula. He sent the flitter plunging into the cloud.

His radar screen now became murky and uncertain but he watched it constantly. The fogged stars in here that shone out like eerie witch-fires were easy to avoid, but there might be dark bodies and he would have little enough warning of them.

The flitter was two-thirds of the way through the cloud, when Mason uttered a sudden exclamation. The radar screen, clearing for a second, showed a symmetrical formation of several dozens of blips, not moving but poised immobile here in the nebula not far from him.

"Ships—cruisers—a full squadron!" Mason muttered. "Hiding here in the nebula—"

The radar screen distorted and fogged again. The hidden ships might not have seen him on their radar in that brief moment of clearing, but if they had seen him—

He sent the flitter rushing ahead at highest speed, expecting at any moment a burst of missiles. Nothing happened. Then he had not been spotted?

"But whose ships are they? Lyran cruisers watching for outlaw ships? No, they couldn't watch with their radar fogged—"

An alarming possibility burst upon him.

"By Heaven, that could be it!"

The flitter burst out of the nebula into open space again. Before him stretched a vast region of scattered stars and clotted star-clusters thinning in number as they approached the fringe of the galaxy. Here was the no-man's-land of the galaxy, the Marches of Outer Space.

Somewhere in this nameless frontier region was Ryll Emrys, the fugitive scientist whom Orion wanted back so badly.

"*And* Brond Holl's own enemies," thought Mason grimly. "Well, I asked for it."

He sent the flitter on a straight course toward Quroon.

CHAPTER THREE

DEEP INSIDE a dense cluster of stars there burned a brilliant, emerald-colored sun with a single world. That big green sun and its planet were guarded on every side by the thickly-swarming hosts of stars whose interacting gravitational fields created a navigation danger made worse by the presence of great drift-streams.

To the lush warm world of the green sun, inhabited only by small and primitive humanoids, had come some of the first explorers who had reached this fringe of the galaxy. That had been long ago in the days when the human race was bursting out from Sol in explosive fashion. But in those great days, when star-kingdoms were rising and grabbing for worlds in the constellational wilderness, this cluster was too dangerous to be tempting. The colonizers, the kingdom-makers, had ignored this fringe region and had gone toward richer parts of the galaxy.

Later, fugitives from the laws of the star-kings had come to the world of this green star Quroon. More and more of them had come, human and humanoid, Terrans and Orionids and Cassiopeians, until there had grown up that strange outlaw civilization ruled by the captains whose armed star-cruisers were the only law out here on the Rim. Often, the kings of Cassiopeia and Lyra and Draco had talked of banding together to crush the outlaws of the Marches, but always their rival claims to the territory had prevented such action.

Mason, navigating the flitter at reduced speed through the bewildering blaze of the cluster suns, thought that eventually one of the star-kingdoms would try to grab the Marches.

"And a nice job they'll have, when they try it," he thought.

The powerful magnetic and gravitational fields of the thronging stars had his instruments cockeyed. He more than once almost took routes between star-systems that would have led into blind alleys of drift.

But he had Brond Holl's memories to guide him, and he tacked through the cluster by familiar star-marks, always drawing nearer that emerald sun.

He knew that there were automatic radar-warning stations located on planets and dead stars that he passed, flashing word of the coming of his small ship to Quroon. If more than one ship, the captains of the Marches would have been on the way to challenge him, but he met no challenge until he was through the last star-pass and running down on the green sun.

A thin, nasal voice spoke suddenly out of his communic. "Cut your speed," it said. "Say who you are and say it fast. You're in missile range."

Mason knew that voice well. Rather, Brond Holl had known it well. He spoke back flatly into the communic.

"Terran flitter, coming in. And a devil of a watch you're keeping to let me get this close, Hoxie."

A crow of surprise and pleasure came from the communic. "Brond Holl, by all that's holy! We got the flash that you'd broken out at Sirius, but we didn't think you'd ever make it here."

"I'm sure that broke a lot of hearts," said Mason sourly.

Speak like Brond Holl, think like him, be him—or you won't last an hour here at Quroon!

He swept in toward the single world of the green sun, cutting speed steadily until he was racing down past the two greenish moons toward the night side of the planet.

The lights of Quroon City, stretching away in a small and formless swarm, came into view on the dark surface. Mason cut downward short of them, dropping toward the starport beacons.

On the starport, a score or more of ships flashed back the green light of the two racing moons. Mason's mouth tightened. It looked as though all the captains were in, and that should make things interesting.

THE FLITTER came to rest not far from the radar and missile-gun towers. Mason looked to the handgun he had taken off the crewman back at Sirius Sixteen, then cracked the airlock and stepped out.

He was used to strange star-worlds, and anyway the viridescent radiance of the two moons and the heavy, sweet and rotten smell that came from the jungle all around the spaceport were not new to him. They were in Brond Holl's memories, and he remembered very well the strange, polypous jungles of Quroon, whose towering growths were halfway between plant and animal, like the sea-anemones of old Earth.

He remembered, too, the man who was coming toward him through the moonlight from the radar tower. An old Terran, with white hair and a face seamed by a strenuous and unvirtuous lifetime, his rheumy eyes now lighting up with welcome.

"So you made it after all," he crowed delightedly. "Well, well, things'll be a bit more lively at Quroon with Brond Holl back."

Mason gave him the scowl that he felt sure the real Brond Holl would have done. He said, "What's the matter, Hoxie? Hasn't there been enough bloodshed lately to amuse you?"

"Ho, you're a rare young hellion, Brond," said old Hoxie, not at all offended. "I was just like you years ago—I'd take nothing from anybody. Those were the days when Quroon was fun."

"Listen," growled Mason, "don't you go arranging any fights for me just so you can enjoy watching."

"You've got me wrong, Brond," said Hoxie, in an injured tone. He took Mason's arm, starting back toward the tower, talking volubly. "I'm just glad to see you back, that's all. All the boys will be glad to see you back. Except maybe Fayaman."

He darted a sidelong glance at Mason as he spoke the name, a sly, quick look.

Beneath the radar tower was a ground-car and Hoxie led Mason solicitously toward it.

"I'm taking you into the City myself, Brond. My second will keep the radar watch. I want to see their faces when you show up."

"You didn't call Garr, then?" asked Mason.

Hoxie uttered a nasal laugh. "No, *sir*, I didn't. I wanted it to be a real surprise."

As the car started forward, Mason urgently reviewed the knowledge that had come to him out of the tapes of Brond Holl's memories.

Old Hoxie was an ancient sinner who had always rather admired the tough, reckless Brond Holl.

Fayaman, a Draconid who had been drummed out of Draco's navy years ago, was Brond Holl's enemy to the hilt. There had been a quarrel between them once over loot and Fayaman was not the type to forgive.

Garr Atten was a much more formidable proposition. Garr, who had been by tacit consent the leader of the captains of the Marches for years, had never had much love for Brond Holl either.

Mason turned his attention back to Hoxie. The old Terran was talking loquaciously as he drove down the road through the jungle. On either side of the passing car loomed up the strange polypoid growths, decked with cup-like leaves and flowers, swaying and writhing slowly in the moonlight. From their shadows came the multifarious sounds of small forms of life that he knew were as strange as the polypous plants.

"Garr's going in for trade, and even work, now," old Hoxie was complaining. "A hell of a thing for Quroon to come to. Time was, there was fun and plunder here but now Garr raises the devil if anyone goes raiding—as *you* will maybe find out."

And again he gave Mason the sly, sidelong glance. But Mason refused to be prodded, his mind was too busy with his own problems. He had to find out if Ryll Emrys was here, but he couldn't ask right out.

"What's been going on since I left?" he asked Hoxie.

"That's what we'd all like to know, Brond," Hoxie answered.

"What do you mean?"

The old Terran looked at him shrewdly. "Garr's up to something, and won't say what. He's excited, and talks big about making the Marches a real independent kingdom. He says we're to hold off from any more raiding, and wait." Hoxie grunted. "The men are tired of waiting."

That meant little to Mason, and gave him no clue to what he wanted most to know. He tried again.

"Has anybody new come in since I left?"

Hoxie shrugged. "The usual people that get in trouble at home and have to run for the Marches—but nobody special. Except a fellow who got run out of Lyra for something, name of Chane Fairlie. He brought his woman along—and she's a looker. The boys all have their eye on her, especially Fayaman."

Mason didn't think this could be the fugitive Orion scientist.

"How long ago did Fairlie show up here?" he asked.

"Only a few weeks ago," Hoxie mumbled.

That didn't fit at all, Mason thought, so it could not be Ryll Emrys. It *could* be the secret agent from Orion, their ace V'rann whom they had sent after Ryll Emrys, but such an agent wouldn't encumber himself with a woman. Still he'd better take a sharp look at Fairlie.

THE LIGHTS of Quroon City rose up ahead of them, and the car entered the unpaved streets of the town.

Mason had been in many a strange city on far star-worlds, but never in such a one as this. Physically, it was unimpressive—a collection of one-story structures of black stone, built every which way along casually rambling streets, with the smaller dwellings extending away amid tall polyp-trees from the bright-lighted street that was the main axis. Here there were drinking-places, shops and dives to serve the most motley population that Mason had ever seen.

Human and humanoid, men and near-men from hundreds of star-worlds far across the galaxy, and women and near-women too. Hair and scale and feather, beaked faces and nose-less faces and wicked but quite human faces. Primitive little humanoid aborigines of Quroon itself, big and furry white humanoids from cold planets who panted in the humid night, proud-crested men from the old races of Rigel who walked like tigers, lithe and serpentine men from beyond the Polar Suns who had never been sons of Adam, and all of them with two things in common—all walked erect on two legs and all had got into trouble somewhere else in the galaxy.

Speculative eyes of human woman, cat-eyes and pupil-less round black eyes and blank, pale eyes that did not seem to see, stared at Mason as he and Hoxie got out of the car. He was known, and he heard the name of "Brond Holl" passing to and fro.

"Come on," said Hoxie, enjoying himself. "You came just the right time. The captains are meeting tonight."

"Why?" demanded Mason sharply.

"I told you they're tired of waiting for Garr to tell his plans, didn't I? That's why."

They pushed through the motley crowd, and Mason let Hoxie lead the way to what appeared to be the biggest drinking place in Quroon. But from the interior came no music or laughter—only the sound of an angry, bellowing voice. He went in, behind Hoxie.

The room was big and stone-paved and stone-walled, a black room whose shadows not all the suspended krypton-lights could dispel. There were tables grouped in a rough ring, and men and not-men at the tables, and others standing in a crowd around the walls, and all of them listening to the man who was speaking angrily to them.

It was Garr Atten who was speaking, and it seemed a little touching to Mason that Garr Atten should be trying to found a star-kingdom when his throne-room was a tavern drinking-room on an outlaw world.

"I'm damned if I don't give up and let you all go to the devil in your own way, if that's what you want!" Garr Atten was roaring.

He was a giant Hydran well past youth, red haired and with a battered, bronzed face and tawny eyes that were flaming with leonine rage. He stood, great fists clenched, glaring around the crowd.

"I've told you that I've got plans, and you can trust me or not, just as you wish," he bellowed.

A handsome, pale man with sleepy black eyes spoke up for the sullen crowd. "We trust you, Garr. But we'd like to know a little about it."

Mason's eyes flew to that speaker. He knew him very well indeed, from Brond Holl's memories. He was Fayaman of Draco, and he was a man to watch.

"Yes, there's your old friend," said Hoxie in a chuckling whisper. He added, "That's the new man, Chane Fairlie, beside him. Ain't that woman of his something? Her name's Lua."

Mason saw a man with the faintly bluish skin and blue-black hair of a Lyran, a tough-looking man with a square face. Behind him stood a Lyran girl, beautiful as only the blue-tinted women of Lyra were, her soft face anxious and half-fearful in expression as she listened to the rising clamor of voices.

A big Betelgeusan humanoid, a striking figure with his body-fur of bright yellow, was speaking. His enormous eyes were fixed on Garr Atten, but the words he spoke were mild.

"Now, Garr, when you said you could make the Marches a free kingdom, we all said we'd follow you. And we will."

A tall humanoid captain from Rigel, his feathered crest ruffed erect, spoke up. "It's just that we're all tired of not doing anything."

Garr Atten was not placated. "What do you want to do—go raiding into Lyra and Cassiopeia again?" he roared. "Bring a half-dozen star-kings down in full force to smash us? I tell you, times have changed. You try that, and you'll end up like—"

Mason stepped out from behind the men in front of him, at that moment. The movement caught Garr's eye. The big Hydran stared at him, his mouth opened in surprise.

"Like Brond Holl?" said Mason pleasantly. "Is that what you were going to say? Your moral example has gone sour, Garr. The bad penny has turned up again."

He heard the buzz of voices, the startled exclamations, but paid no heed to them. He had to play Brond Holl to the hilt if his true identity was not to be suspected, and before these tough star-captains of the Marches there was only one way to play it.

Fayaman, his white face suddenly a shade whiter, was glaring at Mason. With a smothered oath, he jumped to his feet. His hand snaked toward the missile-pistol hidden inside his shirt.

Mason had expected something like that, and already had his hand on the hilt of his own missile-pistol. He said evenly,

"Try it, Fayaman. I want you to. I'm pretty sure you tipped off Cassiopeia to capture me, and this will give me all the excuse I need."

There was a petrified silence, and then Garr Atten strode furiously out with his own weapon in his hand.

"Either one of you starts a fight, I'll kill the survivor," he bellowed. He looked bleakly at Mason and said, "Have you any proof that Fayaman did that?"

"No one else here hated me enough to do it," Mason snapped.

"That's not proof," said the giant Hydran. "So you've come back, Brond. I won't say I'm glad, you always were a hell-raiser, but the Marches are free to any fugitive as they always have been. But you bring any trouble here now when we're going to pull off the biggest thing in the galaxy, and it'll be the end of you!"

MASON STOOD SULLENLY, as though debating in his mind whether to challenge Garr Atten or not. Actually, he was relieved that the Hydran captain had prevented a fight. The last thing he wanted was to get sidetracked into a row with Brond Holl's personal enemies, but he had needed to act, as the real Brond Holl would have done.

He took his hand off his weapon, and said sulkily, "I'm not bringing any trouble, but I've still got my ideas about who made me rot a year in Sirius Prison."

Garr Atten addressed him with grim emphasis. "Brond, you get it into your head right now that things have changed. You go off on another looting expedition, and I'll send a warning to all the star-kingdoms myself."

"What are we to do, then—take to farming?" growled Mason.

"There's plenty of trade with the humanoids out here in the Marches—use your ships for that, not for plundering," said Garr.

Old Hoxie raised his nasal voice. "Seems like I've lived past my time, when the captains of the Marches ain't allowed to take a little loot where they find it."

A murmur of agreement went up from many in the big room. And a flaming spark came into Garr Atten's tawny eyes.

"You fools! We've got a chance to make ourselves a real star-kingdom, not a runaway's hideout. The biggest chance anyone ever had. And you'd throw it away for a little loot. I say, No."

"You still haven't told us how you're going to accomplish all this," grumbled one man.

"You'll know when there's no danger of any of you spilling it," Garr answered roughly. "Till then, you wait."

They were not happy, Mason saw, these hard-bitten outlaw captains. But also none of them felt like challenging the redoubtable Hydran leader right now. He was forcing them to take his plans on trust.

What was Garr Atten planning? How could he expect to establish a kingdom that the galactic governments would recognize? Mason's brain began to turn over fast. It might—it just might be, that he had here a clue to the object of his mission.

The captains were turning away, the gathering breaking up. Mason strode across the room, ignoring the hostile stare of Fayaman, and went up to Garr Atten.

"I've got some news I think you ought to know," he said.

The Hydran scowled at him. "What?"

"I can blab it all over Quroon at the top of my voice if that's what you want," Mason said. "Is it?"

Garr Atten turned dull red in the face. "Brond, you've been asking for me to break your neck ever since you got here. Keep on, and I'll oblige. All right, come on and tell me your precious news in private."

He headed for the door. Mason followed him, noting that Fayaman was still watching, with an expression that seemed strangely familiar to Mason. He tried to remember where he had seen it before, and out of his personal memory banks there popped the image of a huge gray cat fixing that exact hungry and intense stare upon a young rabbit in the grass. He had a moment of hot irritation. Sooner or later this cat was going to spring and he would be forced to do something about it, no matter what vastly more important things he was concerned with. He wished Fayaman at the figurative bottom of the Coalsack.

He did not see Fairlie and the girl Lua until he was outside, and then he saw them going away down the street arm in arm; the girl looking at Fairlie as though hanging on his every word, her hips moving with provocative grace under bright silk, her long hair swinging down her back. Mason envied Fairlie briefly, and then forgot them both for the moment.

Garr Atten led the way through the swarming street. It was a way Brond Holl remembered well, past the glaring lights with the stream of human-inhuman-unhuman faces moving under them like the many colored masks of a strange chorus in a play, past darker places where the windows of the houses were shuttered and the lights discreetly dim, past a belt of the tall and grotesque polyp trees that in their strange semi-animal way writhed away from each passerby, their great sweet-stinking pennants of bloom nodding and shaking.

THE PLACE they went to was a sprawling place of black stone set by itself at the edge of town in a polyp grove. The jungle seemed to claw at it with thick fingers. Millions of tiny night-voices of minute creatures clamored at it from every creeper and grass blade. Mist rose from the ground and tried to hide it in a silver veil. But it was there, looking as stubborn and immovable as the man who had built it.

The servants who let them in were familiar to Brond Holl, too, but Mason could not repress a personal quiver of distaste. These native humanoids of Quroon were more -oid than human, little scampering creatures with prominent teeth and unpleasantly naked skin. Garr Atten sent them off and led Mason into a big bare room, quite austerely furnished in comparison with the luxury the other captains indulged in.

"All right, Brond," he said. "We're alone here. What is it?"

The screech and shrill of the little insect voices drifted in from the night outside, riding the currents of warm air through the windows. Mason sweated. He wiped his sleeve across his forehead and said,

"I thought you might be interested to know that there's a full squadron of somebody's cruisers hanging in Dumbbell Nebula. I almost rammed them in the cloud, coming through."

He startled Garr Atten and before the man's usual tight control took over, he said fiercely, "By God, if Orion—"

He stopped there suddenly.

"Why," asked Mason innocently, "would Orionid cruisers be sitting in the nebula out there with their eyes full of dust? What are they waiting for—a signal to attack?"

"Maybe," said Garr Atten curtly, thinking many thoughts very rapidly as he walked up and down. "Maybe."

The hot damp air was heavy in Mason's lungs. His nerves pricked him with sudden needles. The monotonous voices of the insect night-singers outside rasped his ears. Too much, too little—one word, a false look, a mere breath could lose him both his answer and his life.

He made his voice harsh, challenging—Brond Holl's voice.

"Why did you say *Orion?* You didn't even have to stop to think. What do you know, Garr, that the rest of us don't know?"

Garr Atten looked at him heavily, preoccupied. "Nothing I can tell you now. You'll have to wait—"

Mason walked up to him. "Wait," he said. "That's fine. Me and the rest of them, we wait with a squadron of cruisers hanging over our heads until you get ready to tell us what they're there for. I don't think the others would buy it, Garr. I think they'd want to know how far their necks are stuck out, and what for."

Something quick and quiet happened to Garr Atten's face. It made Mason's back feel cold in all that sticky heat.

"Don't try to blackmail me, Brond," he said. "I don't like it. I want you to keep this information from the others, yes. But you're not going to use it to force me to tell you anything."

How far do I push it? Mason thought. How far would Brond Holl go if I were Brond Holl and thinking only of my own neck and not of what I'm really thinking about?

Damn the heat and the crickets, or whatever the nasty little brutes are on this stinking world—

"I'm not going to trust my safety to you without a word of explanation, either," he said to Garr Atten. "Those cruisers—"

He stopped in mid-flight, listening.

Listening to something—

Listening to nothing.

The night-singer insects had all stopped singing. Beyond the open window the jungle-garden was silent, as though it held its breath.

"Those cruisers," Mason continued smoothly, "are a long way off." He moved to a writing-table in the corner. "I can make you a rough chart of their position—"

He saw a puzzlement, and then a sudden understanding, in Garr Atten's eyes. "Yes, I wish you'd do that," Garr Atten said, and leaned over his shoulder and watched with absorbed interest as Mason wrote, *Someone's in the garden—*

Garr Atten reached out and touched the lamp. The room turned black. In the same instant Mason heard Garr Atten whisper, "Move!"

But he was already moving. He flung himself halfway across the room and before he hit the floor a tiny star, intense and blinding as a nova, flared briefly by the writing table and vanished, taking with it most of the table and a part of the neighboring stone wall—all without so much as a whisper of sound.

Energy-missile, lethal and silent.

MASON SCUTTLED the rest of the way across the room, drawing his own weapon. There was the light *spung!* of an ejector mechanism and then a second star burst and died beyond the window. Garr Atten, firing back. He was unhurt, then. Good. The assassin had missed—

Good. Yes, indeed. Good for Hugh Mason, too, because they two had stood together at the table and the energy pill might have been aimed at either one of them. So who had fired it?

Fayaman, wanting to get Brond Holl?

One of the captains, wanting to get Garr Atten out of the way, with his insistence on a new regime of law and order?

Or someone by the name of V'rann, wanting to get a masquerading spy of Earth by the name of Hugh Mason?

Mason scrambled out into the hall, with Garr Atten so close on his heels they almost tripped each other. Behind them in the room there was sudden light, and as they ran along the hall the door they had just passed through vanished in a noiseless flare.

"The other side of the house," said Mason. "Get out and circle around—"

Garr Atten gave him an odd look, but he said nothing. They ran through a longish hall where half a dozen of the humanoid servants had made themselves into a tight ball in the corner, their alarmed little faces peering. They went out onto a terrace of black stone slippery with dew, and then circled back around the corner of the house. The little singers of the night were still crouched silent among their leaves and grass-blades, waiting for the giants to stop shaking their world. The air was rank with that smell of mingled life and death common to jungle no matter where you find it. And there was death lurking somewhere in the shadows under the tall polyp trees, where the greenish moonlight lay mixed with mist like sweet poison in a cup.

Garr Atten gestured silently and they separated, each one now his own citadel of defense, creeping in shadow while the cold dew soaked into his garments, listening, halting, starting at the writhing quiver of a polyp tree he passed, darting swift as deer across the moonlit places with every nerve taut and screaming in the expectation of sudden light and the impact of destruction.

They stalked someone, and the someone stalked them.

The wall of the house, with the window by which the assassin had stood, showed black and bare in the moonlight. Mason stood in the shadow between two towering polyp trees, not close to either one of them, and listened. As he listened, he wiped his hands on his coverall to get the greasy sweat off them, shifting his weapon from hand to hand. His hands were cold, and so was the rest of him despite the humid warmth.

There was a deep silence, and it was as though this whole world had been dead for a million years.

Then suddenly Mason heard the stir and murmur of a polyp tree a score of yards from him, making a vague sound on the air as it writhed and twisted.

Instantly, knowing that the sound meant that someone had slipped close to the grotesque tree, Mason dived away from where he was and hit the wet grass a dozen feet away.

There was a burst of silent light where he had been.

He rolled over and triggered a silent shot with his own missile-pistol, at the place where the polyp tree had stirred.

His missile hit the tree, exploding in another soundless star. But there was a man close to the tree, a man whose weapon was raised for another shot at Mason, and the star touched his side.

Darkness again, and a sound like a grunt, and then the noisy crash of the severed polyp-tree falling.

Mason scrambled to his feet and ran forward. With his free hand he snatched out his pocket-light and flashed it.

Chan Fairlie's body lay there, face up, his eyes wide and sightless, one hand still clutching his gun. The other hand, and arm, and part of his body, had been touched by the star and weren't there.

Mason's thoughts raced as he looked down at the stony blue face of the dead Lyran.

Had Fairlie been the agent from Orion? Had he been—V'rann?

"If he was," Mason thought, "he'd suspect that Brond Holl's timely escape might be a trick to get a disguised Terran agent here. But he brought that woman here with him, and that doesn't fit—"

His mind leaped to another thought. That Lyran girl who had come to the Marches with Fairlie—she was still alive. He could find out from her—

He spun suddenly around as he heard a step. His light caught the towering figure of Garr Atten, coming between the writhing trees.

"I thought he'd got you," said Garr. "Who the devil—" Then he was silent a moment as Mason swung the light onto the dead face. Finally he said, "Chane Fairlie. But he's been here only a few weeks, why should he try to—"

He broke off and asked Mason keenly, "You never knew him before you came here, Brond?"

"No," answered Mason truthfully.

Garr Atten nodded. "He showed no sign of recognizing you tonight. So he couldn't have had any grudge against you. It was me he was trying to kill."

"If he's only been here a little while, why should he?"

Garr said somberly, "He could have been put up to it by one of the captains. By someone who wants what I've got."

"What *have* you got, Garr?" Mason asked boldly.

The Hydran looked at him somberly. "You kept me from getting killed in there, Brond. I owe you something. I'll tell you."

His big frame seemed to loom gigantic in the green misty moonlight, and his voice throbbed harshly.

"I've got a man. Brond. A man who came here while you were in prison—and who holds the secret of a power such as the galaxy has never seen."

Mason kept his face unmoved, but his brain shouted, *Ryll Emrys!*

"And with that power," Garr Atten said, "I can make the Marches a free kingdom. I tell you, I can smash all the star-kings like eggshells if they try to stop me!"

A cold feeling came back over Mason, as he looked at the craggy face dark with passion and purpose. He remembered Oliphant's dying warning of a weapon of cosmic power, and it was as though for a moment he saw the galaxy and all its empires and star-kingdoms on the brink of an abyss.

"But there's little time," Garr Atten said tightly. "Too little! With Orion's cruisers watching out there, and my own captains against me, I've got to strike now or never."

CHAPTER FIVE

THE PLANET was rolling toward dawn. Already a dimming had crept over the blazing splendor of the cluster-sky, the hosts of stars paling as a sickly green light welled up from the horizon. Then there was an upflinging of spears of green radiance, and the emerald sun rose and glared a hot light over the polypoid jungles around Quroon City.

Garr Atten's humanoid servants had taken the dead man away for burial, chattering among themselves like apes. Garr himself paced to and fro in the big bare room that had nearly seen his death, and Mason watched him.

"They've been demanding and demanding to know what I plan," muttered Garr. "All right, I'll tell them. You can pass the word that the captains are all to meet here this evening."

Mason was eager to go, for he had his own plans and he needed to be fast. He started toward the door.

"Remember, you're to say nothing yet about those Orion cruisers," rumbled the Hydran.

Mason nodded. "I won't."

Garr Atten stared at him. Suddenly he came and stood in front of Mason and looked searchingly into his face. He said,

"In some ways, Brond, you're no damned good. But I don't remember you as a liar. Will you tell me something?"

"What?"

"This," said Garr. "One true word. Are you for me or against me?"

Mason felt a queer emotion. He was on a mission for the Terran Empire, for the peace of the galaxy, and he would break men like matches to accomplish it. This Hydran was an outlaw, and a dreamer, but he was also a man.

"I'll give you a true word, Garr," he said. "I think you're fit to be a star-king, and I'm not against you unless I have to be."

Garr grunted. "A man who asks for truth is a fool. I was almost ready to trust you completely. Well, pass the word to the captains."

Mason went through the dazzling green sunrise back to the main street. There was still noise and activity in the drinking-places, and he looked into them until he found Hoxie.

The old Terran outlaw's eyes lit up when Mason delivered Garr's message.

"I'll sure tell all the boys," he said. "So Garr's finally going to tell us something, eh? About time."

"Where does Chan Fairlie live?" Mason asked.

Hoxie grinned. "So you're after that woman of his too? Well, that ought to make Fayaman love you even more—like I told you, he's always hanging around her."

He told him, and Mason went away from there. He went to one of the streets of black stone houses and huts that rambled casually toward the jungle, and he found Lua, the Lyran girl, sitting in front of one of them carefully combing her long black hair.

The grotesque green polypoid trees swayed and writhed away from him as he came, and she looked up at him swiftly and startledly. Her dark eyes were wide in her clear, faintly blue face, and the striped silk pants and jacket she wore were tight on her, and Mason thought that old Hoxie was right and that this was a woman there was bound to be trouble about. He meant to find out if she was anything more than that.

"Chan Fairlie's dead," he told her, hitting her between the eyes with it because he didn't know any other way.

She leaped to her feet and stood, her face shocked and unbelieving. She looked at him, for a long moment, and then said,

"Who killed him? You—"

"Yes," Mason said. "He came to assassinate Garr Atten, and would have killed me in the bargain, and I had to—"

He got as far as that, and then he was too busy to say more, for she was at him like a wildcat, her fingers raking his face, while her other hand grabbed for the weapon at his belt.

He stopped that, and pinioned her arms between his hands, and shook her. He said roughly,

"Murderers are liable to get killed. You ought to have thought of that before you came here with him."

Lua suddenly stopped struggling, and burst into tears. "What will become of me here now?"

Mason said acidly, "I'm glad your grief isn't so permanent that you can't think of yourself."

He let go of her, and stepped back a pace. And the Lyran girl was now neither a sexy piece nor an angry wildcat, but just a scared girl, her cheeks smeared with tears and her mouth quivering.

"Who was Fairlie?" demanded Mason. "Who was he *really?*"

SHE STARED at him. "I don't know what you mean. He came to Linnabar, where I was dancing in a starport pleasure-palace. He wanted me to go with him, he told me he was a star-trader and owned a small ship. I went. Then later he admitted that he was an outlaw, that he'd stolen the little ship, and that he was on his way to the Marches where the law couldn't reach him."

It could all be true, Mason thought, but if Fairlie had been just an outlaw fleeing to the Marches, why had he tried to kill Garr?

On the other hand, if Fairlie had been V'rann, the agent of Orion, he could have posed as a Lyran outlaw and picked up the girl as a piece of protective camouflage. And V'rann would have had good reason to suspect that "Brond Holl" was a Terran agent, and want to kill him.

"What will become of me now?" Lua asked dolefully, again.

Mason grunted. "I don't think you'll find it too hard to find another—protector, here."

"Fayaman of Draco has been nice to me," said Lua, a thoughtful look in her eyes.

Mason told himself disgustedly that she was a cheap little tramp, but he stuck to his main problem of establishing Fairlie's identity. Of course if Fairlie had been V'rann, his blue Lyran look had been all disguise, but modern make-up tricks were so good it took laboratory techniques to detect them. He hadn't had a laboratory, and he hadn't even had the time, since Garr had had his servants bury Fairlie at once.

Mason stepped toward the open door of the small black stone house.

"What are you going to do?" asked Lua uneasily.

He didn't answer her, but went on in and left her looking after him half-fearfully.

Only three of the shadowy, dank rooms of the stone house had been lived in. The kitchen was a mess, and he decided that cooking and housekeeping were not among Lua's talents. But in the sleeping-room, her tawdry silks and bangles were laid out neatly with loving care.

He rummaged swiftly through Chan Fairlie's effects. They were just the sort of stuff an outlaw on the run would take with him—spare weapons, charts, bottles, and some tri-dimen photos of girls that should have made Lua jealous if she had seen them. There was not a thing here to show that Fairlie *had* been V'rann of Orion. On the other hand, if Fairlie *had* been V'rann, an ace secret agent like that would be too clever to carry anything around that would give him away.

As Mason stood frowning, he suddenly heard the sharp voice of Fayaman from outside.

"Lua, I've just heard that Garr Atten is finally going to tell us his plans today, and—"

Lua's voice, rising to shrillness, interrupted. "Chan's dead! Brond Holl killed him, he said. And he's in there now!"

Mason strode out into the dazzling green sunlight. With an oath, Fayaman turned from the girl, his hand darting toward the front of his shirt.

Mason said, "I'd just like to know, Fayaman, how surprised you really are by that news. If you put Fairlie up to trying to kill Garr, you can't be surprised at all."

"What the devil are you talking about?" demanded Fayaman, his marble-white face tight and dangerous.

"He said Chan tried to kill Garr," wailed Lua, "He said that's why he killed Chan." Tears started again in her eyes as she added, "And he shook me."

Fayaman hesitated, not grabbing for the weapon inside his shirt. There was a shade of indecision in his face now.

"It's true," Mason nodded. "Garr doesn't figure that Fairlie, a newcomer, would think up the assassination himself. Garr is very keen to know who put Fairlie up to it."

Fayaman's hesitation deepened, and slowly he took his hand away from his shirt. After a moment, he said,

"I see. You make a big play of saving Garr, to get in close with him. You're clever, Brond. The trouble is, you're never quite clever enough."

"I wasn't, when I went off raiding and left you behind to send out the tip that got me captured," Mason said harshly. "I won't give you a chance like that again. I'll make sure of you before I go."

Fayaman smiled thinly. "Any time, Brond. Any time at all."

Mason went past them, and noticed that already Lua was snuggling against Fayaman like a puppy trying to pick up a new master.

He didn't think he had got very far. He would have liked to believe that Chan Fairlie had been V'rann, because that would mean V'rann was dead, but he had no proof of it at all. And if it wasn't true, if V'rann was someone else here, he was walking on a live mine. An agent of Orion here, and a squadron of Orionid cruisers waiting out in the nebula, could add up to hell breaking loose when the missing Ryll Emrys was located.

He thought about it, and went back to find Hoxie again. The old Terran had some news by now, and he hailed Mason with a crow of welcome.

"So you killed Chan Fairlie! Well, well, things are livening up at Quroon again. I guess you and Fayaman will be having it out for that wench now."

He clapped Mason on the back admiringly. "Come on home with me, Brond. You've been gone so long your house is a wreck by now. I've got a few good bottles."

MASON WENT, and sat in Hoxie's house drinking with him until his head buzzed. He forced himself to think clearly, for he had to pump Hoxie without arousing suspicion. He wanted badly to know what other newcomer to the Marches might possibly be V'rann.

"No, we don't get the bold and lusty boys we used to get here," Hoxie said regretfully, wiping his mouth. "Garr's too finicky, he don't want murderers and such. As if a few honest murders mattered."

"You mentioned a chap named Zin Diri who came and then left," Mason reminded.

"*He* wasn't any good outlaw material," said Hoxie. "A thin, twitchy fellow who said he was from Argo though he didn't look it to me. But that was months ago—Garr gave him a lift to somewhere else."

That didn't sound as though it could be V'rann, thought Mason. But he suddenly realized that it could have been Ryll Emrys.

But V'rann? Mason realized that he was obsessed with an uneasy conviction that the Orion agent was still alive. And with Garr Atten about to reveal his secret within a few hours—

A thought came abruptly to Mason. If V'rann was here, hiding in some guise, there was one way he *could* be spotted, after the meeting of the captains with Garr this night. V'rann would surely have a way planned to learn what Garr said, and V'rann would act swiftly and that was his, Mason's, chance.

Mason decided it was the only idea he had, and he might as well follow it. To avoid further drinking with the hard-headed old Terran, he pretended to go to sleep.

"Prison must have weakened you down, to pass out so soon, Brond," he heard Hoxie saying, and then his pretended sleep became real.

Hoxie, looking no whit the worse, woke him hours later. "Time for Garr's meeting. You sure don't want to miss that."

The green sun had set and the hosts of stars were leaping out again in the darkening sky when he and Hoxie came to Garr Atten's house. Armed men were posted here and there outside it, but let them through.

"Guess Garr don't want anybody but us to hear his big secret yet," mumbled the old Terran.

Mason thought he was right, and he also thought that if V'rann was living he'd not be stopped by a few guards from hearing.

In the big, bare room, Garr Atten stood and faced his captains grimly. They were all there, human and humanoid, and they were silent but their faces were keen with excitement. And the eyes of Fayaman were bright as those of a questing hound.

Garr's voice was bitter. "You wouldn't trust me, and so I've got to take the chance of losing everything by a leak of information. All right, it's what you want."

He looked them over somberly before he spoke again. "For years, we've had the dream of making the Marches a free and independent kingdom. It's never been possible because if we proclaimed a free kingdom, all the star-kings on this side of the galaxy would pounce in to stop us. And we wouldn't have the strength to repel them. But if we had a weapon strong enough to hold them all off, we *could* make the Marches a nation."

He paused again, and then said,

"A few months ago a refugee named Zin Diri came here. He seemed a decent man and I gave him refuge. He was grateful. He was so grateful that after a while he began to worry, and finally he told me something. He said his real name was Ryll Emrys, and that he'd been a scientist in the Empire of Orion. He said he'd made a far-reaching scientific discovery, but that he'd been horrified when the Orionids got wind of it and

47

wanted him to adapt it as a weapon of conquest for the King of Orion. He was so horrified, Ryll Emrys said, that he fled secretly and finally made it to the Marches.

"But now he was worried. He felt that sooner or later, Orion would find out where he was. And when they did, they'd come in force to get him, and would smash all of us to splinters when we tried to oppose them. He was grateful for the sanctuary we had given him, and was agonized that his presence here might mean doom for us."

Garr Atten's tawny eyes flashed. "I saw our big chance, then. I told Ryll Emrys, 'Give *us* this new weapon of yours. If it's as powerful as you say, we can use it to hold off Orion or anyone else. But he recoiled from that idea at first. He said he'd run away so the thing never would be used for war, he couldn't do it. I pointed out to him that while Orion would use the thing for galactic conquest, we only wanted it to defend ourselves and establish the Marches as a kingdom that could be a refuge for other people like him.

"That finally brought Ryll Emrys to a decision. He agreed to build the thing for me. It had to be on an uninhabited world, though. So I took him deeper into the cluster, to that region where the drift is so bad that Devil's Channel is the only way through it. There's a dying star-system in there beyond the Channel, with no life on any of its planets, though to judge from the ruins on the innermost world, it had humanoid life once. Ryll Emrys set up his work there. I've gone in to him many times, taking him the materials he needed. He's got *one* weapon ready—but we'll need more, many more, before we can face the border star-kings, not to mention Orion. That's why I need all the time I can get."

Mason, like the others, had listened in tense silence. But now he heard Hoxie ask the question that was in the minds of all the captains.

"But what *is* this weapon, Garr? What was it that Ryll Emrys discovered?"

Garr answered slowly. "He discovered something scientists have been looking for since the old Earth days. He found a way to neutralize external gravitational pull, in any or all directions."

They looked blank, and Garr Atten added a pregnant sentence.

"He can do that on a planetary scale."

MASON WENT COLD. The nightmare possibilities of such a thing rushed upon his trained mind, while the outlaw captains were still staring puzzledly at Garr Atten.

"But what does it *do?*" demanded Hoxie.

Garr Atten's voice rumbled like distant thunder. "Can't you understand? Neutralization on a scale like that can eliminate all pulls on a planet except in one direction. You can move a planet in any course you want—it'll *fall* in that direction, faster, and faster."

His face was flaming. "Do you get it now? Ryll's apparatus makes that dead planet a missile. If we build the same apparatus on other dead worlds, we'll have as many planetary missiles as we want. And will the border star-kings or the King of Orion himself come to crush us, when we have fists that can smash star-systems?"

Mason felt aghast. He had utterly underestimated the potential of Ryll Emrys' mysterious discovery. He had never expected a thing of incredible possibilities for destruction such as this. No wonder that Janissar of Orion had sent a squadron across the galaxy, to wait and spring and snatch a thing of such awful power.

But the outlaw captains were flaring with the same excitement that blazed on Garr Atten's face. Shouting voices filled the room. Only a few faces had a tinge of awe, of dread.

"By all the gods of Rigel, with a thing like that we could take over the galaxy!" cried Shaa.

"No," said Garr Atten. "You can forget that idea. Most of us are here because the damned grasping star-kings' ambitions drove us out one way or another, and we're not going to become like them. I swore to Ryll Emrys that I'd only use it for defense, and that goes."

His eyes swept them fiercely. "Now listen to me. I'll go at once to consult Ryll about the men and materials we'll need to build the thing on more dead worlds. We'll need all the time we can get to do that. If one of you blabs this thing in the meantime, I'll kill him. Understand?"

They left the house an hour later, a taut, excited group. Mason was among the first out, and instantly he slipped away in the humid darkness and turned down a side way and started running.

He felt as though he was running a footrace with cosmic disaster. The stars of the cluster blazed over his head. And when he thought of what was on a dead world amid those stars, the threat to galactic peace that was hidden there, he ran faster through the dark back streets to Hoxie's dark house.

He had noted when they left that the old Terran's battered jet car was outside the house, and he prayed that it might still be there. It was, and Mason jumped in and sent the car hurtling out of Quroon City, running without lights by back streets until he reached the jungle road that led to the spaceport.

He kept looking back, but there was no one behind him yet. There would be someone soon, he thought, if V'rann was still living. The secret had been told, and the first thing V'rann would do would be to send a message to the Orionid Cruisers out there in Dumbbell Nebula. And he had found out from Hoxie that there was no long-range communic equipment in the town itself, so V'rann would have to come out here to use the communic of a ship or of the radar tower.

Mason pulled off the road and stopped the car amid the dark polypoid trees, when he reached the starport. He got out, and drew his missile-pistol, and crouched down in the shadows just beside the starport edge.

He waited.

The big ships out on the tarmac glittered brightly as two jade-green moons came chasing each other up over the horizon.

The lights up in the radar tower shone steadily. There was no sound except the night-singing insects of the jungle, coming from everywhere but not from close by him.

Then there was another sound, and Mason tensed. It was the purr of a motor, coming down the road from Quroon City.

Its lights flaring, the car roared past him and raced out onto the starport.

CHAPTER SIX

MASON DARED not shoot for he could not see who was in the car, and it might be Garr Atten. Garr had said that he was going at once to see Ryll Emrys. He dared not take the chance.

Instead, Mason ran out onto the tarmac after the car. It was racing down a long line of the outlaw starships, and turned out of sight between two of them. Mason's feet pounded the tarmac hard, as he sprinted along beneath the looming flangs of the ships, their grim missile-launchers protruding from them to catch the moonlight.

He ran between two of the great craft, and then he saw the car. It was parked, with lights out now, beside a ship. Mason knew that ship at once, from the rocket-blast insignia picked out upon its bows. He knew it from the memories of Brond Holl, who had had every reason to remember that particular craft.

Fayaman's ship.

Was Fayaman really V'rann? It couldn't be.

It could very well be. More than one empire's intelligence knew the tricks of disguise and impersonation. If he, Mason, could be Brond Holl, the ace of Orion might just as likely be Fayaman.

He ran up to the ship. The airlock door was closed and locked, and he tugged at the handle in vain.

Mason, desperate as the moments ran away, leaped back a little. He triggered fast, and three quick silent stars of white light burned, and when they went out the airlock was gone and part of the metal wall around it.

He plunged forward, through the gaping opening.

The lighted main lateral companionway was right in front of Mason, and as he leaped in through the jagged wide opening he saw Fayaman coming running down the steps. His white face was very deadly, and his weapon was in his hand and they both shot at the same time.

In their haste, both missed. Fayaman's missile-pellet went right past Mason's head and on out into the darkness through the opening.

But Mason's missile, grazing past Fayaman, struck the wall beside him.

The silent white star blazed exultantly and wrapped Fayaman in a halo of radiance, and he fell.

There was not too much left of him when Mason went forward and looked down at him. Suddenly he looked upward. He had heard something.

The murmur of a voice, up in the communic room.

In agonized haste, Mason dashed up the steps. He heard the voice more clearly, and he knew it now, and it was speaking very rapidly of a dead world and the way to reach it.

He burst into the communic room and it was Lua, the Lyran girl, who was talking fast into the mike of the long-range communic.

Mason grabbed her, and reached with one hand and shut off all switches, and then swung Lua around to face him.

She laughed in his face. "You're a bit too late. I got through to the squadron."

She was not any longer the half-scared girl he had talked to that morning. The soft, timid look was all gone from her, and her face was as keen and ruthless as a beautiful sword-blade, and her eyes had nothing but mockery and contempt for him.

Mason knew now, and he whispered her name.

"V'rann."

She laughed again. "Yes, Terran. I don't know *your* name, but when Brond Holl broke prison so providentially I suspected a Terran agent would show up here wearing his face. And you confirmed my suspicions this morning."

The mockery in her eyes deepened. She was a secret agent and she had crowned her career with its greatest exploit, and in the blaze of her triumph neither the death of two men nor her own possible fate mattered one little bit to her.

"You never thought that Orion's ace agent could be a woman, did you?" she taunted. "You suspected Fairlie, but not me. Why, man, Fairlie was only an underling obeying my orders. And bungling them, too—as he did when I sent him to kill you and Garr."

Mason said slowly, "And Fayaman knew who you were, and was in on it with you."

"Fayaman," she said scornfully, "was a fool. It was easy to win him over by promising that Orion would give him a kingdom here if we got Ryll Emrys. He actually believed it!"

"You're happy, aren't you," said Mason. "You know what you've maybe turned loose on the galaxy, and you're happy about it."

"I know that it will make Orion supreme and nothing else matters!" she flashed.

THERE CAME into the ship from outside a throb of racing motors, growing rapidly louder.

"That'll be Garr and the rest," Mason said. "You should have known the radar tower would hear your message, and call him."

She shrugged. "I did know it. I never expected to get away. But of course I had to tell Fayaman I'd use a secret wave that wouldn't be heard. He believed that too."

Mason's hands tightened on her arms, and she looked at him with cold amusement. He said grimly,

"Don't be too happy, V'rann. That squadron of Orionid cruisers has quite a way to come. We may do something before they reach Ryll Emrys."

The mockery left her face at that, and a sudden alarm and ruthless purpose shone from it.

"Oh, no," she said. "Whatever clever idea you have won't work, once I tell Garr and the others that Brond Holl is a Terran agent."

The roar of motors was now loud outside, as the cars pulled up beside Fayaman's ship. There was a rush of feet below.

"I was thinking of that," said Mason.

He drew back his fist and suddenly hit her on the chin, hard.

V'rann's eyes glazed and she sagged against him and he lowered her to the floor. There was an angry, excited shouting and then Garr Atten, weapon in hand, came into the communic room with Hoxie and Shaa and a crowd of others behind him.

Garr's face was terrible. He looked at the unconscious girl and then at Mason, and he said,

"Radar tower called me about that message she got off. Then she's an Orionid spy?"

Mason nodded. "Yes. And she pulled it off. Right now, the Orionid squadron that's been hiding in Dumbbell Nebula is on its way to that dead planet and Ryll Emrys. Fayaman told her at once."

Garr's mighty shoulders sagged, and a dull look came over his face. He stood, the weapon in his hand hanging limply. The outlaw captains looked from one to another with stricken eyes, and nobody spoke at all until old Hoxie's nasal voice broke the silence.

"Then that's goodbye to our super-weapon and our star-kingdom."

Mason went up to Garr Atten. He spoke to him and his voice had the lash of a whip.

"It's maybe just as well," said Mason. "The devil of a star-king you'd have made, when you give up this easily."

Garr raised his massive head and a leaping flame of rage was in his tawny eyes. He half-raised his weapon, and then his expression changed and he looked at Mason with narrowed eyes.

"We're nearer that dead planet than the Orionid cruisers are, by a long way," said Mason. "We've almost as many armed ships here as they have. We could give them enough fight to hold them up while we take off Ryll Emrys and destroy his apparatus so they can't get it."

Mason felt that it was a desperate gamble, but if it succeeded he might be able still to get Ryll Emrys away from the Marches and suppress a secret that could rip the galaxy asunder.

But Garr Atten was no puppet to be manipulated by any man. His moment of shock and dismay had passed.

"We can do better than that," he said. "Devil's Channel is the only way through the drift to that planet. We can hold them in there long enough for Ryll Emrys to use his apparatus and move the whole planet out of there, hide it deeper in the cluster where they'll never find it."

His voice suddenly blared loud. "You've all been spoiling for action. Here's your chance for a bellyful of it. If we hit that squadron hard, we save the thing that'll someday make the Marches a free kingdom. How about it?"

There was no doubt about it at all, among the human and humanoid captains of the Marches. Their voices rang fierce and instant affirmation.

"All right, get your crews together on the double," said Garr. "I want every ship off here in an hour. Get going!"

They got going, with a rush of trampling feet and a yelping like wolves let loose to run.

Hoxie looked down at the unconscious V'rann and said, "How about this devil's wench? She's mighty pretty, but so's a snake."

"Time enough to deal with her when we get back—if we do," said Garr. "This ship can't go anywhere with its airlock blasted. Lock her up in a cabin and put a guard outside it."

MASON FELT a relief when he saw V'rann, still out cold, tossed into a bunk in a windowless cabin, and the metal door locked upon her. She might come to later and yell her head off about Brond Holl being a Terran agent, but by that time they'd be gone and the decision would be coming up.

Very quickly the whole starport swarmed with cars and trucks and running men and humanoids, and motley women screeching with excitement and fear. Lights flared, and voices bawled orders through talkers, and then finally the takeoff sirens let go in frantic warning and Garr Atten's ship led the way up off the planet.

Mason was in the control-room with Garr. So was old Hoxie, his face gleaming with vulturine happiness at the prospect of a fight. But there was no happiness in Mason. The chances of beating back a naval squadron did not seem good to him, and even if they did it the power of Ryll Emrys would swiftly become known and would be a prize that half the star-kings in the galaxy would grab for.

Twenty-three ships rose up into the green glare of Quroon and swung sharply away. Mason knew there were more ships than that in the Orionid squadron and they were faster and better armed. But he could see no apprehension at all in the grim, battered face of Garr Atten, as he stared through the scanner-window.

They were going deeper into the cluster and a wild glare beat upon them from the close-packed hive of suns. Across the peacock glory of the swarming stars there trailed mighty nebulosities, cosmic folds as vast as the mantle of God, and the constant patchy blurring and streaking of the radar screen showed heavy drift in many places. But the hardy captains of the Marches kept building speed, flying headlong now toward the star-mark of a triplet of glaring white suns.

They raced past that triple glory and then turned sharply toward a region of drift so dense that it made ordinary shoals look like clear space. Mason could visually catch the constant sparkling of scintillations all across the firmament, and he knew he saw a wilderness of great and small chunks of debris catching and winking back the star-blaze as they danced and rolled and tumbled in the void.

"It's a *little* bit fast for Devil's Channel," said Hoxie, and Garr spoke back to him without turning.

"Don't worry. My pilot knows the Channel. I've been in here a good many times."

Mason hoped the pilot knew. All around them the space between the close-clustered suns was webbed thick with the winking points of light and the radar screen showed only one passage, a narrow, winding gut, through the blur of the drift.

The ship rushed on, and on the screen showed the blips that were the other ships of their little fleet, running equally fast behind them.

"We've beat the Orionids here," said Garr. "Now to set it up."

He had given his orders before they left Quroon, and the ships behind now acted upon them. They decelerated, and started moving toward the drift around them. They were to stop and hover by the drift, where Orionid radar could not spot them, and ambush the squadron when it came through.

But Garr Atten's ship did not decelerate. It raced on down the channel at full speed, until it came out of the drift and into open space. Close ahead glowed the dying red fires of an ancient star, and around it swung eleven dim planets. Their pilot cut speed now, and swung in toward the dun-colored world that was innermost.

Peering down as they swept in for landing, Mason saw an arid, lifeless landscape. There was nothing but sand and eroded rock and an atmosphere whose winds lifted the dust in little whirls and eddies. Then he saw scattered piles of red stone too symmetrical to be natural.

"There hasn't been any life on any of this system's worlds for a long time," muttered Garr Atten. "But there was life on this one long ago. Humanoid, to judge from the ruins."

The ship raced down to a landing. A bitterly cold breath rushed in upon them when the airlock was cracked open.

"Not you, we have to move too fast," said Garr when Hoxie made to follow them.

Mason followed the Hydran out onto brown sandy ground, and looked across a vista of infinite desolation. The dying sun peered down upon them and the little winds whimpered and fretted, and the piles of crumbled stone lay in the sad red light like forgotten tombstones.

"This way," said Garr.

HE LED THE WAY, and as they tramped around the ship Mason saw a quarter-mile away in the ruins the loom of a massive truncated cone of red stone. It was massive as a pyramid of old Earth, and carved steps led up to the flat top. On that top rose an incongruously modern square structure of bright metal and glass, and upward and outward from all around it glistening limbs of metal reached in every direction skyward like arms raised in prayer.

"Is that it?" said Mason, unable even yet to believe wholly.

"That's it," said Garr. "And hurry!"

There was more than one reason to hurry, Mason found out swiftly. The cold, thin air was so poor in oxygen that his nose and throat and lungs began to sear and burn.

"It's why we had to build that air proof lab up there for Ryll and the men I gave him to work with him," said Garr, coughing.

They climbed the steps, up the side of the mighty cone of stone, and reached the airlock door of the metal-and-glass cube. They had been seen, so the airlock was open, and quickly they went through it.

There was a great, quiet room that was the interior of the whole cube. Around it towered glittering machines that to Mason's eyes looked unfamiliar, and also very puny and small. There was no reactor for power, though he guessed that was in the cone beneath them somewhere. But even though he knew that this thing operated by the simple projection of some radiation that neutralized the force called gravitation, it did not seem to him that these little machines could ever move a world.

There were a half-dozen men here waiting for them, and they were of many races, but the foremost of them had the pinkness of an Orionid. And Ryll Emrys did not look like a man who could move a world. He was thin and small and middle-aged, a man who looked as though he had borne a weight too big for him for too long a time and had been crushed by it. There was fear and an old pain in his deep eyes.

"What is it, Garr?" he cried, his voice shrill. "You weren't to come back so soon—has something gone wrong? Tell me…"

Garr told him. And it seemed to Mason that he saw the foreshadowing of cosmic catastrophe in the agony that came into Ryll Emrys' eyes.

"I knew it would be so," he whispered, when Garr had finished. "I knew they would hunt until they found me, and that someday the thing I foolishly made would be let loose in war."

"They haven't got you yet, and they haven't got *this,*" said Garr forcefully, striking his fist against one of the shining machines. "You can move this planet, Ryll. Move it! Take it away from here, deeper into the cluster, while we stop that squadron."

Ryll Emrys looked at him with haunted eyes. "It'll do no good. The kings of the galaxy will never rest until they have this secret."

"We can stop them from getting it," Garr said. "That's in the future. Right now you must move the planet away from here, in case some of the Orionids get by us. You're space-proof in here, and leaving the sun won't bother you."

Ryll Emrys turned away from them, and walked past his staring, silent assistants, and then came back. His face was tragic but he spoke calmly.

"I brought those ships into the Marches to destroy you, Garr. Whatever you want, I'll do. I'll take the planet away."

"Take it fast!" said Garr. "We'll be back later—if we're alive."

He turned and Mason followed him out into the bitter, rasping air again. They ran down the side of the great cone, and toward the ship.

Within minutes, the ship swung sharply up and away. And looking back, Mason saw that now the great arms of metal that reached skyward from the cone were alive with a throbbing radiance that wove a net of almost invisible light far out across the dead planet.

"I don't see it moving any," muttered Hoxie.

"It will," said Garr. "It's already falling, toward the one direction in which gravitation isn't neutralized. Slowly, at first, like any falling thing. But building speed every second—"

The ship raced toward the wide, winking haze of the drift, and into the narrow Channel. Now Garr spoke an order, and their speed lessened rapidly until they were hardly moving.

Cautiously, the pilot edged the ship toward the drift. And presently the craft was right beside the mighty field of tiny to massive chunks of debris that wheeled forever here. To the radar of oncoming ships, their craft could not be distinguished from the drift.

They waited, as the ships of the captains of the Marches were waiting all along the sides of the Channel.

It seemed to Mason that they waited for several eternities, before the pilot silently pointed to the big radar screen.

Garr Atten, his face as expressionless as bronze, nodded. He picked up the mike that would take his voice to the communic room and from it to all his other ships. He said,

"Hit them."

CHAPTER SEVEN

THEY HIT THEM. From all the outlaw ships clinging along the edges of the drift, the faster-than-light missiles sped up the Channel toward the oncoming Orionid squadron.

Mason, staring tensely that way with Garr and old Hoxie, glimpsed a far crackling of sudden little points of white light that shone out briefly against the winking haze of the drift, and then were gone.

"By Heaven, we got a quarter of 'em!" yelled Hoxie, his voice cracking.

In the radar screen, a half dozen of the oncoming blips that were the cruisers of Orion had suddenly vanished. The other blips were slowing down in the channel starting to turn and swing into as dispersed formation as was possible.

Mason thought that the Orionid commander had been coming too slowly. At high speed he might have run the squadron through the gauntlet of outlaw ships, and taken his losses, but his cautious slowness in navigating the Channel had worked against him.

"Keep firing, and work toward them along the edge of the drift!" Garr shouted into his mike. "Press up the Channel!"

The Orionids were at a bad disadvantage. They were out in the open space of the Channel where radar could easily spot them, while the outlaw ships were hard to separate by radar from the blurred jumble of the drift.

Two more of the Orionid ships vanished in distant flares. Then suddenly, on the radar, the blips ceased forming up in the Channel, and instead moved fast toward the jumbled blur that was the drift.

"They're going to try to break past us through the drift!" Mason warned.

Garr nodded grimly. "They'll wish they hadn't. So will some of us. But we know more about flying the drift than they do."

He spoke sharply into his mike. Streaking down and across Devil's Channel came the ships of the Marches, and with Garr's ship leading a loose formation they left the Channel and plunged into the drift.

By ordinary star-ship standards both outlaws and Orionids were now moving at a mere crawl, the tiniest fraction of light-speed. No higher speed was possible in the drift. Yet even so, the sight that met Mason's eyes as he peered through the windows was appalling.

Jagged hunks of metal and stone and nameless cosmic debris as big as houses rushed past them and swarms of smaller particles that ranged down from pebbles to sand grains. The pilot played his controls like a frenetic musician, dancing the ship this way and that through the whirling maze. The radar was a useless blur and alarm signals kept screaming of imminent danger like hysterical old women. And still Garr's ship pressed forward, with the other captains of the Marches following, to intercept the Orionid cruisers that were trying to shortcut through this maze.

A long metal bulk loomed up ahead, running toward them through the rivers of stone, and Garr yelled coordinates into the intercom and the missiles leaped from the launchers below. But the Orionid cruiser had seen them; it veered simultaneously in evasive action.

It veered regardless of the drift that was more deadly than any missile, and a rolling, tumbling swarm of jagged stone slashed through it and sent it reeling away, a twisted wreck.

"Grab onto them and pound them!" Garr bellowed into the mike, and the long ships of the Marches leaped through the deadly labyrinth like hounds through a jungle.

Mason had seen star-ships in action before, and had served in one of them, but he had never seen anything like this. In here, where radar and target-trackers were useless, ships fought each other by visual contact in close combat, dodging through the swirling debris and attacking each other, and dodging and hitting again.

The men of the Marches of Outer Space had had to dodge and hide in the drift more than once in their lives. They knew this kind of crazy flying better than any conventional navy could, and it was their one big advantage over the faster and more heavily armed Orionid ships. Out in open space the squadron of Orion would blow them to atoms before they could close the range, but here in the drift it was different.

ALL AROUND them deadly flares burst and died. Most missiles launched by either side missed and exploded against some chunk of debris, but here and there a ship vanished in a radiant halo. Mason saw two of the outlaw ships go like that, but five Orionids had gone and still the men of the Marches fought and dodged and fought again.

Old Hoxie was yelling and swearing in a high, shrill voice, and he began to crow in triumph.

"We're giving them a bellyful! They wanted to fight in the drift and they're damned well getting more than they wanted—"

Mason saw that it was true enough for now the Orionid cruisers were falling back, trying to withdraw from the drift but getting hit harder and harder. Then he heard the communic suddenly squawking.

Garr Atten, who had been bellowing his orders into the intercom, turned and roared at Hoxie.

"Shut up! I can't hear the communic and someone's calling—"

Hoxie shut up and they heard the slurred, heavy voice of Shaa of Rigel shouting from his ship somewhere in the maze.

"Garr, I've been trying to reach you! One of the Orion cruisers broke out of the fight and slipped away west through the drift. I've been fighting two others and couldn't turn to follow."

Garr's dripping face flashed with alarm. He yelled into the mike,

"Keep hammering them, you've got them on the run! But one has got through and I'm going after him!"

He swung around to the pilot. The man had overheard and was already bringing the ship around fast. He zigzagged it through the drift until they broke into Devil's Channel again.

Mason's eyes and Garr's clung to the radar screen. The channel was empty of blips.

"That cruiser's on its way to Ryll Emrys' planet!" Garr cried, "We've got to catch it."

The ship streaked down the Channel westward, building up to milli-light-speeds on the highest scale of acceleration. But Mason knew that an Orionid navel cruiser was far faster, and it had a start, and had Janissar of Orion and V'rann won after all?

They burst out of the Channel, and rushed through open space toward the dying red sun. The radar showed no ship anywhere and the agony on Garr's face deepened. And then as they raced closer, old Hoxie pointed a trembling hand and quavered,

"Good God. Look at that! Look—"

They were all looking, and a cold awe and dread fell upon Mason as he saw a thing no man had ever seen before.

The dun-colored planet that had been the innermost world had moved out of its orbit during all this time. It was riding majestically outward in a tangent, and would soon cut across the orbit of the second planet a little ahead of that second dead world.

A secret of nature had been found by a questing mind, and a power had been unloosed, and now a man was charioteering a planet. And in front of Mason loomed the terrible foreshadowing of the things to come when that power should be loosed by the star-kings in galactic war.

"They've already landed!" Garr was shouting. "Their ship will be near the tower—all batteries ready but for God's sake don't hit the tower!"

They swooped past the icy second world toward the dun planet that had gone rogue. With a scream the atmosphere went past them as they decelerated, and then beneath them were the desert and the crumbling stones and the looming cone with its uplifted metal arms spraying forth the eerie radiance that controlled the movement of this world.

An Orionid ship was trying to get off the ground a mile from the tower, trying to avoid getting caught flatfooted. It started to roll as it rose upward, to bring its missile-launching batteries into play in quick rotation. But it was too late, Garr's ship had already loosed its missiles and the Orionid cruiser was smothered in bursting flares. The flares died, and only bits of wreckage fell to the ground.

They dropped fast to a landing near the tower, and Mason followed Garr as the big Hydran ran down to the airlock. He was shouting,

"They'll have men in the tower—all hands out!"

They burst out into the cold searing air, and ran toward the tower. Up there on the flat top of the cone, in front of the glass-and-metal cube that was Ryll Emrys' laboratory, uniformed men ran out and fired down at them.

The small missiles burst amid them like brilliant, dancing will-of-the-wisps, and men went down in scorched heaps. Mason had his own gun out and shot upward and so did others. And Orionids fell, up there.

"No shooting!" yelled Garr Atten, in an agony of apprehension. "If Ryll and his machines are destroyed, we've lost everything!"

They went on up in a run. The airlock door of the cube-shaped laboratory had already been forced open by the men of Orion and now they could not close it. Garr and Mason and their followers went in with a rush.

THE GREAT ROOM was strewn with bodies. The men who had worked for Ryll Emrys here lay dead about it, and they had not been killed by missiles but by the knives and metal bars that were held by the uniformed Orionids in the room.

"No shooting!" Garr shouted again as they closed in.

Mason had seen that in a far corner of the room an Orionid officer was stooping over Ryll Emrys, who sat in a corner and did not move.

Trying to reach him, Mason slugged with the barrel of his gun, and felt the blade of a knife graze like hot iron along his shoulder.

The room, the very focus and shrine of the most super-modern science of the galaxy, was being fought in with the most primitive of weapons because neither outlaws nor Orionids dared take the chance of destroying the things around them.

Mason glimpsed Garr going down as a metal bar cracked across the side of his head. The officer had left Ryll Emrys and was running into the melee, shouting to his men, and without a leader the outlaws were wavering.

Mason leveled his weapon. He was the one man of them who was not afraid of destroying the machines around them, who wanted those machines destroyed before they tore the galaxy in twain. He shot, and shot.

His tiny missiles sent dancing death-stars amid the Orionids, and the uniformed men, unable to stand before the weapon and forbidden to reply to it in kind, broke and ran for the door.

Mason started out after them and then he saw the Orionids had their hands raised in surrender.

"Take them to the ship and tie them up," Mason told Garr's men. "Here comes Hoxie—he'll take charge."

He ran back into the laboratory. He bent first over Garr Atten. The Hydran's skull was tough or he would have been a dead man. He would be unconscious for a while, but Mason thought he would come out of it.

He ran on to Ryll Emrys. Ryll was conscious, and looked up at him with a fixed, shadowed gaze. He had a deep knife-wound in his breast, and it had been this wound that the Orionid officer had been trying to bandage when the fight started.

"When they came in and killed my men," Ryll whispered to Mason, "I ran into the fight. They didn't want to kill me. But they have."

Mason knew they had, for with that wound Ryll Emrys could not live. He thought that the scientist had deliberately sought death as a way out of his problem.

"Is Garr dead?" whispered the scientist.

"No," said Mason. "He got a bad blow, but he'll be all right."

"He was my friend," said Ryll Emrys. "I brought him only trouble. And now he will take and use this thing I built, and in the end it will bring him and all the galaxy destruction and disaster."

Mason bent lower. "Listen, Ryll. You don't have to worry about that. I'm going to do my best to destroy this whole installation. I'm a Terran agent, and the Terran Empire doesn't want this thing loose either."

Hope flared up in Ryll Emrys' darkening gaze, like a dying flame. "If you do that, you'll prevent me leaving a terrible legacy to men! For the secret will die with me, if the apparatus is totally destroyed—"

He broke off, and then said, "No, you could not destroy it utterly. Even from fragments, men might piece it together again. But I can annihilate it completely. Take me to the control panel."

Mason lifted and supported the man, and felt him dying in his grasp as he helped him to the great panel of incomprehensible controls and meters. Yet a fierce purpose nerved Ryll Emrys, and one by one he named the controls and told Mason how to change their settings.

He was silent then, sagging in Mason's grasp but still watching the great banks of indicators. Finally he whispered,

"It's done. This world will not now cross in front of the second planet. It is on a collision course. Take Garr and leave quickly."

Mason carried him to a chair. But Ryll Emrys was already dead.

He went over to Garr and got the massive figure of the unconscious Hydran on his shoulder. Staggering from the weight, and with the air rasping his lungs more and more, he went out of the room of death into the sad red daylight.

Hoxie and two of Garr's men were coming up the side of the cone toward him. The two men took Garr, and Hoxie asked,

"Ryll Emrys?"

"Dead," said Mason. "And we'll all be if we don't get off soon. Ryll set the controls to put this planet on collision course."

Appalled, Hoxie looked skyward. And up there in the sky the second planet gleamed like a brightening moon.

The old Terran yelled with terror in his voice. "Hurry, then!"

A HALF HOUR LATER their ship rose up fast and raced away from a planet that was moving doomward.

Mason and Hoxie and others of the crew looked down at the dun-brown planet that now was moving on a changed tangential path, toward the second planet.

Shaa's voice came from the communic. "Garr, we sent the last of the Orionids flying! Only six of them left—but we lost five."

Mason answered. "Garr's out of action, but he'll come round soon. Brond Holl speaking. Join us, but don't go near that planet."

The ships drew together, and poised in space, and the men in them looked down in an awed silence as the dun-colored world and the brighter one slowly converged.

The two planets met.

Burst asunder, riven and shattered, they reeled in a fiery, unstable mass. And then the mass slowly broke into crumbling fragments, and soon a great new swarm of cosmic debris moved in a new orbit around the dying sun, and two lifeless worlds had perished.

And Ryll Emrys and his secret had perished, and Mason hoped it was forever. But the strongest trait of the sons of Adam was the insatiable curiosity that had taken them from old

Earth to the stars. Would that curiosity unlock again someday the door just closed?

Old Hoxie sighed. "Well, that's that. And we might as well all go home."

As the outlaw ships flew back through the Channel, and out of the drift toward Quroon, Mason locked himself into the communic room. He sent coded messages far away, and presently the answers came.

By the time he came out of there, they were running down on Quroon. Hoxie told him,

"Garr's come out of it."

Mason went and found Garr Atten sitting in his cabin, a bandage around his head and a stony look on his face. He looked up at Mason and said,

"So Ryll and his work are gone. And our chance for a free kingdom with him. Well, we did our best."

Mason told him, "I said before that you give up too easily, Garr. There's still a chance—just a chance, mind you—that we'll see the Kingdom of the Marches set up after all."

Garr Atten said sourly, "It's nice of you to try to cheer me up, Brond, but don't be a damn fool."

"Listen, Garr," said Mason. "Orion may not be at all convinced that Ryll's secret has really perished. They're extremely likely to move in and try to take the whole Marches by forced annexation, to find out. If they do, the border star-- kings will declare war at once, to stop them."

Garr nodded. "It's liable to happen. And precious little comfort for us there'll be in that."

"I've been talking with some Terran Empire officials," Mason said. "They agree with me that a crisis like that can be averted, *if* an independent kingdom is set up in the Marches. Terra would recognize such a kingdom and guarantee its frontiers—and neither Janissar of Orion or the lesser star-kings would dare bother the Marches then."

Garr Atten had listened with growing amazement, and now he got to his feet.

"They're going to decide fast back at Sol, and they'll let me know as soon as the Council has met," concluded Mason.

"They'll let *you* know! *You've* been talking to the Terran Empire officials!" burst out Garr. "Why, you're—"

"I'm not Brond Holl, Garr," said Mason. "I'm a Terran agent."

ONLY THREE DAYS later the word came to Quroon. It came to Mason, waiting in the communic room of Garr's ship. He went out of the ship at once and drove through the green blazing sunlight to Quroon City, and walked into the big drinking-place where Garr and his remaining captains waited.

Garr would not ask the question, but Hoxie said eagerly, "Well, what's the word?"

Mason smiled. "Two hours ago, by formal Council vote, the Terran Empire recognized the new Kingdom of the Marches of Outer Space. As soon as the usual plebiscite here indicates that the people here want it so, Garr Atten will be recognized as lawful sovereign."

He got no farther than that, for the roar that went up from the outlaw captains drowned his voice.

Mason thought of the first time he had seen Garr Atten, dreaming of kingship in this tavern drinking room, and of how a man's dreams could come true in strange ways.

Later, Mason said to Garr, "I'll be leaving soon—I want my own face back. But what about V'rann?"

Garr raised his voice for them all to hear and said sternly, "We'll have laws here now, and people will obey them. She instigated attempted murder and she'll do a sentence for it in prison here before she goes back to Orion."

Hoxie groaned. "That's it—that's the last straw. A *prison* here at Quroon!"

THE END

If you've enjoyed this book, you will not want to miss these terrific titles…

ARMCHAIR SCI-FI, FANTASY, & HORROR DOUBLE NOVELS, $12.95 each

D-41   **FULL CYCLE** by Clifford D. Simak
          IT WAS THE DAY OF THE ROBOT by Frank Belknap Long

D-42   **THIS CROWDED EARTH** by Robert Bloch
          REIGN OF THE TELEPUPPETS by Daniel Galouye

D-43   **THE CRISPIN AFFAIR** by Jack Sharkey
          THE RED HELL OF JUPITER by Paul Ernst

D-44   **PLANET OF DREAD** by Dwight V. Swain
          WE THE MACHINE by Gerald Vance

D-45   **THE STAR HUNTER** by Edmond Hamilton
          THE ALIEN by Raymond F. Jones

D-46   **WORLD OF IF** by Rog Phillips
          SLAVE RAIDERS FROM MERCURY by Don Wilcox

D-47   **THE ULTIMATE PERIL** by Robert Abernathy
          PLANET OF SHAME by Bruce Elliot

D-48   **THE FLYING EYES** by J. Hunter Holly
          SOME FABULOUS YONDER by Phillip Jose Farmer

D-49   **THE COSMIC BUNGLARS** by Geoff St. Reynard
          THE BUTTONED SKY by Geoff St. Reynard

D-50   **TYRANTS OF TIME** by Milton Lesser
          PARIAH PLANET by Murray Leinster

ARMCHAIR SCIENCE FICTION CLASSICS, $12.95 each

C-13   **SUNKEN WORLD**
          by Stanton A. Coblentz

C-14   **THE LAST VIAL**
          by Sam McClatchie, M. D.

C-15   **WE WHO SURVIVED (THE FIFTH ICE AGE)**
          by Sterling Noel

ARMCHAIR MASTERS OF SCIENCE FICTION SERIES, $16.95 each

MS-5   **MASTERS OF SCIENCE FICTION, Vol. Five**
          Winston K. Marks—Test Colony and other tales

MS-6   **MASTERS OF SCIENCE FICTION, Vol. Six**
          Fritz Leiber—Deadly Moon and other tales

THE GALAXY SHUDDERS AT A TERROR FROM HALF A MILLION YEARS AGO...

Speculate for a moment about the enormous challenge to archeology if relics were found of an alien race, extinct for half a million years! A race that was so scientifically far in advance of our own that they held undreamed of scientific secrets—including the secret of the restoration of life! But the world would soon tremble at the restoration of just one member of this ancient race—brought back after 500,000 years of death…

Expect a muscle-tightening, sweat-producing, mind-prodding adventure in the far-off future when you read this taut science fiction classic by Raymond F. Jones

CAST OF CHARACTERS

DR. DELMAR UNDERWOOD
Could this brilliant physicist find a way to save the galaxy from destruction at the hands of a madman?

TERRY BERNARD
This archeologist was overwhelmed by the magnitude of the mystery they had uncovered.

DR. ILLIA MOROV
She alone possessed the ability to perform a crucial operation, and a world awaited the results.

DEMARZULE
This inhuman monster was reanimated—quite innocently—from a small container of protoplasm!

JANDRO
Organs in his alien body were the key components needed to defeat Demarzule, but could he survive?

DREYER
His ability to decipher ancient alien inscriptions was crucial to the survival of the Galaxy.

THE ALIEN

By
RAYMOND F. JONES

ARMCHAIR FICTION
PO Box 4369, Medford, Oregon 97504

*For more information about Armchair Books and products, visit our
website at…*

www.armchairfiction.com

Or email us at…

armchairfiction@yahoo.com

CHAPTER ONE

OUT BEYOND the orbit of Mars the *Lavoisier* wallowed cautiously through the asteroid fields. Aboard the laboratory ship few of the members of the permanent Smithson Asteroidal Expedition were aware that they were in motion. Living in the field one or two years at a time, there was little that they were conscious of except the half-million-year-old culture whose scattered fragments surrounded them on every side.

The only contact with Earth at the moment was the radio link by which Dr. Delmar Underwood was calling Dr. Illia Morov at Terrestrial Medical Central.

Illia's blonde, precisely coiffured hair was only faintly golden against the stark white of her surgeons' gown, which she still wore when she answered. Her eyes widened with an expression of pleasure as her face came into focus on the screen and she recognized Underwood.

"Del! I thought you'd gone to sleep with the mummies out there. It's been over a month since you called. What's new?"

"Not much. Terry found some new evidence of Stroid III. Phyfe has a new scrap of metal with inscriptions, and they've found something that almost looks as if it might have been an electron tube five hundred thousand years ago. I'm working on that. Otherwise all is peaceful and it's wonderful!"

"Still the confirmed hermit?" Illia eyes lost some of their banter, but none of their tenderness.

"There's more peace and contentment out here than I'd ever dreamed of finding. I want you to come out here, Illia. Come out for a month. If you don't want to stay and marry me, then you can go back and I won't say another word."

SHE shook her head in firm decision. "Earth needs its scientists desperately. Too many have run away already. They say the Venusian colonies are booming, but I told you a year ago that simply running away wouldn't work. I thought by now you would have found it out for yourself."

"And I told you a year ago," Underwood said flatly, "that the only possible choice of a sane man is escape."

"You can't escape your own culture, Del. Why, the expedition that provided the opportunity for you to become a hermit is dependent on Earth. If Congress should cut the Institute's funds, you'd be dropped right back where you were. You can't get away."

"There are always the Venusian colonies."

"You know it's impossible to exist there independent of Earth."

"I'm not talking about the science and technology. I'm talking about the social disintegration. Certainly a scientist doesn't need to take that with him when he's attempting to escape it."

"The culture is not to blame," said Illia earnestly, "and neither is humanity. You don't ridicule a child for his clumsiness when he is learning to walk."

"I hope the human race is past its childhood!"

"Relatively speaking, it isn't. Dreyer says we're only now emerging from the cave man stage, and that could properly be called mankind's infancy, I suppose. Dreyer calls it the 'head man' stage."

"I thought he was a semanticist."

"You'd know if you'd ever talked with him. He'll tear off every other word you utter and throw it back at you. His 'head man' designation is correct, all right. According to him, human beings in this stage need some leader or 'head man' stronger than themselves for guidance, assumption of responsibility, and blame, in case of failure of the group. These functions have never in the past been developed in the individual so that he could stand alone in control of his own ego. But it's coming—that's the whole import of Dreyer's work."

"And all this confusion and instability are supposed to have something to do with that?"

"It's been growing for decades. We've seen it reach a peak in our own lifetimes. The old fetishes have failed, the head men have been found to be hollow gods, and men's faith has turned to derision. Presidents, dictators, governors, and priests—they've all fallen from their high places and the masses of humanity will no longer believe in any of them."

"AND *that* is development of the race?"

"Yes, because out of it will come a people who have found in themselves the strength they used to find in the 'head men.' There will come a race in which the individual can accept the responsibility which he has always passed on to the 'head man,' the 'head man' is no longer necessary."

"And so—the ultimate anarchy."

"The 'head man' concept has obviously outlived it's usefulness. With human beings capable of independent, constructive behavior, actual democracy will be possible for the first time in the world's history."

"If all this is to come about anyway, according to Dreyer, why not try to escape the insanity of the transition period?"

Illia Morov's eyes grew narrow in puzzlement as she looked at Underwood with utter incomprehension. "Doesn't it matter at all that the race is in one of the greatest crises of all history? Doesn't it matter that you have a skill that is of immense value in these times? It's peculiar that it is those of you in the physical sciences who are fleeing in the greatest numbers. The Venusian colonies must have a wonderful time with physicists trampling each other to get away from it all—and Earth almost barren of them. Do the physical sciences destroy every sense of social obligation?"

"You forget that I don't quite accept Dreyer's theories. To me this is nothing but a rotting structure that is finally collapsing from its own inner decay. I can't see anything positive evolving out of it."

"I suppose so. Well, it was nice of you to call, Del. I'm always glad to hear you. Don't wait so long next time."

"Illia—"

But she had cut the connection and the screen slowly faded into gray, leaving Underwood's argument unfinished. Irritably, he flipped the switch to the public news channels.

Where was he wrong? The past year, since he had joined the expedition as Chief Physicist, was like paradise compared with living in the unstable, irresponsible society existing on Earth. He knew it was a purely neurotic reaction, this desire to escape. But application of that label solved nothing, explained nothing—and carried no stigma. The neurotic reaction was the norm in a world so confused.

He turned as the news blared abruptly with its perpetual urgency that made him wonder how the commentators endured the endless flow of crises.

The President had been impeached again—the third one in six months.

There were no candidates for his office.

A church had been burned by its congregation.

Two mayors had been assassinated within hours of each other.

It was the same news he had heard six months ago. It would be the same again tomorrow and next month. The story of a planet repudiating all leadership. A lawlessness that was worse than anarchy, because there was still government—a government that could be driven and whipped by the insecurities of the populace that elected it.

Dreyer called it a futile search for a 'head man' by a people who would no longer trust any of their own kind to be 'head man.' And Underwood dared not trust that glib explanation.

Many others besides Underwood found they could no longer endure the instability of their own culture. Among these were many of the world's leading scientists. Most of them went to the jungle lands of Venus. The scientific limitations of such a frontier existence had kept Underwood from joining the Venusian colonies, but he'd been very close to going just before he got the offer of Chief Physicist with the Smithson Institute expedition in the asteroid fields. He wondered now what he'd have done if the offer hadn't come.

THE interphone annunciator buzzed. Underwood turned off the news as the bored communications operator in the control room announced, "Doc Underwood. Call for Doc Underwood."

Underwood cut in. "Speaking," he said irritably.

The voice of Terry Bernard burst into the room. "Hey, Del! Are you going to get rid of that hangover and answer your phone or should we embalm the remains and ship 'em back?"

"Terry! You fool, what do you want? Why didn't you say it was you? I thought maybe it was that elephant-foot Maynes, with chunks of mica that he thought were prayer sticks."

"The Stroids didn't use prayer sticks."

"All right, skip it. What's new?"

"Plenty. Can you come over for a while? I think we've really got something here."

"It'd better be good. We're taking the ship to Phyfe. Where are you?"

"Asteroid C-428. It's about 2,000 miles from you. And bring all the hard-rock mining tools you've got. We can't get into this thing."

"*Is that* all you want? Use your double coated drills."

"We wore five of them out. No scratches on the thing even."

"Well, use the Atom Stream, then. It probably won't hurt the artifact."

"I'll say it won't. It won't even warm the thing up. Any other ideas?"

Underwood's mind, which had been half occupied with mulling over his personal problems while he talked with Terry, swung startledly to what the archeologist was saying. "You mean that you've found a material the Atom Stream won't touch? That's impossible! The equations of the Stream prove—"

"I know. *Now* will you come over?"

"Why didn't you say so in the first place? I'll bring the whole ship."

UNDERWOOD cut off and switched to the Captain's line. "Captain Dawson? Underwood. Will you please take the ship to the vicinity of Asteroid C-428 as quickly as possible?"

"I thought Doctor Phyfe—"

"I'll answer for it. Please move the vessel."

Captain Dawson acceded. His instructions were to place the ship at Underwood's disposal.

Soundlessly and invisibly, the distortion fields leaped into space about the massive laboratory ship and the *Lavoisier* moved effortlessly through the void. Its perfect inertia controls left no evidence of its motion apparent to the occupants with the exception of the navigators and pilots. The hundreds of delicate pieces of equipment in Underwood's laboratories remained as steadfast as if anchored to tons of steel and concrete deep beneath the surface of Earth.

Twenty minutes later they hove in sight of the small black asteroid that glistened in the faint light of the faraway Sun. The space-suited figures of Terry Bernard and his assistant, Batch Fagin, clung to the surface, moving about like flies on a blackened, frozen apple.

Underwood was already in the scooter lock, astride the little spacescooter, which they used for transportation between ships of the expedition and between asteroids.

THE pilot jockeyed the *Lavoisier* as near as safely desirable, then signaled Underwood. The physicist pressed the control that opened the lock in the side of the vessel. The scooter shot out into space, bearing him astride it.

"Ride em, cowboy!" Terry Bernard yelled into the intercom. He gave a wild cowboy yell that pierced Underwood's ears. "Watch out that thing doesn't turn turtle with you."

Underwood grinned to himself. He said, "Your attitude convinces me of a long held theory—that archeology is no science. Anyway, if your story of a material impervious to the Atom Stream is wrong, you'd better get a good alibi. Phyfe had some work he wanted to do aboard today."

"Come and see for yourself. This is it."

As the scooter approached closer to the asteroid, Underwood could glimpse the strangeness of the thing. It looked as if it had been coated with the usual asteroid material of nickel iron debris, but Terry had cleared this away from more than half the surface.

The exposed half was a shining thing of ebony, whose planes and angles were machined with mathematical exactness. It looked as if there were at least a thousand individual facets on the one hemisphere alone.

At the sight of it, Underwood could almost understand the thrill of discovery that impelled these archeologists to delve in the mysteries of space for lost kingdoms and races. This object, which Terry had discovered, was a magnificent artifact. He wondered how long it had circled the Sun since the intelligence that formed it had died. He wished now that Terry had not used the Atom Stream, for that had probably destroyed the validity of the radium-lead relationship in the coating of debris that might otherwise indicate something of the age of the thing.

Terry sensed something of Underwood's awe in his silence as he approached. "What do you think of it, Del?"

"It's—beautiful," said Underwood. "Have you any clue to what it is?"

"Not a thing. No marks of any kind on it."

The scooter slowed as Del Underwood guided it near the surface of the asteroid. It touched gently and he unstrapped himself and stepped off. "Phyfe will forgive all your sins for this," he said. "Before you show me the Atom Stream is ineffective, let's break off a couple of tons of the coating and put it in the ship. We may be able to date the thing yet. Almost all these asteroids have a small amount of radioactivity somewhere in them. We can chip some from the opposite side where the Atom Stream would affect it least."

"Good idea," Terry agreed. "I should have thought of that, but when I first found the single outcropping of machined metal, I figured it was very small. After I found the Atom Stream wouldn't touch it, I was overanxious to undercover it. I didn't realize I'd have to burn away the whole surface of the asteroid."

"We may as well finish the job and get it completely uncovered. I'll have some of my men from the ship come on over."

It took the better part of an hour to chip and drill away samples to be used in a dating attempt. Then the intense fire of the Atom Stream was turned upon the remainder of the asteroid to clear it.

"We'd better be on the lookout for a soft spot." Terry suggested. "It's possible this thing isn't homogeneous, and Papa Phyfe would be very mad if we burned it up after making such a find."

FROM behind his heavy shield, which protected him from the stray radiation formed by the Atom Stream, Delmar Underwood watched the biting fire cut between the gemlike artifact and the metallic alloys that coated it. The alloys cracked and fell away in large chunks, propelled by the explosions of matter as the intense heat vaporized the metal almost instantly.

The spell of the ancient and the unknown fell upon him and swept him up in the old mysteries and the unknown tongues. Trained in the precise methods of the physical sciences, he had long fought against the fascination of the immense puzzles, which the archeologists were trying to solve, but no man could long escape. In the quiet, starlit blackness there rang the ancient memories of a planet vibrant with life, a planet of strange tongues and unknown songs—a planet that had died so violently that space was yet strewn with its remains—so violently that somewhere the echo of its death explosion must yet ring in the far vaults of space.

Underwood had always thought of archeologists as befogged antiquarians poking among ancient graves and rubbish heaps, but now he knew them for what they were—poets in search of mysteries. The Bible-quoting of Phyfe and the swearing of redheaded Terry Bernard were merely thin disguises for their poetic romanticism.

Underwood watched the white fire of the Atom Stream through the lead glass of the eye-protecting lenses. "I talked to Illia today," he said. "She says I've run away."

"Haven't you?" Terry asked.

"I wouldn't call it that."

"It doesn't make much difference what you call it. I once lived in an apartment underneath a French horn player who practiced eight hours a day. I ran away. If the whole mess back on Earth is like a bunch of horn blowers tooting above your apartment, I say move and why make any fuss about it? I'd probably join the boys on Venus myself if my job didn't keep me out here. Of course it's different with you. There's Illia to be convinced along with your own conscience."

"She quotes Dreyer. He's one of your ideals, isn't he?"

"No better semanticist ever lived." Terry said flatly. "He takes the long view, which is that everything will come out in the wash. I agree with him, so why worry—knowing that the variants will iron themselves out, and nothing I can possibly do will be noticed or missed? Hence, I seldom worry about my obligations to mankind, as long as I stay reasonably law-abiding. Do likewise, Brother Del, and you'll live longer or at least more happily."

UNDERWOOD grinned in the blinding glare of the Atom Stream. He wished life were as simple as Terry would have him believe. Maybe it would be, he thought—if it weren't for Illia.

As he moved his shield slowly forward behind the crumbling debris, Underwood's mind returned to the question of who created the structure beneath their feet, and to what alien purpose. Its black, impenetrable surfaces spoke of excellent mechanical skill, and a high science that could create a material refractory to the Atom Stream. Who, a half million years ago, could have created it?

The ancient pseudo-scientific Bode's Law had indicated a missing planet, which could easily have fitted into the Solar System in the vicinity of the asteroid belt. But astronomers had never accepted Bode's Law— until interstellar archeology discovered the artifacts of a civilization on many of the asteroids.

The Smithson Institute had undertaken the monumental task of exploration more than a generation ago. Though always handicapped by shortage of funds, they had managed to keep at least one ship in the field as a permanent expedition.

Dr. Phyfe, leader of the present group, was probably the greatest student of asteroidal archeology in the System. The younger archeologists labeled him benevolently Papa Phyfe, in spite of the irascible temper which came, perhaps, from constantly switching his mind from half a million years ago to the present.

In their use of semantic correlations, Underwood was discovering, the archeologists were far ahead of the physical scientists, for they had an immensely greater task in deducing the mental concepts of alien races from a few scraps of machinery and art.

Of all the archeologists he had met, Underwood had taken the greatest liking to Terry Bernard. An extremely competent semanticist and archeologist, Terry nevertheless did not take himself too seriously. He did not even mind Underwood's constant assertion that archeology was no science. He maintained that it was fun, and that was all that was necessary.

At last, the two groups approached each other from opposite sides of the asteroid and joined forces in shearing off the last of the debris. As they shut off the fearful Atom Streams, the scientists turned to look back at the thing they had cleared.

TERRY said quietly, "See why I'm an archeologist?"

"I think I do—almost," Underwood answered.

The gemlike structure beneath their feet glistened like polished ebony. It caught the distant stars in its thousand facets and cast them until it gleamed as if with infinite lights of its own.

The workmen, too, were caught in its spell, for they stood silently contemplating the mystery of a people who had created such beauty.

The spell was broken at last by a movement across the heavens. Underwood glanced up; "Papa Phyfe's coming on the warpath. I'll bet he's ready to trim my ears for taking the lab ship without his consent."

"You're boss of the lab ship, aren't you?" said Terry.

"It's a rather flexible arrangement—in Phyfe's mind, at least. I'm boss until he decides he wants to do something."

The headquarters ship slowed to a halt and the lock opened, emitting the fiery burst of a motor scooter, which Doc Phyfe rode with angry abandon.

"You, Underwood!" His voice came harshly through the phones. "I demand an explanation of—"

That was as far as he got, for he glimpsed the thing upon which the men were standing, and from his vantage point it looked all the more like a black jewel in the sky. He became instantly once more the eager archeologist instead of expedition administrator, a role he filled with irritation.

"What have you got there?" he whispered.

Terry answered. "We don't know. I asked Dr. Underwood's assistance on uncovering the artifact. If it caused you any difficulty, I'm sorry; it's my fault."

"PAH!" said Phyfe. "A thing like this is of utmost importance. You should have notified me immediately."

Terry and Underwood grinned at each other. Phyfe reprimanded every archeologist on the expedition for not notifying him immediately whenever anything from the smallest machined fragment of metal to the greatest stone monuments were found. If they had obeyed, he would have done nothing but travel from asteroid to asteroid over hundreds of thousands of miles of space.

"You were busy with your own work," said Terry.

But Phyfe had landed, and as he dismounted from the scooter, he stood in awe. Terry, standing close to him, thought he saw tears in the old man's eyes through the helmet of the spaceship.

"It's beautiful!" murmured Phyfe in worshipping awe. "Wonderful. The most magnificent find in a century of asteroidal archeology. We must make arrangements for its transfer to Earth at once."

"If I may make a suggestion," said Terry, "you recall that some of the artifacts have not survived so well. Decay in many instances has set in—"

"Are you trying to tell me that this thing can decay?" Phyfe's little gray Van Dyke trembled violently.

"I'm thinking of the thermal transfer. Doctor Underwood is better able to discuss that, but I should think that a mass of this kind, which is at absolute zero, might undergo unusual stresses on coming to Earth normal temperatures. True, we used the Atom Stream on it, but that heat did not penetrate enough to set up great internal stresses."

Phyfe looked hesitant and turned to Underwood. "What is your opinion?"

Underwood didn't get it until he caught Terry's wink behind Phyfe's back. Once it left space and went into the museum laboratory, Terry might never get to work on the thing again. That was the perpetual gripe of the field men.

"I think Doctor Bernard has a good point," said Underwood. "I would advise leaving the artifact here in space until a thorough examination has been made. After all, we have every facility aboard the *Lavoisier* that is available on Earth."

"Very well," said Phyfe. "You may proceed in charge of the physical examination of the find, Doctor Underwood. You, Doctor Bernard, will be in charge of proceedings from an archeological standpoint. Will that be satisfactory to everyone concerned?"

It was far more than Terry had expected.

"I will be on constant call," said Phyfe. "Let me know immediately of any developments." Then the uncertain mask of the executive fell away from the face of the little old scientist and he regarded the find with humility and awe. "It's beautiful," he murmured again, *"beautiful."*

CHAPTER TWO

PHYFE remained near the site as Underwood and Terry set their crew to the routine task of weighing, measuring, and photographing the object, while Underwood considered what else to do.

"You know, this thing has got me stymied, Terry. Since it can't be touched by an Atom Stream that means there isn't a single analytical procedure to which it will respond—that I know of, anyway. Does your knowledge of the Stroids and their ways of doing things suggest any identification of it?"

Terry shook his head as he stood by the port of the laboratory ship watching the crews at work outside. "Not a thing, but that's no criterion. We know so little about the Stroids that almost everything we find has a function we never heard of before. And of course we've found many objects with totally unknown functions. I've been thinking—what if this should turn out to be merely a natural gem from the interior of the planet, maybe formed at the time of its destruction, but at least an entirely natural object rather than an artifact?"

"It would be the largest crystal formation ever encountered, and the most perfect. I'd say the chances of its natural formation are negligible."

"But maybe this is the one in a hundred billion billion or whatever number chance it may be."

"If so, its value ought to be enough to balance the Terrestrial budget. I'm still convinced that it must be an artifact, though its material and use are beyond me. We can start with a radiation analysis. Perhaps it will respond in some way that will give us a clue."

When the crew had finished the routine check, Underwood directed his men to set up the various types of radiation equipment contained within the ship. It was possible to generate radiation through almost the complete spectrum from single cycle sound waves to hard cosmic rays.

The work was arduous and detailed. Each radiator was slowly driven through its range, then removed and higher frequency equipment used. At each fraction of an octave, the object was carefully photographed to record its response.

After watching the work for two days, Terry wearied of the seemingly non-productive labor. "I suppose you know what you're doing, Del," he said. "But is it getting you anywhere at all?"

Underwood shook his head. "Here's the batch of photographs. You'll probably want them to illustrate your report. The surfaces of the object are mathematically exact to a thousandth of a millimeter. Believe me, that's some tolerance on an object of this size. The surfaces are of number fifteen smoothness, which means they are plane within a hundred thousandth of a millimeter. The implications are obvious. The builders who constructed that were mechanical geniuses."

"DID you get any radioactive dating?"

"Rather doubtfully, but the indications are around half a million years."

"That checks with what we know about the Stroids."

"It would appear that their culture is about on a par with our own."

"Personally, I think they were ahead of us," said Terry. "And do you see what that means to us archeologists? It's the first time in the history of the science that we've had to deal with the remains of a civilization either equal or superior to our own. The problems are multiplied a thousand times when you try to take a step up instead of a step down."

"Any idea of what the Stroids looked like?"

"We haven't found any bodies, skeletons, or even pictures, but we think they were at least roughly anthropomorphic. They were farther from the Sun than we, but it was younger then and probably gave them about the same amount of heat. Their planet was larger and the Stroids appear to have been somewhat larger as individuals than we, judging from the artifacts we've discovered. But they seem to have had a suitable atmosphere of oxygen diluted with appropriate inert gases."

THEY were interrupted by the sudden appearance of a laboratory technician who brought in a dry photographic print still warm from the developing box.

He laid it on the desk before Underwood. "I thought you might be interested in this."

Underwood and Terry glanced at it. The picture was of the huge, gemlike artifact, but a number of the facets seemed to be covered with intricate markings of short, wavy lines.

Underwood stared closer at the thing. "What the devil are those? We took pictures of every facet previously and there was nothing like this. Get me an enlargement of these."

"I already have." The assistant laid another photo on the desk, showing the pattern of markings as if at close range. They were dearly discernible now.

"What do you make of it?" asked Underwood.

"I'd say it looked like writing," Terry said. "But it's not like any of the other Stroid characters I've seen—which doesn't mean much, of course, because there could be thousands that I've never seen. Only how come these characters are there now, and we never noticed them before?"

"Let's go out and have a look," said Underwood. He grasped the photograph and noted the numbers of the facets on which the characters appeared.

In a few moments the two men were speeding toward the surface of their discovery astride scooters. They jockeyed above the facets shown on the photographs, and stared in vain.

"Something's the matter," said Terry. "I don't see anything here."

"Let's go all the way around on the scooters. Those guys may have bungled the job of numbering the photos."

They began a slow circuit, making certain they glimpsed all the facets from a height of only ten feet.

"It's not here," Underwood agreed at last. "Let's talk to the crew that took the shots."

They headed towards the equipment platform, floating in free space, from which Mason, one of the Senior Physicists, was directing operations. Mason signaled for the radiations to be cut off as the men approached.

"Find any clues, Chief?" he asked Underwood. "We've done our best to fry this apple, but nothing happens."

"Something *did* happen. Did you see it?" Underwood extended the photograph with the mechanical fingers of the spacesuit. Mason held it in a light and stared at it. "We didn't see a thing like that. And we couldn't have missed it." He turned to the members of the crew. "Anyone see this writing on the thing?"

They looked at the picture and shook their heads.

"What were you shooting on it at the time?"

Mason glanced at his records. "About a hundred and fifty angstroms."

"So there must be something that becomes visible only in a field of radiation of about that wave length," said Underwood. "Keep going and see if anything else turns up, or if this proves to be permanent after exposure to that frequency."

Back in the laboratory, they sat down at the desk and went through the file of hundreds of photographs that were now pouring out of the darkroom.

"Not a thing except that one," said Terry. "It looks like a message intended only for someone who knew what frequency would make it visible."

UNDERWOOD shook his head. "That sounds a little too melodramatic for me. Yet it is possible that this thing is some kind of repository, and we've found the key to it. But what a key! It looks as if we've got to decipher the language of the Stroids in order to use the key."

"The best men in the field have been trying to do that for only about seventy-five years. If that's what it takes, we may as well quit right now."

"You said that this was nothing like any other Stroid characters that you had seen. Maybe this belongs to a different cultural stratum. It might prove easier to crack. Who's the best man in the field on this stuff?"

"Dreyer at the semantics lab. He won't touch it any more. He says he's wasted fifteen years of his life on the Stroid inscriptions."

"I'll bet he will tackle this, if it's as new as you think it is. I've seen some of those antiquarians before. We'll get Phyfe to transmit some copies of this to him. Who's the next best man?"

"Probably Phyfe himself."

"It won't be hard to get him started on it, I'll bet."

It wasn't. The old scientist was ecstatic over the discovery of the inscriptions upon the huge gem. He took copies of the pictures into his study and spent two full days comparing them with the known records.

"It's an entirely new set of characters," he said after completing the preliminary examination. "We already have three sets of characters that seem to be in no way related. This is the fourth."

"You sent copies to Dreyer?"

"Only because you requested it. Dreyer admitted long ago that he was licked."

DURING the week of Phyfe's study, the work of radiation analysis had been completed. It proved completely negative with the single exception of the 150 A. radiation, which rendered visible the characters on the gem. No secondary effects of any significance whatever had been noted. The material reflected almost completely nearly every frequency imposed upon it.

Thus, Underwood found himself again at the end of his resources it was impossible to analyze material that refused to react, which was refractive to every force applied.

Underwood told Terry at the conclusion of a series of chemical tests, "If you want to keep that thing out here any longer, I'm afraid you've got to think of some more effective way of examining it than I have been able to do. From a physical standpoint this artifact is in about the same position as the language of the Stroids had been semantically—completely intractable."

"I'm not afraid of its being sent back to the museum now. Papa Phyfe's got his teeth into it and he won't let go until he cracks the key to this lingo."

Underwood didn't believe that it would ever be solved, unless by some lucky chance they came upon a sort of Rosetta Stone which would bridge the gap between the human mind and that of the alien Stroids. Even if the Stroids were somewhat anthropomorphic in makeup as the archeologists believed, there was no indication that their minds would not be so utterly alien that no bridge would even be possible.

Underwood felt seriously inclined to abandon the problem. While completely fascinating, it was hardly more soluble than was the problem of the composition of the stars in the days before the spectroscope was invented. Neither the archeologists, the semanticists, nor the physicists yet had the tools to crack the problem of the Stroids. Until the tools became available, the problem would simply have to go by the boards.

The only exception was the remote possibility of deliberate clue left by the Stroids themselves, but Underwood did not believe in miracles.

His final conviction came when word came back from Dreyer, who said; "Congratulations, Phyfe," and returned the copies of the Stroid characters with a short note.

"Well, that does it," said Underwood.

Phyfe was dismayed by Dreyer's reply. "The man's simply trying to uphold a decaying reputation by claiming the problem can't be solved. Send it to the museum and let them begin work on it. I'll give it my entire time. You will help me, if you will, Doctor Bernard."

TERRY himself was becoming somewhat dismayed by the magnitude of the mystery they had uncovered. He knew Phyfe's bulldog tenacity when he tackled something and he didn't want to be tied to semantics for the rest of the term of the expedition.

Underwood, however, had become immersed in X-ray work, attempting to determine the molecular structure of the artifact from a crystallographic standpoint, to find out if it could be found, it might be possible to disrupt the pattern.

After he had been at it for about a week, Terry came into the lab in a disgruntled mood at the completion of a work period.

"You look as if Papa gave you a spanking," said Underwood. "Why the downcast mood?"

"I think I'll resign and go back to the museum. It's useless to work on this puzzle any longer."

"How do you know?"

"Because it doesn't follow the laws of semantics with respect to language."

"Maybe the laws need changing."

"You know better than that. Look, you are as familiar with Carnovan's law as I am. It states that in any language there is bound to be a certain constant frequency of semantic conceptions. It's like the old frequency laws that used to be used in cryptographic analysis except a thousand times more complex. Anyway, we've made thousands of substitutions into Carnovan's frequency scale and nothing comes out. Not a thing. No concept of ego, identity, perfection, retrogression, or intercourse shows up. The only thing that registers in the slightest degree is the concept of motion, but it doesn't yield a single key word. It's almost as if it weren't even a language."

"Maybe it isn't."

"What else could it be?"

"Well, maybe this thing we've found is a monument of some kind and the inscriptions are ritualistic tributes to dead heroes or something. Maybe there's no trick at all about the radiation business. Maybe they used that frequency for common illumination and the inscription was arranged to show up just at night. The trouble with you strict semanticists is that you don't use any imagination."

"Like to try a hand at a few sessions with Papa Phyfe?"

"No, thanks, but I do think there are other possibilities that you are overlooking. I make no claim to being anything but a strictly ham semanticist, but suppose, for example, that the inscriptions are not language at all in the common sense."

"They must represent transfer of thought in some form."

"True, but look at the varied forms of thought. You are bound down to the conception of language held as far back as Korzybski. At least to the conception held by those who didn't fully understand Korzybski. You haven't considered the concept of music. It's a very real possibility, but one which would remain meaningless without the instrument. Consider also—Wait a minute. Terry! We've all been a bunch of thoroughbred dopes!"

"What is it?"

"Look at the geometrical and mechanical perfection of the artifact. That implies mathematical knowledge of a high order. The inscriptions could be mathematical measurements of some kind. That would explain the breakdown of Carnovan's principles. They don't apply to math."

"But what kind of math would be inscribed on a thing like that?"

"Who knows? We can give it a try."

IT was the beginning of their sleeping period, but Terry was fired with Underwood's sudden enthusiasm. He brought in a complete copy of all the inscriptions found upon the facets of the black gem. Underwood placed them on a large table in continuous order as they appeared around the circumference.

"It's mud to me," said Terry. "I'm the world's worst mathematician."

"Look!" exclaimed Underwood. "Here's the beginning of it." He suddenly moved some of the sheets so that one previously in the middle formed the beginning of the sequence. "What does it look like to you?"

"I've seen that until I dream of it. It's one Phyfe tried to make the most of in his frequency determinations. It looks like nothing more than some widgets alongside a triangle."

"That's exactly what it is, and no wonder Phyfe found it had a high frequency. That is nothing more or less than an explanation of the Stroid concept of the differential. This widget over here must be the sign of the derivative corresponding to our dy/dx."

Hastily, Underwood scrawled some symbols on a scratch pad, using combinations of "x"s and "y"s and the strange, unknown symbols of the Stroids.

"It checks. They're showing us how to differentiate! Not only that we have the key to their numerical system in the exponentials, because they've given us the differentiation of a whole series of power expressions here. Now, somewhere we ought to find an integral expression, which we could check back with differentiation. Here it is!"

TERRY, left behind now, went to the galley and brewed a steaming pot of coffee and brought it back. He found Underwood staring unseeingly ahead of him into the dark, empty corners of the lab.

"What is it?" Terry exclaimed. "What have you found?"

"I'm not sure. Do you know what the end product of all this math is?"

"What?"

"A set of wave equations, but such wave equations as any physicist would be thought crazy to dream up. Yet, in light of some new manipulations introduced by the Stroids, they seem feasible."

"What can we do with them?"

"We *can* build a generator and see what kind of stuff comes out of it when we operate it according to this math. The Stroids obviously intended that someone find this and learn to produce the radiation described. For what purpose we can only guess—but we might find out."

"Do we have enough equipment aboard to build such a generator?"

"I think so. We could cannibalize enough from equipment we already have on hand. Let's try it."

Terry hesitated. "I'm not quite sure, but—well, this stuff comes about as near as anything I ever saw to giving me what is commonly known as the creeps. Somehow these Stroids seem too—too *anxious*. That sounds crazy, I know, but there's such alienness here."

"Nuts. Let's build their generator and see what they're trying to tell us."

CHAPTER THREE

PHYFE was exuberant. He not only gave permission to construct the generator, he demanded that all work aboard the lab ship give priority to the new project.

The design of the machine was no easy task, for Underwood was a physicist and not an engineer. However, he had two men, Moody and Hansen, in his staff who were first rate engineers. On them fell the chief burden of design after Underwood worked out the rough specifications.

One of the main laboratories with nearly ten thousand square feet of floor space was cleared for the project. As the specifications flowed from Underwood's desk, they passed over to Moody and Hansen, and from there out to the lab where the mass of equipment was gathered from all parts of the fleet.

An atomic power supply sufficient to give the large amount of energy required by the generator was obtained by robbing the headquarters ship of its auxiliary supply. Converter units were available in the *Lavoisier* itself, but the main radiator tubes had to be cannibalized from the 15A equipment aboard.

Slowly the mass of improvised equipment grew. It would have been a difficult task on Earth with all facilities available for such a project, but with these makeshift arrangements it was a miracle that the generator continued to develop. A score of times Underwood had to make compromises that he hoped would not alter the characteristics of the wave which, two weeks before he would have declared impossible to generate.

When the equipment was completed and ready for a trial check, the huge lab was a mass of haywiring into which no one but Moody and Hansen dared go.

The completion was an anticlimax. The great project that had almost halted all other field work was finished—and no one knew what to expect when Hansen threw the switch that fed power from the converters into the giant tubes.

As a matter of fact, nothing happened. Only the faint whine of the converters and the swinging needles of meters strung all over the room showed that the beam was in operation.

On the nose of the *Lavoisier* was the great, ungainly radiator a hundred feet in diameter; which was spraying the unknown depths of space with the newly created power.

Underwood and Terry were outside the ship, behind the huge radiator, with a mass of equipment designed to observe the effects of the beam.

In space it was totally invisible, creating no detectable field. It seemed as inactive as a beam of ultraviolet piercing the starlit darkness.

UNDERWOOD picked up the interphone that connected them with the interior of the ship. "Swing around, please, Captain Dawson. Let the beam rotate through a one hundred and eighty degree arc."

The Captain ordered the ship around and the great *Lavoisier* swung on its own axis—but not in the direction Underwood had had in mind. He failed to indicate the direction, and Dawson had assumed it didn't matter.

Ponderously, the great radiator swung about before Underwood could shout a warning. And the beam came directly in line with the mysterious gem of the universe, which they had found in the heart of the asteroid.

At once, the heavens were filled with intolerable light. Terry and Underwood flung themselves down upon the hull of the ship and the physicist screamed into the phones for Dawson to swing the other way.

But his warnings were in vain, for those within the ship were blinded by the great flare of light that penetrated even the protective ports of the ship. Irresistibly, the *Lavoisier* continued to swing, spraying the great gem with its mysterious radiation.

Then it was past and the beam cut into space once more.

On top of the ship, Underwood and Terry found their sight slowly returning. They had been saved the full blast of the light from the gem by the curve of the ship's hull, which cut it off.

Underwood stumbled to his feet, followed by Terry. The two men stood in open-mouthed unbelief at the vision that met their eyes. Where the gem had drifted in space, there was now a blistered, boiling mass of amorphous matter that surged and steamed in the void. All semblance to the glistening, faceted, ebon gem was gone as the repulsive mass heaved within itself.

"It's destroyed!" Terry exclaimed hoarsely. "The greatest archeological find of all time and we destroy it before we find out anything about it—"

"Shut up!" Underwood commanded harshly. He tried to concentrate on the happenings before him, but he could find no meaning in it. He bemoaned the fact that he had no camera, and only prayed that someone inside would have the wit to turn one on.

As the ship continued its slow swing like a senseless animal, the pulsing of the amorphous mass that had been the jewel slowly ceased. And out of the gray murkiness of it came a new quality. It began to regain rigidity—and transparency!

UNDERWOOD gasped. At the boundary lines of the facets, heavy ribs showed the tremendously reinforced structure that formed the skeleton. And each cell between the ribs was filled with thick substance that partially revealed the unknown world within.

But more than that, between one set of ribs he glimpsed what he was sure was an emptiness, a doorway to the interior!

"Come on," he called to Terry. Look at that opening!"

They leaped astride the scooters clamped to the surface of the lab ship and sped into space between the two objects. It required only an instant to confirm his first hasty glimpse.

They navigated the scooters close to the opening and clamped them to the surface. For a moment, Underwood thought the gem might be some strange ship from far out of the Universe, for it seemed filled with mechanism of indescribable characteristics and unknown purposes. It was so filled that it was impossible to see very far into the interior even with the help of the powerful lamps on the scooters.

"The beam was the key to get into the thing," said Terry. "It was intended all along that the beam be turned on it. The beam had to be connected with the gem in some way."

"And what a way!"

The triangular opening was large enough to admit a man. Underwood and Terry knelt at the edge of it, peering down, flashing their lights about the revealed interior. The opening seemed to drop into the center of a small room that was bare.

"Come into my parlor, said the spider to the fly," quoted Terry. "I don't see anything down there, do you?"

"No. Why the spider recitation?"

"I don't know. Everything is too pat. I feel as if someone is watching behind us, practically breathing down our necks and urging us on the way he wants us to go. And when we get there we aren't going to like it."

"I suppose that is strictly a scientific hunch which we ignorant physicists wouldn't understand."

But Terry was serious. The whole aspect of the Stroid device was unnerving in the way it led along from step to step, as if unseen powers were guiding them, rather than using their own initiative in their work.

Underwood gave a final grunt and dropped into the hole, flashing his light rapidly about. Terry followed immediately. They found themselves in the center of a circular room twenty feet in diameter. The walls and the floor seemed to be of the same ebony-black material that had composed the outer shell of the gem before its transmutation.

THE walls were literally covered from the floor to the ten foot ceiling with inscriptions that glowed faintly in the darkness when the flashlights were not turned on them.

"Recognize any of this stuff?" asked Underwood.

"Stroid III," said Terry in awe. "The most beautiful collection of engravings that have ever been found. We've never obtained a consecutive piece even a fraction this size before. Dreyer has got to come now."

"I've got a hunch about this," said Underwood slowly. "I don't know a thing about the procedures used in deciphering an unknown lingo, but I'll bet you find that this is an instruction primer to their language, just as the inscriptions outside gave the key to their math before detailing the wave equations."

"You might be right!" Terry's eyes glowed with enthusiasm as he looked about the polished walls with the faintly glowing characters inlaid in them. "If that's the case, Papa Phyfe and I ought to be able to do the job without Dreyer."

They returned to the ship for photographic equipment and to report their finding to Phyfe. It was a little difficult for him to adjust to the view that something had been gained in the transformation of the gem. The sight of that boiling, amorphous mass in space had been to him like helplessly standing on the bank of a stream—and watching a loved one drown.

But with Terry's report on the characters in Stroid III which lined the wall of the antechamber, which they had penetrated, he was ready to admit that their position had improved.

Underwood was merely a bystander as they returned to the gem. Two photographers, Carson and Enright, accompanied them along with Nichols, assistant semanticist.

Underwood stood by, in the depths of speculation, as the photographers set up their equipment and Phyfe bent down to examine the characters at close range.

Terry continued to be dogged by the feeling that they were being led by the nose into something that would end unpleasantly. He didn't know why, except that the fact of immense and meticulous preparation was evidenced on all sides. It was the reason for that preparation which made him wonder.

PHYFE said to Underwood, "Doctor Bernard tells me your opinion is that this room is a key to Stroid III. You may be right, but I fail to find any indication of it at present. What gives you that idea?"

"The whole setup," said Underwood. "First, there was the impenetrable shell. Nothing like it exists in Solarian culture today. Then there was the means by which we were able to read the inscriptions on the outside. Obviously, if heat and fission reactions as well as chemical reactions could not touch the stuff, the only remaining means of analysis was radiative. And the only peoples who could discover the inscriptions were those capable of building a generator of 150 A. radiations. We have there two highly technical requirements of anyone attempting to solve the secret of this cache—ability to generate the proper radiation, and the ability to understand their mathematics and build a second generator from their wave equations.

"Now that we're in here, there is nothing more we can do until we can understand their printed language. Obviously, they must teach it to us. This would be the place."

"You may be right," said Phyfe. "But we archeologists work with facts, not guesses. We'll know soon enough if it's true."

UNDERWOOD felt content to speculate while the others worked. There was nothing else for him to do. No way out of the anteroom was apparent, but he was confident that a way to the interior would be found when the inscriptions were deciphered.

He went out to the surface and walked slowly about, peering into the transparent depths with his light. What lay within this repository left by an ancient race that had obviously equaled or surpassed man in scientific attainments? Would it be some vast store of knowledge that would come to bless mankind with greater abundance? Or would it, rather, be a new Pandora's box, which would pour out upon the world new ills to add to its already staggering burden?

The world had about all it could stand now, Underwood reflected. For a century, Earth's scientific production had boomed. Her factories had roared with the throb of incessant production, and the utopia of all the planners of history was gradually coming to pass. Man's capacities for production had steadily increased for five hundred years, and at last the capacities for consumption were rising equally, with correspondingly less time spent in production and greater time spent in consumption.

But the utopia wasn't coming off just as the Utopians had dreamed of it. The ever present curse of enforced leisure was not respecting the new age any more than it had past ages. Men were literally being driven crazy with their super-abundance of luxury.

Only a year before, the so called Howling Craze had swept cities and nations. It was a wave of hysteria that broke out in epidemic proportions.

Thousands of people within a city would be stricken at a time by insensate weeping and despair. One member of a household would be afflicted and quickly it would spread from that man to the family, and from that family it would race the length and breadth of the streets, up and down the city, until one vast cry as of a stricken animal would assault the heavens.

Underwood had seen only one instance of the Howling Craze and he had fled from it as if pursued. It was impossible to describe its effects upon the nervous system—a whole city in the throes of hysteria.

Life was cheap, as were the other luxuries of Earth. Murders by the thousands each month were scarcely noticed, and the possession of weapons for protection had become a mark of the new age, for no man knew when his neighbor might turn upon him.

Governments rose and fell swiftly and became little more than figureheads to carry out the demands of peoples cloyed with the excesses of life. Most significant of all, however, was the inability of any leader to hold any following for more than a short time.

Of all the inhabitants of Earth, there were but a few hundred thousand scientists who were able to keep themselves on even keel, and most of these were now fleeing.

As he thought of these things, Underwood pondered what, the opening of the repository of a people who sealed up their secrets half a million years ago would mean to mankind. This must be what Terry felt, he thought.

For perhaps three hours he remained on the outside of the shell, letting his mind idle under the brilliance of the stars. Suddenly, the phones in his helmet came alive with sound. It was the voice of Terry Bernard.

"We've got it, Del," he said quietly. "We can read this stuff like nursery rhymes. Come on down. It tells us how to get into the thing."

Underwood did not hurry. He rose slowly from his sitting position and stared upward at the stars, the same stars that had looked down upon the beings who had sealed up the repository. This is it, he thought. Man can never go back again.

HE lowered himself into the opening.

Doctor Phyfe was strangely quiet in spite of their quick success in deciphering the language of the Stroids. Underwood wondered what was going through the old man's mind. Did he, too, sense the magnitude of this moment?

Phyfe said, "They were semanticists as well. They knew Carnovan's frequency. It's right here, the key they used to reveal their language. No one less advanced in semantics than our own civilization could have deciphered it, but with a knowledge of Carnovan's frequency, it is simple."

"Practically hand-picked us for the job," said Terry.

Phyfe's sharp eyes turned upon him suddenly behind the double protection of his spectacles and the transparent helmet of the spacesuit.

"Perhaps," said Phyfe. "Perhaps we are. At any rate, there are certain manipulations to be performed which will open this chamber and provide passage to the interior."

"WHERE'S the door?" said Underwood.

Following the notes he had made, Terry moved about the room, directing Underwood's attention to features of the design. Delicately carved, movable levers formed an intricate combination that suddenly released a section of the floor in the exact center of the room. It depressed slowly then revolved out of the way.

For a moment no one spoke while Phyfe moved to the opening and peered down. A stairway of the same glistening material as the walls about them led downward into the depths of the repository.

Phyfe stepped down and almost stumbled into the opening. "Watch for those steps," he warned. "They're larger than necessary for human beings."

Giants in those days came to Underwood's mind. He tried to vision the creatures that had walked upon this stairway and touched the hand rail that was shoulder high for him.

The repository was divided into levels and the stairway ended abruptly as they came to the level below the anteroom. The chamber in which they found themselves was crowded with artifacts of strange shapes and varying sizes. Not a thing of familiar cast greeted them. But opposite the bottom of the stairway was a pedestal and upon it rested a book-like object that proved to be hinged metallic sheets, covered with Stroid III inscriptions, when Terry climbed up to examine it. He was unable to move it, but the metal pages were locked with a simple clasp that responded to his touch.

"It looks as if we've got to read our way along," said Terry. "I suppose this will tell us how to get into the next room."

Underwood and the other expedition members moved cautiously about, examining the contents of the room. The two photographers began to make an orderly pictorial record of everything within the chamber.

Standing alone in one corner, Underwood peered at an object that appeared to be nothing but a series of opaque, polychrome globes tangent to each other and mounted on a pedestal.

Whether it were some kind of machine or monument, he could not tell.

"You feel it, too," said a sudden quiet voice behind him. Underwood whirled about in surprise. Phyfe was there behind him, his slight figure a shapeless shadow in the spacesuit.

"Feel what?"

"I've watched you, Doctor Underwood. You are a physicist and in far closer touch with the real world than I. You have seen me—I cannot even manage an expedition with efficiency—my mind lives constantly in the past, and I cannot comprehend the significance of contemporary things. Tell me what it will mean, this intrusion of an alien science into our own."

A sudden, new, and humbling respect filled Underwood. He had never dreamed that the little archeologist had such a penetrating view of himself in his relation to his environment.

"I wish I could answer that question," said Underwood, shaking his head. "I can't. Perhaps if we knew, we'd destroy the thing—or it might be that we'd shout our discovery to the Universe. But we can't know, and we wouldn't dare be the judges if we could. Whatever it is, the ancient Stroids seem to have deliberately attempted to provide for the survival of their culture." He hesitated. "That, of course is my guess."

In the darkened corner of the chamber, Phyfe nodded slowly. "You are right, of course. It is the only answer. We dare not try to be the judges."

UNDERWOOD saw that he would get nowhere in his understanding of the Stroid science by merely depending on the translations given him by Terry and Phyfe. He'd have to learn to read the Stroid inscriptions himself. He buttonholed Nichols and got the semanticist to show him the rudiments of the language. It was amazingly simple in principle and constructed along semantic lines.

The going became rapidly heavier, however, and it took them the equivalent of five days to get through the fairly elementary material disclosed in the first level below the antechamber.

The book of metal pages did little to satisfy their curiosity concerning either the ancient planet or its culture. It instructed them further in understanding the language, and addressed them as Unknown friends— the nearest human translation.

As was already apparent, the repository had been prepared to save the highest products of the ancient Stroid culture from the destruction that came upon the world. But the records did not even hint as to the nature of that destruction and they said nothing about the objects in the room.

The scientists were a bit disappointed by the little revealed to them so far, but, as expected, there were instructions to enter the next lower level. There, an entirely different situation confronted them.

The chamber into which they came after winding down a long, spiral stairway, narrow, yet with the same high steps as before, was spherical in shape and seemed to be concentric with the outer shell of the repository. It contained a single object.

The object was a cube in the center of the chamber, about two feet on a side. From the corners of the cube, long supports of complicated spring structure led to the inner surface of the spherical chamber. It appeared to be a highly effective shock mounting for whatever was contained within the cube.

THE sight before the men was impressive in simplicity, yet was anticlimactic, for there was nothing here of the great wonders that they had expected. There was only the suspended cube and a book.

Quickly, Phyfe advanced along the narrow catwalk that led from the opening to the cube. The book lay on a shelf fastened to the side of the cube. Phyfe opened it to the first sheet and read haltingly and laboriously:

"Greetings, Unknown Friends. Greetings to you from the Great One. By the token that you are now reading this, you have proven yourselves mentally capable of understanding the new world of knowledge and discovery that may be yours.

"I am Demarzule, the Great One, the greatest of great Sirenia—and the last. And within the storehouse of my mind is the vast knowledge that made Sirenia the greatest world in all the Universe.

"Great as it was, however, destruction came to the world of Sirenia. But her knowledge and her wonders shall never pass. In ages after, new worlds will rise and beings will inhabit them, and they will come to a minimum plane of knowledge that will assure their appreciation of the wonders that may be theirs from the world of Sirenia.

"You have minimum technical knowledge, else you could not have created the radiation necessary to render the storehouse penetrable. You have a minimum semantic knowledge, else you could not have understood my words that have brought you this far.

"You are fit and capable to behold the Great One of Sirenia!"

As Phyfe turned over the first metal sheet, the men looked at each other. It was Nichols, the semanticist, who said, "There are only two possibilities in a mind that would write a statement of that kind. Either it belonged to a truly superior being, or to a maniac. So far, in man's history, there has not been encountered such a superior being. If he existed, it would have been wonderful to have known him."

Phyfe paused and peered with difficulty through the helmet of the spacesuit. He continued, "I live. I am eternal. I am in your midst, Unknown Friends, and to your hands falls the task of bringing speech to my voice, and sight to my eyes, and feeling to my hands. Then, when you have fulfilled your mighty task, you shall behold me and the greatness of the Great One of Sirenia."

Enright, the photographer said, "What the devil does that mean? The guy must have been nuts. He sounds like he expected to come back to life."

The feeling within Underwood was more than bearable. It was composed of surging anticipation and quiet fearfulness, and they mingled in a raging torrent.

The men made no sound as Phyfe read on, "I shall live again. The Great One shall return, and you who are my Unknown Friends shall assist me to return to life. Then and only then shall you know the great secrets of the world of Sirenia, which are a thousand times greater than your own. Only then shall you become mighty, with the secrets of Sirenia locked in my brain. By the powers I shall reveal, you shall become mighty until there are none greater in all the Universe."

PHYFE turned the page. Abruptly he stopped. He turned to Underwood. "The rest of it is yours," he said.

"What—?"

Underwood glanced at the page of inscription. With difficulty he took up the reading silently. The substance of the writings had changed and here was a sudden wilderness of an alien science.

Slowly he plodded through the first concepts, then skimmed as it became evident that here was material for days of study. But out of his hasty scanning there came a vision of a great dream, a dream of conquest of the eons, the preservation of life while worlds waned and died and flared anew.

It told of an unknown radiation turned upon living cells, reducing them to primeval protoplasm, arresting all but the *symbol* of metabolism.

And it spoke of other radiation and complex chemical treatment, a fantastic process that could restore again the life that had been only *symbolized* by the dormant protoplasm.

Underwood looked up. His eyes went from the featureless cube to the faces of his companions.

"It's alive!" he breathed. "Five hundred million years—and it's alive! These are instructions by which it may be restored!"

None of the others spoke, but Underwood's eyes were as if a sudden, great commission had been placed upon him. Out of the turmoil of his thoughts a single purpose emerged, clear and irrevocable.

Within that cube lay dormant matter that could be formed into a brain—an alien but mighty brain. Suddenly, Underwood felt an irrational kinship with the ancient creature who had so conquered time, and in his own mind he silently vowed that if it lay within his power, that creature would live again, and speak its ancient secrets.

CHAPTER FOUR

"DEL!" The shock of surprise and the flush of pleasure heightened the beauty of Illia's delicate features. She stood in the doorway, the aureole of her pale golden hair backlighted by the illumination from within the room.

"Surprised?" said Underwood. He always found it difficult to speak for a moment after the first sight of Illia. No one would guess a beauty like her to be the top surgeon of Medical Center.

"Why didn't you let me know you were coming? It's not fair—"

"—not to give you time to build up your defenses?"

She nodded silently as he took her into his arms. But quickly she broke away and led him to the seat by the broad windows overlooking the night lights of the city below.

"Have you come back?" she said.

"Back? You put such a confusing amount of meaning into ordinary words, Illia."

She smiled and sat down beside him, and swiftly changed the subject. "Tell me about the expedition. Archeology has always seemed the most futile of all sciences, but I've supposed that was because I could find nothing in common between it and my medical science, nothing in common with the future. I've wondered what a physicist could find in it."

"I think you'll find something in common with our latest discovery. We have a living though dormant creature on an equal or superior plane of intelligence with us. Its age is around half a million years. You will be interested in the medical aspects of that, I am sure."

FOR a moment Illia sat as if she hadn't heard him. Then she said. "That could be a discovery to change a world, if you're sure of what you've found."

Underwood felt irritation more because he had been trying to fight down the same idea himself than because she had spoken it. "Your semantic extensions would turn Phyfe's whiskers white. We haven't found any such world shaking discovery. We've found a creature out of another age and another culture, but it's not going to disrupt or change our society."

"If it's a scientifically superior culture, how do you know what it will do?"

"We don't, but to apply so many extensions only confuses our interpretation more. I mention it because we are going to need a biological advisor. I thought you might like to be it."

Her eyes were staring far out across the halo of the city's lights. She said, "Del, is it human?"

"Human? What's human? Is intelligence human? Can any other factor of our existence be defined as human? If you can tell me that, perhaps I can answer. So far, we only know that it is a sentient creature of high scientific culture."

"Then that alone makes its relationship with us a sympathetic one?"

"Why, I suppose so. I see no reason why not."

"Yes. Yes, I agree with you! And don't you see? It can be a germ of rejuvenation, a nucleus to gather the scattered impulses of our culture and unify them in an absorption of this new science. Look what biological knowledge the mere evidence of suspended animation indicates."

"All right." Underwood laughed faintly in resignation. "There's no use trying to avoid such a discussion with you, is there, Illia? You'd take the first flower of spring and project a whole summer s glory from it, wouldn't you?

"But am I wrong in this? The people of Earth need *something* to cement them together in this period of disillusionment. This could be it."

"I know," said Underwood. "We talked it over out there before we decided to go ahead with the restoration. We talked and argued for hours. Some of the men wanted to destroy the thing immediately because it is impossible to forecast the effect of this discovery from a strictly semantic standpoint. We have no data.

"Terry Bernard definitely fought for its destruction. Phyfe is afraid of the possible consequences, but he maintains that we haven't the right to destroy it because it is too great a heritage. I maintain that from a purely scientific standpoint we have no right to consider anything but restoration, regardless of consequences.

"And there is something more—the personal element. A creature whose imagination and daring were great enough to preserve his ego through an age of five hundred thousand years deserves something more than summary execution. He deserves the right to be known and heard. Actually, it seems ridiculous to fear anything that can come of this. Well, Phyfe and Terry are expert semanticists, and they're afraid—"

"Oh, they're wrong, Del! They *must* be wrong. If they have no data, if they have only a hunch, a prejudice, it's ridiculous for them as scientists to be swayed by such feelings."

"I don't know. I wash my hands of all such aspects of the problem. I only know that I'm going to see that a guy who's got the brains and guts this one must have had, has his chance to be heard. So far, I'm on the winning side. Tomorrow I'm going to see Boarder and the Director's Committee with Phyfe. If you're interested in taking the job I mentioned, come along."

THE ENTHUSIASM of the directors was even greater than that of Illia, if possible. None of them seemed to share the fears of some of the expedition members. And, somehow, in the warm familiarity of the committee room, those fears seemed fantastically groundless. Boarder, the elder member of the committee of directors, could not hold back his tears as he finished the report and Underwood had given verbal amplification.

"What a wonderful thing that this should have happened in our lifetime," he said. "Do you think it is feasible? The thing seems so—so fantastic, the restoration of a living creature of half a million years ago."

"I'm sure I don't know the answer to that," said Underwood. "No one does. The construction of the equipment described by the Stroid, though, is completely within range of our technical knowledge. I'm certain that we can set it up exactly according to specifications. It is possible that too much time has passed and the protoplasm has died. It is possible that Demarzule thought in terms of hundreds of years, or, at the most, a few thousand, before he would be found. There is no way to know except to construct the equipment and carry out the experiment, which I will do if the Directors wish to authorize the expenditure."

"There is no question of that!" said Boarder. "We'd mortgage the entire Institution if necessary! I'm wondering what laboratory space we can use. Why not put it in the new Carlson Museum building? The specimens for the Carlson can stay in the warehouse for a while longer."

Boarder looked about the circle of Directors facing him. He saw nods and called for a vote. His proposal was upheld.

With approval given, Phyfe returned to the expedition to supervise the transfer of the repository of Demarzule to Earth, while Underwood began infinitely detailed planning for the construction and setup of equipment as specified by the instructions he had brought from the Stroid repository.

The great semanticist, Dreyer, was asked to help in a consulting capacity for the whole project; specifically, to assist in retranslation of the records to make absolutely certain of their interpretation of the scientific instructions.

Dreyer was a short, squat man who had never been caught without a thick black cigar from which billowed endless columns of pale blue smoke. His face was round and baby-calm. He gave the impression of having achieved the impossible goal of complete serenity in a world that swirled with unceasing turmoil.

HE listened quietly when approached, and when Phyfe and Underwood had finished their stories, he said, "Yes, I shall be glad to help. This is a thing of great importance."

But Underwood was forced to shed his mind of sociological and semantic implications of the job they were doing. The technical work involved was of tremendous complexity and magnitude. A mountainous quantity of complicated equipment had to be designed and built, but as Underwood deciphered the instructions of the Stroids and had it verified by Dreyer, he could find no short cuts nor did he dare attempt any.

The Carlson Museum had been designed along the lines of an ancient Greek temple and was set prominently on a low hill apart from other groups of buildings of the Smithson. Its glistening marble columns made a landmark for miles. It was rather symbolical in a way, Underwood thought, that such an imposing edifice should be appointed for the resurrection of the ancient Great One.

The central hall of the museum was cleared of display cases, which had already been set up. Electronic and biological equipment began to flow in as Underwood sent strange fabrication orders to scattered shops and plants throughout the country.

WHEN it was announced that the Carlson would not open on the date previously set, the worldwide news associations were interested and Underwood was suddenly besieged by reporters. He briefly outlined their discovery. It would make some good science supplement yarns, Underwood supposed, and by the time the reporters got through with the stories they would have a whole race of monsters out of space being restored in the Carlson.

Underwood told them as much.

But Davis of the Science Press shook his head. "No, that's not the angle. Archeology always makes good stories, but this is the first time archeology has ever produced any live specimens. We'll build the creature up big from the sympathetic angle. What did you say the inscription called him? The Great One?"

Underwood nodded.

"That's it! The mysterious, all knowing brain that has lain dormant in the void for ages, waiting for the touch of a merciful hand to restore life to that mighty intellect and receive in payment the magnificent store of knowledge locked within it. That's the angle we'll use."

Underwood mentally gagged and returned to his work.

Slowly the equipment took shape within the large hall. The center of construction was the ceramic bath, which would hold the mass of protoplasm in its nutrient solution and keep it in controlled temperatures and pressures. The complex observation panel was being assembled beside it. From this point every physiological function of the developing mass could be observed as it progressed. Scores of meters would give electronic readings, which could be interpreted, in terms of developing functions. It was almost like watching the development and growth of a fetus, for that appeared almost to be the course of growth that was to be expected.

Automatic valves would control the injection into the bath of nutrient materials with an accuracy of a thousandth of a milligram. A dozen operators would be trained, were now being selected, for the precise task of watching the bath during every second of the growth of the organism.

The upper half of the walls of the bath was transparent, as was the cover. Inside, under the cover, the broad reflecting cone of the radiator would spray the long dormant protoplasm with life-giving radiation. Giant generators required to provide this radiation filled other parts of the hall.

IT was five months after the actual discovery of the repository that the restoration equipment was completed and tested and ready for use. Public interest in the project had been aroused by the sensational news reports, and a constant stream of people passed the Carlson to glimpse the activities going on inside.

The news stories built up the Stroid as the magnificent benefactor of mankind, as Davis had promised. They presented a sympathetic aspect of a creature imprisoned and doomed throughout the ages, and now being released from bondage and ready to pour out blessings upon his benefactors.

Underwood didn't pay much attention to the news stories, but the increasing swarms of people began to get in his way and hampered operations. He was forced to ask the directors to fence off a large area about the Carlson.

During this time the *Lavoisier* had been slowly swinging in an orbit about the Earth to keep the repository, taken bodily into its hold, at the temperature of space, until time for the transfer of the protoplasm to the nutrient bath.

Now, with everything completed at the Museum, Underwood and Phyfe returned to the repository to direct the removal of the container of protoplasm, leaving Terry Bernard in charge at the museum. The operators and technicians were ready to take over their duties.

Removal of the protoplasm to Earth was a critical operation. The bath at the Carlson had been brought down to absolute zero and would be brought up a few degrees at a time.

Boarder and the other directors of the Institution did not share Underwood's reluctance for publicity. They were accustomed to the ways of the publicity writers, for much of the income of the Institute depended upon such publicity which drew substantial contributions.

So it was that the arrival of the *Lavoisier* was widely announced. A crowd of ten thousand gathered to watch the removal of the protoplasm that had once been a great and alien being.

Underwood stood in the control room watching the landing area beside the Carlson as the ship settled deep into Earth's atmosphere. Gradually he made out the identity of the black smear covering the landscape about the white stone building that gleamed like a Grecian temple.

TERRY, beside him, exclaimed, "Look at that mob! The whole town must be out to welcome our guest."

"If they don't get out of the landing area, they'll be smeared over the landscape. Collins, contact the base and get that field cleared!"

The communications officer put the call in. The laboratory ship circled idly while the mob moved slowly back to permit the ship to touch down beside the building.

Underwood raced out of the ship and into the building. His technicians were standing by. Each one in turn reported his position operating properly. Then Underwood called back to the ship and ordered the portable lock released.

At once the massive cargo hold was thrown open and the thick-walled lock, bearing the container of protoplasm, was wheeled out.

The crowd caught sight of it as it rolled swiftly into the building. Someone in the far ranks sent up a cry. "Hail the Great One! Welcome to Earth!"

Hundreds took up the shout, then thousands of throats until a sea of sound washed against the ears of those within the building. Underwood paused and turned to look out as the sound caught him. A faint chill went through him.

"The fools," he said angrily to Terry. "They'll drive themselves into hysteria if they keep that up! Why didn't the directors keep this whole business quiet? They ought to have known how it would affect a mob of bystanders."

From a distance, Illia and Dreyer watched silently. Underwood hurried away to give attention to the cargo. The lock was wheeled close to the bath and a passage was opened as the two containers were brought adjacent. On sterile slides, the frozen protoplasmic mass slid forward and came to rest at last within the machine for which it had waited half a million years.

There was utter lack of response to that final placement of the mass. Yet those who watched knew that the great experiment had begun. In six months, they would find out if they were successful.

Underwood sent the carriage back to the ship, and the *Lavoisier* moved to the Institute's spaceport. Then Boarder entered with a score of photographers and newsmen in his wake. They took pictures of the equipment and technicians, and of the protoplasm lying inert within the bath, in which the nutrient liquids would be placed after a temperature of a hundred degrees had been reached.

Underwood did not have time to pay any attention to the newsmen. He tried to be everywhere at once, inspecting meters and gauges, assuring himself that all was functioning well. Every piece of equipment was triply installed for safety in case of breakdown. The instructions warned that, once started, the process of restoration must not be interrupted or death to the Great One would result.

When he had finished his inspection, Underwood felt suddenly exhausted. He turned away to avoid the newsmen whom Boarder was now lecturing on the subject of the strange repository in space and its even stranger inhabitant.

Underwood spied the aged figure standing almost unseen near the recess between two panels. It was Phyfe and he spoke slowly as Underwood approached.

"It is begun," the old archeologist said slowly. "And it can never be undone."

Underwood felt again that chill of apprehension and looked sharply at Phyfe, but the latter was staring straight ahead—straight at the inert block of protoplasm.

CHAPTER FIVE

PHYFE asked to be relieved of his duties as head of the expedition still in the field in order that he might devote his entire time to a study of Stroid records and manuscripts now in existence. Terry Bernard gave up field work to assist him in order to be near the site of restoration. With them was Dreyer, who attacked with feverish effort the translation of the language that had defied him so long.

Underwood was concerned with the resurrection itself. He sensed that the very secret of life was involved in the work he was doing. The instruction book left by the Stroid was in the nature of an operating manual, however; rather than a theoretical text, and now that the experiment was actually under way, Underwood abandoned everything in an attempt to study fully the processes that were taking place.

So occupied were they with their own studies that the scientists scarcely noticed the public reaction to the creature they were attempting to restore.

The first outward sign had been that wild cry of welcome the day the protoplasm was brought to Earth.

The next was the Sunday sermon preached by one of the multitude of obscure religious leaders in a poorly attended meeting in a luxurious church in that same city.

William B. Hennessey had been a publicity man in his early years before the full breakdown began to show, and he was conscious of good publicity values. But perhaps he half believed what he wrote and the mere preaching of it convinced him it was so. It is probable that there were other preachers who took the same theme that Sunday morning, but William B. Hennessey's was the one that got the news publicity.

He said, "How many of this congregation this morning are among those who have given up in the race of life, who have despaired of values and standards to cling to, who have forsaken the leadership of all who would lead you? Perhaps you are among the millions of those who have given up all hope of solving the great problems of life. If you are, I want to ask if you were among those who witnessed the miraculous arrival of the Gift out of the Ages. Were you among those who saw the Great One?"

William B. Hennessey paused. "For centuries we have looked for leadership in our own midst and not found it. They were, after all, merely human. But now, into the hands of our noble scientists, has been imparted the great task of awakening the sleeping Great One, and when they have completed their work, the Golden Age of Earth will be upon us.

"I call upon you to throw off the shackles of despair. Come out of the prison of your disillusionment. Make ready to greet the Great One on the day of his rising. Let your hearts and minds be ready to receive the message that he shall give, and to obey the words of counsel you shall surely be given, for truly from a greater world and a brighter land than ours has come the Great One to preserve us!"

WITHIN an hour Hennessey's words were flashed around the world.

Terry was the only one of the scientists on the project who heard about it. He went over to the museum in the afternoon and found Underwood and Dreyer at the test board.

"Some crackpot preacher this morning gave out a sermon on Oscar here." He jerked a thumb toward the bath. "He says we've got the solution to all the world's ills. He's calling on the people to worship Oscar."

"You might know some fool thing like that would happen."

Dreyer emitted a single, explosive puff of cigar smoke. "A religious cult based upon this alien intelligence. We should have predicted that development. I wonder why our computations failed to indicate it."

"I think it's dangerous," said Terry. "It could turn into serious business."

"What do you mean? I don't get it," said Underwood.

"Don't you see the implications? The whole trouble with our culture is disillusionment, lack of leadership. If this thing turns out to be sentient, intelligent—even superior—why, it could become anything the people wanted to make it, president, dictator, god, or what not."

"Oh, take it easy," Underwood said. "This is just one little tinhorn preacher who probably didn't have more than a hundred in his congregation. The news broadcasts must have treated it as a humorous commentary on our experiments. Just the same, we should never have allowed the news to be broadcast. It all started with that hysterical mob the day we brought the protoplasm here."

Dreyer shook his head amid the smoke aura. "No. It began long ago when the first cave man plastered up his clay gods and found them cracked in the SUR and washed away with the rains. It began when the first cave chieftain was slain by a rival leader and his disillusioned followers looked about for a new 'head man.' It has been going on ever since."

"IT'S no concern of ours," said Underwood.

Dreyer went on slowly, "As one by one the gods and chieftains fell, men cast about for new leaders who would bear the burdens of mankind and show the way to that illusive paradise that all men sought. Through the ages there have always been those who would let themselves be lifted up and called great, who would undertake to lead. Some had their eyes on faraway starry places that man could never reach and their disciples fell away, heartbroken and discouraged. Others sought their goal by mastery over foreign men and nations and bathed their followers in blood and disaster. But always their star fell and men never found the elusive goal which they could not name nor define."

"And so the Age of Disillusion," said Underwood bitterly.

"But disillusion is a healthy thing. It leads to reality."

"How can you call this healthy?" Underwood demanded. "Men believe in nothing. They have lost faith in life itself."

"Faith in life? I wonder what that means," said Dreyer, musingly. "Watch your extensions, Dr. Underwood."

Underwood flushed, recalling Illia's remark that Dreyer would tear off every other word and throw it back at him. "All right, then. There are no governments, no leaders, no religions to lean upon in times of need, because men have no confidence in such sources."

"All of which is a sign that they are approaching a stage in which they will no longer need such support. And, like a baby in his first steps, they stumble and fall. They get bruised and cry, as I detect that many of our scientists have done, else they would not have run away to Venus and other places."

Underwood blinked from the sting of Dreyer's rebuke. "That's the second time I've been accused of running away," he said.

"No offense," Dreyer said. "I am merely stating facts. That you do not believe them is not to your condemnation, only a commentary on the state of your knowledge. But our discussion is on the restoration of the alien, and your knowledge may have far-reaching effects in the disposition of this project."

"Policy is controlled by the directors, who will be guided by your recommendations—"

Dreyer shook his head. "No, I think not, unless it pleases them. Should I ever recommend destruction of the alien, I would have to work through you. And that would take much convincing, would it not?"

"Plenty," said Underwood. "Are you recommending that now?"

"Not yet. No, not yet."

Slowly, Dreyer moved away toward the massive bath that housed the alien, Demarzule, Hetrarra of Sirenia, the Great One.

UNDERWOOD watching the beetle-back of the semanticist felt deflated by the encounter. Dreyer seemed always so nerve-rackingly calm. Underwood wondered if it were possible to acquire such immunity to turmoil.

He turned back to Terry, who had stood in silent agreement with Dreyer. "How are you and Phyfe coming along?"

"It's a slow business, even with the help of the key in the repository. That was apparently pure Stroid III, but we have two other languages or dialects that are quite different and we seem to have more specimens of those than we do of Stroid III. Phyfe thinks he's on the way to cracking both Stroid I and II, though.

Personally, I'd like to get back out to the asteroids, if it weren't for Demarzule. I wasn't meant to be a scholar."

"Stick with it. I'm hoping that we can have some kind of idea what the Stroid civilization was like by the time Demarzule revives."

"How is it coming?"

"Cell formation is taking place, but how organs will ever develop is more than I can see. We're just waiting and observing. Four motion picture cameras are constantly at work, some through electron microscopes. At the end of six months we'll at least have a record of what occurred, regardless of what it is."

The mass of life grew and multiplied its millions of cells. Meanwhile, another growth, less tangible but no less real, was swiftly rising and spreading through the Earth. The mind of each man it encompassed was one of its cells, and they were multiplying no less rapidly than those of the growth within the marble museum building. The leadership of men by men had proven false beyond all hope of ever restoring the dream of a mortal man who could raise his fellows to the heights of the stars. But the Great One was something else again. Utterly beyond all Earthly build and untainted with the flaws of Earthmen, he was the gift of the gods to man—he was a god who would lift man to the eternal heights of which he had dreamed.

The flame spread and leaped the oceans of Earth. It swept up all creeds and races and colors.

Delmar Underwood looked up from his desk in annoyance as a pompous, red-faced man of short, stout build was ushered in by his secretary. The man halted halfway between the door and the desk and bowed slightly.

He said, "I address the Prophet Underwood by special commission of the Disciples."

"What the devil—?" Underwood frowned and extended a hand toward a button. But he didn't ring. The visitor extended an envelope.

"And by special authorization of Director Boarder of the Institute!"

STILL keeping his eyes on the man, Underwood accepted the envelope and ripped it open. In formal language and the customary red tape manner, it instructed Underwood to hear the visitor, one William B. Hennessey, and grant the request that Hennessey would make.

Underwood knew him now. His throat felt suddenly dry. "What's this all about?"

The man shrugged disparagingly. "I am only a poor Disciple of the Great One, who has been commissioned by his fellows to seek a favor at the hands of the Prophet Underwood."

As Underwood looked into the man's eyes, he felt a chill, and a wave of apprehension swept over him with staggering force.

"Sit down," he said. "What is it you want?" He wished Dreyer were here to place some semantic evaluation upon this crazy incident.

"The Disciples of the Great One would have the privilege of viewing the Master," said Hennessey as he sat down near the desk. "You scientists are instruments selected for a great task. The Great One did not come only to a select few. He came to all mankind. We request the right to visit the temple quietly and view the magnificent work you are doing as you restore our Master to life so that we may receive of his great gifts."

Underwood could picture the laboratory filled with bowing, praying, yelling, fanatic worshippers crowding around, destroying equipment and probably trying to walk off with bits of holy protoplasm. He pressed a switch and spun a dial savagely. In a moment the face of Director Boarder was on the tiny screen before him.

"This fanatic Hennessey is here. I just wanted to check on the possible liability before having him thrown out on his ear."

Boarder's face grew frantic.

"Don't do that! You got my note? Do exactly as I said. Those are orders!"

"But we can't carry on an experiment with a bunch of fanatics yapping at our heels."

"I DON'T care how you do it. You've got to give them what they want. Either that or fold up the experiment. The latest semiweekly poll shows they effectively control eighty million votes. You know what that means. One word to the Congressional scientific committee and all of us would be out on our ear."

"We could shut the thing up and call it off. The protoplasm would just quietly die and then what would these birds have to worship?"

"Destruction of government property *can* carry the death penalty," said Boarder ominously. "Besides, you're too much of the scientist to do that. You want to see the thing through just as much as the rest of us do. If I had the slightest fear that you'd destroy it, I'd yank you out of there before you knew where you were—but I haven't any such fears."

"Yes, you're right, but these—" Underwood made a grimace as if he were trying to swallow an oyster with fur on.

"I know. We've got to put up with it. The scientist who survives in this day and age is the one who adjusts to his environment." Boarder grinned sourly.

"I went out to space to escape the environment. Now I'm right back in it, only worse than ever."

"Well, look, Underwood, why can't you just build a sort of balcony with a ramp running across the lab so that these Disciples of the Great One can look down into the bath? You could feed them in at one end of the building and run them out the other. That way it wouldn't upset you. After all, it's only going to last six months."

"When the Stroid revives, they'll probably want to put him on a throne with a radiant halo about his head." Boarder laughed. "If he represents the civilization whose artifacts we've found on the asteroids, I think he'll take care of his 'Disciples' in short order. Anyway, you'll have to do as they demand. It won't last long."

Boarder cut off and Underwood turned back to the bland Hennessey, who sat as if nothing would ever disturb him.

"You see," Hennessey said. "I knew what the outcome would be. I had faith in the Great One."

"Faith! You knew that the scientific committee would back you up because you represent eighty million neurotic crackpots. What will you do when your Great One wakes up and tells you all to go to hell?"

Hennessey smiled quietly. "He won't. I have faith."

CHAPTER SIX

TWO DAYS later, Underwood received a call from Phyfe, asking for an appointment. It was urgent; that was all Phyfe would tell him.

The archeologist had not heard of the demands of the Disciples. He was surprised to see the construction under way in the great central hall where the restoration equipment was installed.

He found Underwood with Illia in the laboratory examining films of the protoplasmic growth.

"What are you building out there?" he asked. "I thought you had all the equipment in."

"A monument to human stupidity," Underwood growled. Then he told Phyfe of the orders he had received. "We're putting in a balcony so that the faithful can look down upon their Great One. Boarder says we'll have to put up with this nonsense for six months."

"Why six months?"

"Demarzule will be revived by then or else we'll have failed. In either case, the Disciples will have come to an end."

"Why?"

Underwood glanced up in irritation. "If he's dead, they won't have anything to worship. And if he lives, he certainly won't have anything to do with them."

"I could ask another 'why,'" said Phyfe, "but I'll put it this way. You know nothing of how he will act if he lives. And if he dies he'll probably be a martyr that will establish a new worldwide religion—with those of us who have had to do with this experiment and its failure being burned at the stake."

UNDERWOOD laid down the sheaf of films. Out among the asteroids he had learned to respect the old archeologist's opinions, but Dreyer had already laid more of a burden upon him than he felt he should bear.

"The technological aspects of this problem are more than you say you have found?"

"Fortunately for us, certain Stroid records were small metallic plates whose molecular structure was altered according to script or vocal patterns. Some of the boys in the lab have developed a device for listening to the audio records. We have actually heard the *voices* of the Stroids! At least there are sounds that resemble a spoken language. But it is what we have found on the written records that brought me here.

"More than eighty-five years ago, the most fortunate find previous to the discovery of the repository was made. An extensive cache of historical records was uncovered by Dickens, one of the early workers in the field. They were almost fused together, and the molecular alteration was barely traceable due to exposure to terrific heat. But we've succeeded in separating the plates and transferring their records in amplified form to new sheets. And we can read them. We have a remarkably complete section of Stroid history just before their extermination, and, if we are reading it correctly, there's a surprising fact about them."

"What is that?"

"They were not native to this Solar System. They were extra-galactic refugees whose home world had been destroyed in something completely revolting an intellect that would foresee the doom of a world and set about to assure its own preservation."

"But that is only your own subjective extension," Illia answered. "There is no such semantic concept in the idea."

"ISN'T there? The egotism, the absolute lack of concern for a creature's fellows—those are semantically contained in it. And that is why I'm more than a little afraid of what we shall find if we do succeed in reviving this creature. How is it developing?"

"It seems to be going through a sort of conventional embryonic growth," Illia answered. "It's already passed a pseudo-blastic stage. So far, it has generally mammalian characteristics; more than that is impossible to say." But what to do about this new evidence is enough for my mental capacity. I can't and won't give a damn about any other aspects."

"You must!" Phyfe's eyes were suddenly afire, demanding, unyielding. "We have new evidence—Terry may have been right when he asked to have the protoplasm destroyed."

Illia froze. "What evidence?"

"What type of mentality would attempt to preserve itself through a planetary catastrophe that destroyed all its contemporaries?" asked Phyfe. "I find some great interstellar conflict and whose enemies eventually traced them and destroyed for the second time the world on which they lived. Out of all that ancient people, destroyed as completely as was Carthage, only this single individual remained.

"Do you see the significance of that? If he lives, he will live again with the same war-born hate and lust for revenge that filled him as he saw his own world fall!"

"It won't survive the knowledge that all that he fought for disappeared geologic ages past," objected Underwood. "Besides, you are contradicting yourself. If he was so unconcerned about his own world, perhaps he had no interest in the conflict. Maybe he was the supreme genius of his day and wanted only to escape from a useless carnage that he could not stop."

"No, there is no contradiction," said Phyfe earnestly. "That is typical of the war leader who has brought his people to destruction. At the moment when disaster overwhelms them, he thinks only of himself. The specimen we have here is a supreme example of what such egocentric desires for self-preservation lead to."

Phyfe abruptly rose from the chair and tossed a sheaf of papers on the laboratory bench. "Here it is. Read it for yourself. It's a pretty free translation of the story we found on Dickens' records."

HE left abruptly. Illia and Underwood turned to the short script he had left behind and began reading.

The hundred mighty vessels of the Sirenian Empire flung themselves across space that was made tangible by their velocity. The impregnable heart of the fleet was deep in the hull of the flagship, *Hebrian*, where the Sirenian Hetrarra, Demarzule, slumped sullenly before the complex panel that reported all the workings of his vast fleet.

Beside him was the old but sinewy figure of Toshmere, the genius who had saved this remnant of the once mighty empire that could have put a million vessels like these into space at one time.

Toshmere said, "Further flight is useless. Our instruments show that the Dragbora are gaining. Their fleet outnumbers us ten to one. Even with my protective screens, we can't hope to resist long. They've got the one weapon we can't withstand. They're determined to wipe out the last of the Sirenian Empire."

"And I'm determined to wipe out the last of the Dragbora!" Demarzule snapped in sudden fury. He rose out of the chair and paced the room. "I shall live! I shall live to see their world blasted to energy and the last Dragbor dead. Is the repository nearly ready?"

Toshmere nodded.

"And you are certain of your method?"

"Yes. Would you care to see our final results?"

Demarzule nodded and Toshmere led the way through the door and down the long corridor to the laboratory where lay Demarzule's hopes of spanning the eons and escaping the enemy who had sworn no quarter.

The Sirenian Hetrarra watched impassively as the scientist put a small animal into a bowl-like chamber. He backed away behind a shield and pressed a switch. Instantly, the animal was bathed in a flood of orange glow and a terrible look of pain crossed the animal's face while hideous cries came from its throat.

"IT is not pleasant," observed Demarzule.

"No," said Toshmere. "But it is necessary that it be done with full consciousness of mind. Otherwise, proper restoration cannot be made."

The ruler was impassive as the animal's cries slowly died while its body melted under the glow of the beam—literally melted until it flowed into a pool at the bottom of the bowl where it quivered with residual life forces.

"Pure protoplasm," explained Toshmere. "It can be frozen to absolute zero and the remaining metabolism will be undetectable, yet life will remain, perhaps for a thousand *ela*, long enough for new worlds to form and old ones die."

"Long enough for the last Dragbor to die—while I, Demarzule, Hetrarra of Sirenia, live on in glory and triumph."

Toshmere smiled a thin smile that Demarzule did not see in his own preoccupation. What a tragedy for the civilizations of the Universe if Demarzule or any remnant of the Sirenian Empire should survive, Toshmere thought. The Dragbora had well considered their plans when they set upon a program of complete extermination for the Sirenians.

His own life would be far more worthy of salvation from the impending doom than that of Demarzule. From the first moment that he had conceived the repository and presented the idea to Demarzule, Toshmere had planned that it would hold not Demarzule, but Toshmere himself.

There was only one way to go ahead with such a gigantic project, however, and that was letting Demarzule believe that it would be for him. Since it could not be prepared in secret, Demarzule would have to assent to the construction. He would do that if he thought it were for himself. The idea would appeal to his egotistical mind; the thought of his own personality spanning the eons, while all the civilization he knew decayed and was swept away, would delight him.

"The revival," said Demarzule. "Let me see how life is to be brought back."

Toshmere swung another projector into line above the bowl and snapped another switch. Invisible rays suddenly bathed the mass of shapeless protoplasm within the bowl. As they watched, it quivered and flowed, swiftly changing shapes, and growth and life took possession of it.

THE ruler of the Sirenians watched the reformation of the animal in the bowl. Limbs and torso formed in shadowy gray outline, then abruptly solidified and the animal leaped up, alive and startled.

Even Demarzule was somewhat taken aback by the seeming miracle. "It is swift," he remarked. "The specimen is unharmed?"

"Completely," said Toshmere. "The process is not so rapid after a long period of time has elapsed. The level of life is very low, but never will it completely disappear. The lower it is, however, the longer it takes for restoration. After many hundred *ela*, it might require as much as a *tor-ele.*"

"But it would be sure to succeed regardless?"

Toshmere nodded.

The hundred ships of the Sirenian bore on their steady course with the enemy constantly gaining even though Galaxies away. At last the lookout spotted a likely System in which the fifth planet showed signs of habitability. Demarzule ordered preparations be made for a halt.

The planet they found was inhabited by the remnants of a dying civilization that had retrograded almost to its infancy. The opposition offered was quickly disposed of and the Sirenian refugees began the frantic and hopeless task of constructing defenses against the coming of the overwhelming force of the Dragbora, defenses they knew were as penetrable as air to the new, fearful weapon strength of the enemy.

But while gigantic screen generators were swiftly reared against the sky and beam emplacements were dug, the best and wisest of the scientists were busy preparing the repository for the Hetrarra, Demarzule.

The huge, crystal-like container, which would be rendered impervious to all known forces except the key frequency whose formula was inscribed upon the outside, was to be lowered thousands of feet into the great ore beds of the planet, in the hope of avoiding the final blast that would shear the planet.

Two men would go into that repository, but only one would survive the eons.

Toshmere was the only one completely acquainted with the entire process so that it would be necessary for him to direct the operation of the instruments. But Toshmere knew that Demarzule had no intention of allowing him to leave the repository with knowledge of its secrets—any more than Toshmere intended that Demarzule should be the one to benefit by those secrets.

For three *tor-ela* the Sirenians worked frantically, putting up then mighty defense works, and then their lookout posted a hundred thousand light years out in space announced the arrival of the terrible Dragboran fleet—just before a tongue of light from that fleet lashed out at him and swept him into the eternities.

TOSHMERE approached Demarzule in his headquarters as the word came. "There is not much time left, Hetrarra. The repository is ready."

Demarzule looked out upon the sprawling works and great machines so pitifully huddled together on an alien planet. This was all that remained of the vast empire, which he had dreamed of extending to the limits of space itself, the empire over which he was to have been supreme Hetrarra. And in a short moment this remnant would be wiped out under the devastating supremacy of the now mightier Dragbora.

He looked at Toshmere hesitantly. In the face of certain death the old, lean, sinewy scientist showed nothing but calm. The Hetrarra took one final glance at the remnants of his Sirenian Empire and nodded.

"I am ready," he said.

They went out to the entrance to the shaft leading toward the heart of the planet. The shaft had been built with the knowledge of only a few Sirenians and none of them were aware of its purpose, thinking rather that it was a means of defense.

Nobody saw the Hetrarra and the genius Toshmere enter the elevator that carried them forever into the depths below the surface of the planet.

Underwood and Illia came to the end of the page and Underwood swore softly as he thumbed through the few remaining sheets. There was no more about the ancient Demarzule and Toshmere.

The writer of the history had apparently been one of the Sirenian scientists, a confident and friend of Toshmere who had been close to him in those last days. He had been one of the few to witness the descent of the two into the depths of the planet, but he knew nothing of what happened when they reached the bottom and sealed the repository.

He did not know which one had survived in that mighty struggle that must have taken place below.

And shortly no one of the Sirenians cared what the fate of their deserting Hetrarra might have been, for the great Dragboran fleet was upon them. With the mighty, unknown weapon that struck terror to the mightiest of Sirenia, they sped out of space and swiftly nullified the Sirenian defenses. It was a carnage that was frightful even to the

Sirenians, so schooled in the methods of shedding blood. Their defenses might not have existed for all the effect they had on their enemy. At first one by one, and then by tens, the operators were touched by death and their machines turned to molten ruin.

At last, when only incandescent metal and sprawling dead lay of the Sirenian fleet, the enemy ships withdrew, and the handful of survivors dared hope that there might be escape for them.

BUT there was none. As the fleet withdrew beyond their vision, a single small ship appeared in the heavens and they screamed with the knowledge of what it was. But they were dead long before the planet exploded into its component fragments, which hurtled in all directions into space.

Underwood put the manuscript down, his mind reluctant to close the scene of vast and terrible battle that had occurred so long ago. It had answered some of the problems raised by a Stroidal archeology. It explained the utter lack of relationship between Stroid III, which was the language of the Sirenians, and Stroid I and II, which were undoubtedly native to the vanished planet.

But this snatch of history prepared by the unknown scientist companion of Toshmere raised the greatest enigma of all.

Illia's eyes looked up into Underwood's. "Who could have won?" she said. "If it was Toshmere, the alien will be all that we hoped he would be. If it is Demarzule, then Terry is right—he should be destroyed."

Underwood glanced out toward the nutrient bath where the alien slept, where the shadowy outlines of a faintly human figure already appeared in the misty depths of the nutrient solution.

"It's got to be Toshmere," he said and hoped he was right.

CHAPTER SEVEN

THE viewing balcony above the floor of the museum hall was completed and the disciples of the Great One began to flow through in a never-ending stream. To Underwood, it was a sickening, revolting sight. As he watched the faces of those who came and worshipped at the shrine, he saw them transformed, as if they had seen some great vision. They came with burdens of care lining their faces—all ages, young and old— and they left with shining eyes and uplifted faces. There were even sick and crippled who came and left crutches, eyeglasses and trusses.

Twice a day, William B. Hennessey stood upon the balcony and uttered a prayer to the Great One, and the stream of fanatic worshipers stopped and bowed down.

One of Underwood's biologists, Craven, was so fascinated by the exhibition of mass hysteria that he asked for permission to make a study of it.

Underwood forced the spectacle out of his mind. He knew he couldn't endure staying there at the museum if he allowed his mind to dwell upon the decadence of mankind.

The mass of protoplasm in the nutrient bath was becoming more and more a typical mammalian embryo, anthropomorphic in most respects, but with differences that Illia and Underwood could not assign to the natural development of the creature, or to the unusual circumstances of its revival, because there was no standard with which to compare it.

Then, one day near the end of the fourth month, Underwood received an urgent call from Phyfe.

"Come over at once!" he said. "We've found the answer in the repository. We know who the Great One is."

"Who?"

"I want you to see for yourself."

Underwood swore as Phyfe cut off. He turned his observations over to the operator on duty and left the building. The lexicography and philography sections of the institute were in an old sprawling block across the city by the spaceport; the semantics section was also housed there. The repository had been taken there for continued examination.

Dreyer and Phyfe met him. The old archeologist was trembling with excitement. "I've found the mummy!" he said.

"What mummy?"

"The mummy of the one in the repository who was killed by the successful one."

"Who was it?"

"You'll see. He left a record for the discoverers of the repository."

THEY went into the enclosure that had been built to house the alien structure. Inside, the repository looked many times the size it had appeared in space. Underwood followed them into the familiar passages. They went down into the main chamber, which had held the protoplasm of the Great One. Then Underwood observed an opening leading lower down.

"You found a way into the rest of the repository?"

"Yes, and how unfortunate we were not to have found our way into that portion first. But come."

Phyfe disappeared through the narrow opening and they passed three levels filled with unknown artifacts. Then at last they came to the smallest chamber formed by the curve of the outside hull. It was too small for them to stand upright and filled rapidly with Dreyer's cigar smoke.

"There it is, right where we found it," said Phyfe.

Underwood looked at the thing without recognition. It appeared as if a rather huge, dried-up bat had been carelessly tossed into the corner of the chamber.

"Completely desiccated," said Phyfe. "He didn't stay here long enough between his death and the destruction of the planet for decay to set in. He simply dried up as the molecules of water were frozen and dispersed. I wish there were some way the biologists could find to restore him. He's so shapeless it's difficult to tell what he looked like."

"But who is he?"

"Here is the record he left. Apparently they had some kind of small electric tool they carried with them to write on metallic surfaces. How they read them is a mystery because we have to have a mass of equipment as big as this chamber to decipher the stuff. Here are photographs of his message that we have rendered visible."

Underwood took the sheaf of photographs. They showed the walls of the chamber including the dried mummy lying inert where it had fallen in pain and death. But standing out in sharp white characters was a lengthy inscription written by the ancient creature of eons ago.

"Can you read it?" asked Phyfe. Underwood scanned the characters and nodded slowly. He had not been able to keep up on the language as Phyfe had, but he could read it now with fair facility.

The first part of the message was a brief reiteration of the history of the ill-fated refugees that he already knew, but then he came to a fresh portion.

"Demarzule has slain me!" the message read.

THE words were like pellets of ice suddenly shot with bullet speed into his face. He looked up at the impassive faces of the other two men and read there the decision they had made.

Then, slowly, his eyes lowered to the sheet again and he went on deliberately with the reading.

"I have attempted to get to the main chamber and destroy the transformation equipment, but I cannot. Demarzule has learned how to operate the equipment. Though there is nothing creative in him, and all his aims are of conquest and destruction, he still has the command of vast stores of Sirenian science.

"I am not a warrior or clever in the ways of fighting. It was not difficult for Demarzule to best me. I die soon, therefore it is for you who may read this in the ages to come. This is my message to you, my warning: Destroy the contents of the protoplasm chamber without mercy. Demarzule is there and he will be the scourge of any civilization in which he arises. He dreams of conquest and he will not rest until he is master of the Universe. He has destroyed galaxies; he will destroy others if he lives again. Kill him! Erase all knowledge of the dreadful Sirenian Empire from your memory!"

"Should you be tempted to restore the Hetrarra and believe your science a match for ours, remember that the knowledge required to enter this repository is only the minimum. It is the lowest common denominator of our civilization. Therefore, kill—"

The record ended with the last scrawled admonition of the ancient scientist, Toshmere.

For long moments, the chamber of the repository was silent. Phyfe made no comment as Underwood finished. He saw the tensing of the physicist's jaw and the staring fixation of his eyes, as if he would penetrate the ages with his naked vision and try to picture the dying scientist scrawling his message on the walls of the death chamber.

Then Phyfe said at last, "We can't risk the revival of Demarzule now, Del. Think what it would mean to turn loose a mentality having command of such a superior science."

"We're not exactly planning to turn him loose," said Underwood defensively. "We'll still have control when he revives. He can be kept in suitable confinement—and finally disposed of, if necessary. It seems worth it if we could tap the science he knows."

"Are you forgetting that we do not have control of him in any sense of the word? The Disciples have. We're under direction of the Institute, which can be wiped out in an instant by the Science Committee. They, in turn, are mere puppets of the Disciples who hold the voting power. When Demarzule revives, he'll have a ready made following who'll regard him not only as Emperor, but as god. I tell you we have no alternative but destruction."

UNDERWOOD'S jaws tightened further. Within his grasp was a science that might represent thousands of years of normal development of the Solar system. He could not give up a gift such as the Sirenian culture offered.

Then his eyes found those of Dreyer, who had said nothing, who sat on his heels placidly in his haze of smoke. And there he read the irrevocable answer.

"All right," he said. "You win—you and old Toshmere. Let's get inside to a phone and I'll give the word to turn the radiation off."

Swiftly now they clambered up the stairs as if to escape some foul tomb of the long-dead. They hurried into the building and into the office of Phyfe. There Underwood called Illia.

She answered instantly, as if she had been waiting for his message, fearfully and without hope.

"It's Demarzule, the conqueror," he said. "Turn off the radiation and drain the tank. We'll stand the consequences of that, but we dare not go on with the restoration."

Illia bit her lip and nodded. "It might have been Earth's great chance," she said, and there was something like a sob in her voice. "I'll turn it off at once."

Phyfe said, "Know what, Underwood? There's going to be trouble over this. I think I'll ask for a transfer back to the expedition. Would you like to come along with us?"

"I suppose so, but I'm afraid the Scientific Committee won't let us get away that easily. You and I are through for the rest of our lives. Didn't you think of that, Phyfe? We'll be lucky if we don't have to spend the rest of out lives in prison. But, Dreyer, you don't need to be caught in this. Get away before they come for us."

"I hadn't considered it that way," said Phyfe, "but I suppose you're right. The Disciples won't be likely to let us get away this easy, will they?"

Before Dreyer could speak, a call came through on the office interphone. Phyfe switched on and the frantic face of Esmond, one of the junior archeologists, appeared.

"Phyfe!" the man exclaimed. "I don't know what it is all about, but the police are on the way down to your office. They have warrants for the arrest of you and Dr. Underwood!"

PHYFE nodded. "Thanks, Esmond. I'll see that there's no trouble for you because of this. I appreciate it. They didn't lose any time, did they?" he said to Underwood. "But as long as Demarzule has been destroyed, we've accomplished what we've tried to do."

"Wait a minute!" said Underwood. "Do we know that Demarzule has been destroyed? Something must have gone wrong; the police came too quickly."

"Look!" Shaken out of his customary calm, Dreyer was pointing through the window across the city.

There, where they knew the Carlson to be, was a great shining bubble of light.

"A force shell!" Underwood exclaimed. "How—?"

"They have evidently been prepared for a long time," said Dreyer.

Underwood tried the phone again and called for Illia, but there was no response from inside the shell of impenetrable energy. A moment of terrible fear caught Underwood up in its turbulence. What of Illia? Was she all right?

"Whatever the answer," Phyfe exclaimed, "it's a ten to one shot that Demarzule is not destroyed. In which case we'd better not be taken!"

"What can we do? They'll have the building surrounded. There'll be no chance of getting out."

"This is an old building. There are rooms and sub-basements that few know about, and the staff are all scientists. They'll be loyal. Come on!"

"No, wait," said Underwood. "Nothing can be gained by my hiding in this rabbit warren underneath the city. There is only one chance of destroying Demarzule, and that is my getting back to the museum and doing it personally."

"You're crazy! The Disciples will never let you back in there. Come on, man, we're wasting time!"

"You two go on and hide, Phyfe. I'll try to lay the blame on you and a group of scientists, and swear my own innocence. It's the only way to get access to Demarzule. Get going. Wait—have you got a burner?"

"In the drawer there. We'd better take it."

UNDERWOOD yanked open the drawer and found the weapon. Then he held the muzzle a short distance from his upper arm and fired. His face twisted involuntarily with pain and Phyfe stared in amazement. "What for?" the archeologist demanded.

Underwood tossed him the weapon as the room filled with the stench of his burned flesh. "You shot me when I refused to order the radiation off. It's a thin story and if they won't believe it I'll be a goner. But if we don't risk it, Demarzule will be the next ruler of Earth."

Dreyer nodded. "It's a chance. You'd better take it. Good luck."

A sudden commotion down the hall outside the door warned of the approach of the arresting officers. Phyfe gave a last despairing glance at Underwood, who was clutching the painful burn on his arm. The archeologist turned and darted swiftly through a door at the rear of the office, followed by Dreyer.

Almost instantly the main door was flung wide and two heavily armed officers burst into the room. Their impulsive charge was halted as they stared at the groaning physicist.

"Get help," Underwood said desperately. "I've got to get to the museum. It may not be too late if Dr. Morov turned the beam off. Phyfe forced me to order it stopped. Scientists don't want the Great One revived. He shot me when I refused. Would have killed me if—"

Underwood sagged forward over the desk and fainted from the pain he could no longer endure.

CHAPTER EIGHT

THE BEEFY Committee Chairman regarded Underwood in the crowded hearing room with the self-righteous, detached anger of one who represents approximately a million voters. He told Underwood, "The reprieve you have been granted is not given because your crime is considered any less grievous. Because your act threatened a possession of this government, which may potentially change the entire life of Earth for the better, your crime is deemed punishable by death.

"However, you are the only man capable of directing the project. Therefore, your sentence is commuted and will be resolved if you successfully conclude the project of restoring the Great One. Only by so doing may you prove your innocence. If an accident brings failure, three separate committees of competent scientists will bring a verdict that will determine whether you shall live."

"And what of Dr. Illia Morov?"

"Her sentence is life imprisonment for her attempt to destroy the Great One."

"She obeyed my orders given under duress, as I have explained. I cannot be responsible for the successful restoration if I am to be denied competent assistance. Her knowledge is absolutely essential to the success of the work."

The chairman frowned. "The civil courts have exercised judgment. It may be possible for her to be bound over to us as you were, but her sentence cannot be commuted except by special appeal and retrial. We will see what can be done in the matter."

Underwood choked back the blast he would like to have hurled, his denunciation of everything that symbolized the rotten culture into which he had been driven by accident of birth. He dared hope only that Illia would be granted leniency, that somehow they could think of a way to destroy the alien.

HE had forced his mind shut against all possibilities of antagonism between the culture of Sirenia and that of Earth. Now he was aware of the full potentialities of a mind like Demarzule's, armed with Sirenian super-science, loose among Earthmen, and he was motivated by an urge to destroy that was as great as his former desire to save and restore. Earth was in bad enough shape without a Demarzule.

For himself and for Illia he almost dared hope that they might find escape from the wrath of the Disciples—perhaps to the Venusian colonies—for there was nothing left for them upon Earth.

The Chairman added with deadly significance, "Just to make sure that no risk is being taken with the Great One, you will be constantly attended by an armed guard. You will carefully explain every move, before you make it—otherwise you may not be alive to make it."

That was all then. Underwood was led out under heavy guard between the rows of watchers, most of whom were Disciples. He could almost feel the doubt and hate directed toward him.

When he returned to the museum, guards of the Disciples stood everywhere. The scientists worked with blank, expressionless faces—and guns at their backs.

Craven, the biologist who had made detailed studies of the Disciples, glanced up from his desk uncertainly as Underwood walked in. He had been placed in charge temporarily during the absence of Illia and Underwood.

"I'm sorry about—everything, Del. Especially about Dr. Morov. When I saw her turning off the radiation I knew that something was wrong, but when she said that word had come from you to do it, I knew it was time for us to take over. I'm glad that they found you were not in sympathy with the scientists who wanted the Great One destroyed."

His words refused to fall into place in Underwood's mind so that they made sense. But after a moment it came—though there were personal guards attached to every other scientist in the place, there was none standing watch over Craven. So Craven was one of them, a Disciple. And if Craven, why not others?

But the biologist had been studying the Disciples from a scientific standpoint. Had he succumbed in spite of that or because of it?

It was a problem beyond Underwood's grasp. He evaded a reply with: "How is everything going? Is the cell division increasing? Intensities of radiation and nutrient solution being stepped up according to our plans?"

Craven nodded. "As far as I can tell the Great One is developing properly. You'll want to make a complete check, of course. The daily reports are ready for your inspection."

Underwood grunted and left, followed by the silent, ever-present guard. He went out to the test board where the trio of technicians kept constant watch on the processes. Everything was functioning according to instructions in the repository—instructions prepared by Toshmere.

Everywhere were the guards, and up on the balcony were the unending streams of Disciples of the Great One. It was like a nightmare to Underwood. How had control of the project slipped away? It had happened so rapidly and insidiously that he had not been aware. But that was not it; the truth was that he had never had control. From the moment that the scientists brought the protoplasm of Demarzule to Earth and revealed the story of their find, it had been inevitable.

Inevitable, Underwood thought, and the greatest semantic blunder ever made. It might have been a good thing if it had been Toshmere instead of Demarzule. The world had had no leaders for a century except the bungling, vote-buying politicians. Toshmere might have led them back to a semblance of strength and initiative, but what would the conqueror and destroyer, Demarzule, do?

THE following day, Illia returned. Underwood was shocked by her appearance. She had dreamed of a new and saner world to be brought by the alien out of space, just as Underwood had dreamed of a new world of science to be revealed. And now their dreams had turned into a monster.

The worst of their meeting was that there was nothing they could say to each other. Illia came into the tiny world of nightmare under the force shell in the custody of guards, and one remained constantly by her side as she resumed her duties. Likewise, Underwood's own guard never left him. Underwood had to maintain his pretense of innocence before them.

"It was Phyfe and Dreyer," he said to Illia. "I'm glad you didn't succeed in destroying Demarzule."

She hesitated an instant, then nodded with understanding. "I didn't know what you were doing, but I supposed there was some reason. I didn't suspect their evil plot."

AND that was all. There was nothing more they could say. Nothing of her despair at her white-faced, lusterless appearance. Nothing of her lost dream.

The mass grew and took shape. Limbs and head and torso were distinctly formed and losing their fearsome, embryonic cast. The creature would be of adult form and shape, Underwood saw and would not represent a return to infancy. It was fully eight feet tall and was humanoid to the extent of having four limbs and head and torso, but the X-rays showed radical differences in bone and joint structure. One cranial and two abdominal organs were completely unfamiliar and could be identified by none of the biologists on the project.

For a time Underwood nursed the hope that these structural differences might make it impossible for Demarzule to survive on Earth. But the further the lungs developed, the more evident it became that the Sirenian would adapt to the atmosphere. As to food there was little doubt that nourishment would be no problem. By the sixth month, too, it was hopeless to assume that anything would go wrong with the process of restoration. Toshmere had planned too well.

Underwood wondered what had become of Phyfe and Dreyer, if they had been captured and killed, or if they still lived in the depths of the ancient buildings beneath the city. There had been absolutely no word. He had been kept in complete isolation since their tragic failure. He spoke to no one except the silent guards and his fellow technicians. He knew of none that he could trust, for he was certain that among the scientists working beside him, there were those whose duty it was to spy upon him. Craven, for example, had become more sullen day by day, and now he avoided Underwood almost continually, as if ashamed of the things that he believed in and had done, but unable to renounce them or help himself. The symptoms of hysteria were becoming constantly more evident.

Underwood looked for them in the other scientists, but he was not skilled enough to detect all the signs. The only way was to play safe and take no one into his confidence.

LIFE went on timelessly in the nightmare world. The light of day was completely obscured by the force shell. As Underwood strolled out of the museum building and looked up at its blackness, he recalled how it had saved the world centuries ago, when mankind had once before been on the verge of self-destruction in the dim beginnings of the atomic age. Only by the discovery of the force shell, a field impenetrable by any substance or radiation or force, had men been saved from total annihilation.

But now man was faced by another potent force of destruction—his own desire to submit to any leader who promised relief from independent responsibility and action. The alien would certainly be able to fulfill that promise where no man could, but was it worth the risk of being saddled with a bloody dictatorship?

It was fantastic, Underwood thought, that he could find no way to elude his guards and kill the growing monster. Variations in the strength of the radiation might do it, but there was no possibility of varying the radiation. The guards, whose leaders were technically trained, had access to the records of the scientists, which not only gave the details of previous work, but outlined each step until Demarzule was restored. Underwood dared not attempt departures of procedure from the written notes. The bath itself had been surrounded by a transparent guard impervious to solid shot or radiation weapons—even if he could have obtained any—nor could poisons be placed in the nutrient solution. There was simply nothing that could be done while Demarzule was still in the nutrient bath. But on the day of his arising? A desperate, last-ditch plan formed in Underwood's mind.

He explained to his guard, "When the Great One arises, it would be well for someone to welcome him in his own tongue. Only a few of us scientists are able to, and of those who can, I am the only one here. With your permission, I'll be beside him and welcome him when he rises."

The guard considered. "I'll relay your request to the First High Prophet Hennessey. If it is deemed fitting you shall be appointed to welcome the Great One."

Underwood wished that he had given Hennessey a warmer welcome that first day when the fanatic prophet came to his office, but Hennessey gave permission immediately. Underwood imagined the Prophet taking considerable satisfaction in the irony of Underwood being the first to welcome the Great One.

Mounted beside the narrow catwalk between the observation board and the bath were the controls, which would finally cut the radiation and drain the nutrient solution as the process of restoration came to an end. Here also were the water valves used to flush the bath when it had first been constructed.

In this narrow space, Underwood could escape the watching eye of his guard for an instant. He hoped to be able to cut the radiation and drain the bath prematurely. If that couldn't be done, he might fill the bath with water and drown Demarzule before the guards could intervene or reach the shutoff valve. Underwood had managed to secrete a small bar in his pocket with which he hoped to break the valve after it was opened.

The massive form of Demarzule had been stirring like an embryo for days now, and Underwood watched closely for the first attempt to rise.

That would be the earliest moment that he could hope to make an attempt to destroy the Sirenian.

He wished he could confide in Illia, but there was no chance. He feared she might have some desperate, dangerous plan of her own.

The color of the Sirenian's skin had turned a deep hue-like dark redwood, and that appeared to be its natural tone. The hair upon the head was coppery, darker than the skin. Demarzule's whole appearance was one of might and strength even as he lay quiescent. His features were bold, with wide-set eyes and sharp nose. The mouth was stern, almost harsh.

HYSTERIA among the Disciples was mounting hourly. Instead of flowing through the building along the balcony in their endless stream, they poured in and stayed, hoping to be there for the rising of the Great One. Some were pushed over and killed by the fall to the floor below. They overflowed into the main hall and swarmed about the masses of equipment. This was welcomed by Underwood, who hoped that the pressing mob might damage some of the equipment and thus bring about the end of Demarzule.

In any event, the hysteria was having its effects upon the guards who continued to watch the scientists. Their alertness and efficiency were giving way to the same tension that filled the mobs within the hall like a disease.

Underwood went sleepless for two days at the end, not daring to miss his one chance. And hundreds of the faithful who jammed the hall and thousands more who waited outside had already stood that long waiting for the miracle.

It was in early dawn when Underwood caught the first faint motion that indicated Demarzule was about to rise.

Underwood jerked a finger in the direction of the bath and looked questioningly at the guard. The man nodded and Underwood raced along the narrow catwalk.

There was no question of premature draining of the solution and cutting the radiation. It was time for that now. Demarzule was struggling upward, his lungs gasping in the first breath of Terrestrian atmosphere, which filled the upper part of the enclosure.

Underwood cut the radiation switch and twisted the valve on the water line with a mighty wrench that tore the wheel from the shaft. Water flooded into the chamber.

Demarzule struggled to a sitting position and stared as if dazed, his countenance working fearsomely.

The Disciples saw him. A shout of ecstasy thundered through the great hall and the empty rooms of the museum. And then, suddenly, there was a new sound. A single voice rang out above all the rest.

"Strike now!" it shouted. "Strike down the invader. Destroy the blasphemy of the Great One!"

UNDERWOOD'S head twisted about. There on the balcony in the place lately occupied by the Prophet, Hennessey, was Terry Bernard!

For an instant Underwood could not comprehend the meaning of it. The gun in Terry's hand flashed red. Underwood's guard slumped in his murderous rush and fell from the catwalk. He alone had seen the sudden rise of water and realized its meaning.

The cries and curses and screams and prayers that filled the hall made the previous commotion deathly silence by contrast. Sudden beams of deadly fire shot through the air, and Underwood could make no sense of it all.

Sides in the conflict began to appear. Underwood saw that some of the technicians and scientists had weapons and had disposed of their guards. Now they were firing carefully into the mob about the equipment, picking off the armed leaders.

Inside the impenetrable enclosure, the giant Sirenian staggered uncertainly as if stunned. The water was rising swiftly about his hips. The air, rushing out the oxygen intake pipe, allowed the water to rise in the otherwise hermetically sealed chamber.

A few minutes more and Demarzule would be cut off from the air supply. How long it would take to drown him, Underwood did not know. It would depend largely on his present rate of metabolism, which was a great uncertainty. But could the mob be held off that long? They had to be! He bent down and grabbed up the gun that his pursuing guard had dropped.

In the background of his mind he wondered what this sudden attack meant. How strongly organized was it, and who was behind it? Apparently Terry had given the signal for attack, and many of the scientists on the project had been prepared for it, yet Underwood had been given not the slightest hint that such attack would take place. He wondered why he had been left out.

The screaming of the hysterical Disciples was deafening as those in front tried to force their way back from the line of battle, and those in the rear tried to press forward to glimpse Demarzule.

Underwood leaped down to the floor in the sea of confusion and found himself unable to determine which way the conflict was moving.

None of the scientists were near him, only the maddened, unreasoning Disciples. He decided to stay near the water valve to make certain that it was not shut off by any of the guards.

Then two figures surged up to him and one grasped his arm. "Del! Come on, let's get out of here!"

He turned. Terry's blood streaked face was almost unrecognizable. His other hand clutched Illia's arm.

"You two go on," Underwood shouted. "Get out if you can. I've got to stay—to make sure he drowns."

"THE water's cut off! Can't you see?"

Underwood turned in horror. The water level was falling instead of rising. Someone had cut it off at one of the other valves farther along the line and had opened the drain. Air was being pumped through, for Demarzule was standing rigidly now, looking down upon the surging mass as if contemplating their fate. The bitter animal struggle for survival was gone now from his face, and only a mocking scorn was there as the mob battled before him.

"We've failed!" Underwood exclaimed. "It must have been Craven who shut the water off. We haven't a chance now."

"Not if we stay here. Come on. We can lose ourselves in this crowd and work our way outside. There's a ship waiting to take us across to Phyfe. The *Lavoisier* is manned and ready to go."

"The *Lavoisier*! Where—?"

"Who knows? Go!"

Hopelessly, Underwood allowed himself to be pushed and jammed into the thick of the mob by the frantic Terry. Signs of armed conflict were dying. Underwood supposed that the scientists had been subdued, for now the hall was completely filled with the Disciples. It was impossible, he thought, that they could ever make their way out without being apprehended. But even as doubts came, he knew that he had to get out. He had to live to make another stand against the Sirenian.

He looked back. Demarzule was standing erect now. Slowly his great arms came up and his hands extended as if in blessing and welcome, and the moaning of the ecstatic Disciples rose in wild discordance.

Then out of those alien lips, amplified a thousand fold by the audio system installed within the chamber to catch any uttered words, there came an alien voice that only Underwood could understand. And as the strange words poured forth he shuddered at their implications.

"My people." Demarzule said. "My great and mighty people!"

CHAPTER NINE

UNDERWOOD turned as if driven back by the force of the conquering voice of thunder that came from the throat of Demarzule.

No one was paying any attention to the three scientists now. The faces of the Disciples were upturned toward the Great One, waiting for further pronouncements.

Underwood, Terry and Illia shoved through the wide doors of the hall against the crowd pressing from outside. As they fought through, the enormous voice continued to assail their ears.

"I have triumphed over death," Demarzule exclaimed. "I have conquered the ages, and now I come to you, my people. I have come to lead you to the stars and to the Galaxies beyond the stars, where your very name shall cause the creatures of distant worlds to tremble."

Each word was like a knife stabbing into Underwood, for they showed that Demarzule had already comprehended the situation—and mastered it. And though the people did not understand the words, the tone of his voice carried the meaning almost equally well, and there were none in that mass of worshipping Disciples who doubted that a new day of greatness had dawned for Earth.

All semblance of organization under the small-time prophets and priests such as Hennessey had vanished. There had never been much organization because people did not trust any man sufficiently to compose a very tight or efficient organization.

This was to the benefit of the scientists. It would take time for Demarzule to become aware of the opposition and the identity of the scientists. But he must surely be aware of the attempt on his life, Underwood thought, unless full consciousness had not returned until the water had begun to subside in the chamber, and Demarzule had not realized the significance of it.

But Underwood did not believe that. Demarzule had exhibited such rapid grasp of the attitude of the Disciples that he probably possessed a semantic accuracy in his thinking which would shame the best of Earth's scientists.

The three were making more rapid progress now as they pushed out into the part of the mob that could not see Demarzule. Under the black dome of the force shell, as far as they could see, the area between the building and the outer edge of the shell was filled with struggling humanity. The words of Demarzule could be heard only faintly.

"The north gate," Illia said. "That is the widest. Maybe the guard system has broken down completely—"

TERRY nodded. "It looks like it. That's the closest to our flier, anyway. If we are challenged, let's carry Illia and explain she was injured in the mob. That might get us through. If not, keep your gun ready."

Underwood assented. He felt as if this were some nightmare from which he was struggling to awaken—unsuccessfully. He wondered what had happened to the other scientists on the project, and to those who had attempted the storming of the building. Had they all perished in the short and futile battle?

He had to admit to himself that at times, during those long days under the surveillance of the Disciple guards, he had wondered if there wouldn't have been some chance of utilizing Demarzule's science without danger. That hope, however, had been finally and completely blasted by Demarzule's arising. The Sirenian had not changed in half a million years.

As they savagely thrust through, Underwood considered the course that would probably be followed by Demarzule. He would gather about him a puppet organization of administrators who would take on a priestly sanctification before the people because of their nearness to the Great One. The organization would tighten about the Earth, enfolding the willing devotees, ruthlessly wiping out small centers of opposition that might spring up.

At the command of the Disciples would be the world's weapons and factories. And added to these would be the fearful science—and unknown weapons of the Sirenian.

What force could hold back this avalanche?

The answer was: *None.* There was no force that could touch him, nothing the scientists could do to prevent the unleashed forces of Earth from sweeping the Galaxies.

Flight. That was the only recourse for those who wished to escape the debacle. But it must be more than flight. However hopeless it seemed, those of Earth's scientists who could be gathered must be dedicated to the task of Demarzule's overthrow, the saving of Earthmen from an insane course of conquest.

CLOSE TO the north gate, the distorting energies of the force shell were led around a portion of space to form an opening in the wall. Word of the rising of the Great One had spread like a virus and thousands were gathered beyond the shell, trying in vain to force their way in. All semblance of attempting to guard the entrances seemed to have vanished as the trio forced their way through the opening and out into the sunlight that seemed utterly blinding to Illia and Underwood, who had not seen it for so long.

For a moment Underwood wondered if they could not have remained inside the Carlson and taken a chance on shooting Demarzule when he came out of the protecting shield about the bath. But he knew better. Demarzule would not come out until the room was cleared and the faithful were standing guard with their guns ready to blast any would-be assassin.

No, they were on the only course open to them. They were committed to it now; there was no turning back.

At last they came out into a relatively free space where they could move rapidly. Underwood caught sight of the small three-man flier atop a low rise, a mile from the museum.

"What about the others?" Underwood said as they ran. "Didn't any of them get away?"

"I don't think so," Terry answered. "We didn't expect it. Our object was to destroy Demarzule, and, failing that, to get you two."

The two running men, one with bandaged arm and the other with blood-smeared face, and the white-faced girl were attracting unwelcome attention, but at last they came to the rise where the flier lay, and climbed in. Without a lost motion, Terry worked the controls and they whirled into the air.

From their elevation, Underwood looked back toward the museum, the holy sanctuary of the Disciples. The roads leading to the site were black with humanity as the faithful streamed to the building to witness the Great One and hear his voice.

HE turned to Terry. "Bring me up to date."

"They contacted me—I wasn't suspected by the police, you know—and we organized a small group of the scientists we felt we could trust. We told them all about Demarzule and our blunder in bringing him back. We organized for the purpose of destroying him by any means possible, but of course we had no means. The force shell prevented direct attack on the Carlson, so we tried filtering in with the Disciples. Four of us were caught and killed.

"We didn't try to communicate with you, because we felt it was too dangerous, and knew that you would be doing anything possible. We succeeded in getting enough of our number in for the end of the show and passing weapons to some of the scientists on the project, but we apparently lost all our men without doing damage to the Great One. Only getting ourselves lost in that mob saved us three. I suspect that they feel so secure in the protection of Demarzule now that that is their only reason for not gassing the whole mob in order to get us."

"What's your next move?" asked Illia.

"The *Lavoisier* came in two weeks ago for supplies. Most of the crew is on our side, and the rest aren't there any more. Phyfe and Dreyer are already aboard, as well as the rest of the scientists of our group. All we can do is point the nose up and get going as fast as we can travel. It may be only a matter of hours until Demarzule is aware of us and sends a fleet in pursuit. After we get out into space, the rest is up to the boss." He jerked a thumb in Underwood's direction.

"What do you mean?" asked Underwood.

"I mean that as top-dog physicist and the only one besides us somewhat non-combatant archeologists and semanticists who understands the Sirenian lingo, not to mention your familiarity with Demarzule, you got yourself elected chairman of this delegation."

Underwood laughed shortly and bitterly. "I'm responsible for the mess, so I should be the one responsible for finding a way out. Is that it?"

"We'll turn you over to the psychiatric department if you don't cut that out," said Terry grimly.

"Sorry. I'm grateful, of course, that the rest of you think I could be useful, but I'm afraid my brain is a complete blank on how to get out."

"Maybe you think the rest of us aren't the same way," said Terry. "But you're the most qualified of us all to recognize a means of licking Demarzule when you see it."

Underwood stared ahead of them toward the expanding view of the buildings where the scientists had held out against the Disciples. He tried to picture what the past months had been for them, but he could never know the hundreds of desperate escapes and skirmishes with guards and officers, and swift murders in the depths below the city.

Beside the clustered buildings the great laboratory spaceship, *Lavoisier*, lay on the experimental grounds, shining in the early dawn. Sudden bright spurts of light showed on the field. Illia saw it first. "Gunfire!" she cried.

"They're being attacked!" Terry exclaimed. "We've got to get down there or they may have to leave without us. Get out that pair of heavy burners under your seat, Del. We'll have to go in shooting."

Underwood hauled out the weapons as the flier darted swiftly toward the field. A concentrated knot of offense was being offered from the building entrance nearest the ship, but other officers were surrounding the ship behind the screen of the distant shrubbery.

"I'LL fly over them," said Terry. "Give them a good blast with both guns."

Underwood opened the port against the wind and pointed the noses of the deadly weapons outward. He clicked the trigger and an unending stream of fire hurled toward the earth, sweeping through the lines of attackers as they crouched behind the shrubs and fences. Then, swiftly, Terry spun the ship to avoid the building and they zoomed upward. At that instant a crippling beam came from below.

"We're hit!" Terry exclaimed. "It killed the motor. Hang on for a crash landing. I'll try to make the port of the ship."

Underwood returned his attention to the guns as if nothing had occurred. As the nose dipped, he fired into the building from which the disabling shot had come. He thought he heard a scream of pain, though it might have been only the sound of the wind against the shell of the little flier.

They were falling fast now, heading for the open port of the large spaceship. They could see some of the crew members and scientists emerging, weapons ready to protect their landing. They sped down below the level of the top of the hull and the vast sheets of plate seemed to flow past the port of the flier like a river of steel.

It stopped flowing. They hit hard, and Terry yanked open the door. They tumbled out in the midst of their defenders, while spurts of flame showed in the sunlight all about them.

"Get in!" one of the men shouted. "We almost had to leave without you. They'll be bringing reinforcements." It was Mason, the physicist.

Underwood nodded. "We're ready. Is everyone else aboard who is going?"

"Yes."

There was a sudden cry beside Underwood and one of the crewmen dropped his gun and clutched an arm in pain. Mason and Terry clutched him in supporting arms and dragged him into the vessel. Underwood clasped Illia's hand and hurried through the port. Behind them the last of the men slammed the door and dogged it tight.

"Phyfe's waiting for you in the control room," Mason said. "We'll take care of Peters, here. Terry had better stay for treatment also."

Underwood nodded and raced along the corridor with Illia. They passed other men intent upon their own tasks. Some of them he knew; others he had never seen before. He hoped that Phyfe and Terry had chosen carefully. The remembrance of the biologist, Craven, came to his mind. They came to the entrance to the control room. Captain Dawson was in technical command, waiting for instructions to take off.

Apparently Mason was assuming charge of the takeoff, for his voice came through the audio system as Underwood entered. Phyfe nodded assent to Captain Dawson. "Take it up!"

ALMOST instantly, the ship soared aloft.

"Wait!" Underwood exclaimed, as he entered the control room.

Phyfe and Dawson looked toward the door. "There can be no waiting," said Phyfe. "We had almost given up you and Terry and Illia. The police have been searching for us for weeks, and now that we're out in the open they'll spare no force to take us."

"We can't go without the Stroid records," said Underwood. "Terry tells me I've been elected to head this outfit. If that's so, then my first order is to pick up every scrap of Stroid record and artifact that has ever been found before we take off."

Dreyer came in and looked interestedly as Underwood spoke, but he said nothing.

"WHY?" said Phyfe. "I don't understand."

"There was a weapon," said Underwood, "a weapon that the Sirenians were afraid of, which apparently was responsible for the power of the Dragbora over them. If any trace of that weapon remains in the Universe, our goal is to find it. It may be our one hope of defeating Demarzule."

The others looked at him as if doubting his sanity, yet hoping he was on the trail of a solution;

"But that was five hundred thousand years ago!" said Phyfe. "How could we hope to find such a weapon that disappeared that long ago? We have no clues—"

"We have the Stroid records. That's why I want them."

"But the Sirenians seemed to know nothing about the nature of the weapon."

"We're not so sure of that. But even if that's so, there was the great civilization of the Dragbora. We don't know that it is extinct, and we know nothing of its location—but the weapon may be there. And the clue to *its* location may be in the Stroid records."

Dreyer nodded and gave a violent puff of smoke. "He's right, Phyfe. We hadn't thought of it, but that may be our one chance. At least it gives us an objective instead of just plunging into purposeless flight."

"I suppose so," Phyfe said doubtfully. "But I don't see how—"

"I'll take care of that. Show us where the records are. We'll get the repository first, however; I want the whole thing brought aboard."

Underwood turned swiftly to Dawson and ordered the ship lowered beside the temporary structure housing the repository near the Stroid museum building. Then he stepped to the ship's interphone and explained their maneuver. He called for twenty volunteers to man scooters and weapons to cover those who were to transfer the records.

Below them, on the ground, the police forces who watched their prey escape stood puzzledly as the *Lavoisier* turned and moved slowly across the group of buildings and began dropping again. Three deadly polio fliers hovered in the air about the great spaceship.

It was the fliers that Underwood watched with intent study. The twenty men he had selected out of the volunteers gathered around the viewing plates with him.

"The first objective will be to down those fliers," said Underwood. "Then you will provide constant cover for those of us who leave the ship to bring the records back. Go to your assigned air locks. I'll signal when the fliers are in the best position for one group of you to attack it."

Byers, the engineer mechanic appointed captain of the group, nodded.

"They won't know what hit 'em," he promised.

"I hope so," said Underwood. "All right, take your stations and signal when you're ready."

The men filed out of the room while the big ship slowly settled toward the Earth. The three police fliers continued to move about with deadly inquisitiveness. Then the sudden signal from Earth indicated the men were positioned and ready.

Underwood watched the fliers. One was out of sight of the other two near the nose of the *Lavoisier*, Underwood called sharply: "Number three, attack!"

Almost instantly, a lock opened behind the unsuspecting police flier and three scooters darted out, their riders firing a deadly stream, which came to a focus on the tail of the flier. A sudden blossom of flame sent up a plume of black smoke and the flier nosed Earthward without its occupants knowing what had struck.

But now the second flier was rounding the hull and the three scooters were spotted. The police fired and one scooter plummeted out of sight.

"NUMBER seven!" Underwood ordered.

A lock near the top of the hull opened and a second trio of scooters darted out. The flier was beneath them, and its pilots had time to look up and see the blasting fire that poured through the transparent bubble over them. But they had no time to retaliate.

Fire began rising from the ground forces now and the scooter riders were forced to dodge and twist to avoid being hit. At the same time they dived close to the ground and sprayed the attackers.

From above, however, the third flier joined with devastating fury. Two more scooters dropped. Underwood ordered the remaining scooters to the attack. Simultaneously, they poured from the ship, swept over the remaining flier in a wave of destruction and dropped it onto the ground forces.

The latter spread out now and hunted for cover before the mounting destruction of the scooter riders.

"Align cargo hatch number one by the repository shelter," Underwood instructed the Captain. "We'll load that first."

The ship settled to the surface without a jar. The immediate area around the shelter was cleared. Mason, taking charge of the loading, ordered the hatch swung open. Portable cargo units were passed out and strapped to the periphery of the huge, faceted artifact, whose bulk almost filled the hatchway.

Sporadic fire continued from the hidden police, but the scooter riders were holding it below an effective level without losing any more of their own number.

Mason turned the current into the cargo units, and slowly the huge mass rose from the spot where it rested. Then a G-line attached to it began reeling in, drawing the repository toward the ship.

As the hatch clanged shut over it, Underwood exhaled heavily. "That's the main part of our job! Another half hour to scoop up the records in the building and we'll be through."

Illia gave a sudden shrill cry. "Del! The building—it's on fire!"

The men stared. From the museum where the Stroid records lay, there rose billows of smoke and licking flames.

"They must have known what we were after," said Phyfe, "and they fired the building. There's no chance now of getting any of them."

"Yes, there is! Most of the records are metallic." Underwood stepped to the interphone. "Every man but the takeoff crew in spacesuits. Carry sidearms and be ready to enter the museum at once."

"What are you going to do?" Illia cried.

ALREADY he was at the nearest locker, struggling into the ungainly spacesuit. "These will be enough protection from the fire to enable each man to bring out one load, perhaps."

The old building, as if symbolic of the times, was submitting willingly to the flames. It's ancient, only partly fireproofed construction was giving way, and the fire protection system had failed completely.

Rapidly, Underwood went over the plan Phyfe had given him locating the bulk of the records, then raced toward the cargo hold where the others were nearly ready. He ordered each pair of men to tow a cargo carrier.

It was a weird procession of unworldly figures that made their way clumsily from the ship and up the steps of the burning building.

Underwood and Mason were together, towing their carrier, which rested a foot off the floor. Almost blinded by the smoke, they led the way through the halls and into the stacks where the half-million-year-old records lay on shelves.

"Load up! This is it," Underwood called. Like creatures in some fantastic hell, he saw the others file into the large room behind him. They began emptying over the shelves, filling the carriers with whatever came to hand.

The wooden beams supporting the high, archaic roof structure were dry and roaring with flames. Somewhere out of their line of sight, a beam gave way and a shower of plaster and masonry filled the air.

"There won't be time for any more," Mason said. "Our carrier's full. Let's go."

Underwood shoved the carrier toward the doorway through which they had come. Its inertia was its only opposition.

"You drag the carrier," said Underwood. "I'll get another armful."

While Mason vanished out through the pall of smoke, Underwood scooped up another armful of materials. Then, almost blindly, he sought the exit.

Nearly all the others were loaded and dragging their carriers now. Underwood glanced back. What secrets might yet lie here among the records they must leave behind! He hoped the gods of chance had been merciful enough to guide their hands toward some record that would direct the scientists to the ancient enemy of the Sirenian Empire, the Dragbora, whose dreadful weapon had been so feared by the Sirenian hordes.

Back in the ship, Underwood glanced back longingly at the flame-ravaged building. It was useless to attempt another trip.

THE police had apparently hoped the fire would defeat the purposes of the scientists, but after the successful rescue of tons of records and artifacts, they resumed their attack with increasing fury.

Underwood called to Byers and the scooter riders to come in. Slowly, the protective forces withdrew to the ship, and as they did so, the police began firing into the opening ports. The scooters poured into the ship, more than one bearing a mortally wounded crewman.

Altogether, only fourteen returned.

"That's all," Byers said grimly. "The rest of the boys won't be coming back."

For a drastic moment of uncertainty, Underwood wondered if his demand for the records would be worth that sacrifice. It had to be, he told himself. Without hope of a weapon to defeat the Sirenian, there was no purpose in flight into space.

He returned to the control room and gave the order to lift ship.

CHAPTER TEN

THROUGH the ports Underwood watched the nearby buildings drop away. The Sun's disk shot up over the horizon and bathed them in golden glow. Then the pilot adjusted the controls and sudden, crushing acceleration was applied to the ship, but to the occupants it was imperceptible.

Like the tired old man that he was, Phyfe slumped down in a cushioned seat beside the navigator's table.

"You look as if you'd had a pretty rough time of it since I saw you last," said Underwood.

Phyfe smiled disparagingly. "For fifty years I've been a scholar and archeologist. It's much too late to find myself in the midst of a planetary crisis, and expect to be able to cope with it."

"You've done a fine job so far."

"I could never even lead an expedition very satisfactorily and certainly not a group of this kind. Terry might, but he lacks the physical knowledge you have. Mason might, but he knows nothing of the Sirenians. You're the best qualified of us all for the job."

"I want to be sure the rest think so. It might not be a bad idea to hold an election."

"We should call a meeting of everyone, anyway. Many of the scientists are not adequately acquainted with the problem. They should be organized according to their specialties, and we ought to prepare some system of defense."

With the ship no farther than the orbit of the moon, a meeting was called of the hundred and twenty-five scientists and crewmen of the *Lavoisier*. Phyfe, as nominal chairman, presented Underwood formally as leader of the group. Acceptance was unanimous and enthusiastic, for Underwood was known to nearly all of them by reputation if not personally.

BRIEFLY, he outlined the events concerning the discovery and restoration of Demarzule, the futile attempts of the scientists to stand against humanity's demand for a new god. Then he called on Dreyer to describe the characteristics of the enemy who opposed them.

"In the ages of Earth's past history," Dreyer said, "there have been conquerors, emperors, dictators and tyrants, but there has never been Demarzule, the Sirenian. To the Sirenians, conquest and leadership were as essential as food. There was only one solution for them as they expanded in the Galaxy, and that was complete mastery of the Galaxies— or extinction. It was undoubtedly fortunate for our own world that the Dragbora succeeded in destroying them.

"As to our present problem, Demarzule will sell the peoples of Earth the idea of their complete superiority over all other races in the Universe. They're ripe for acceptance of such doctrine. He'll use the supernatural aspect of his appearance among us and encourage a worshipful attitude. Then he is, I think, certain to begin the construction of battle fleets and the assembly of weapons and armies—not the ships and weapons we know, but the best that Sirenian science could produce half a million years ago.

"Within a few hours from now he'll be sure to learn of our escape and our identity as enemies. It is impossible to believe he will not dispatch pursuit ships to destroy us. Our only chance is to be too far away for them to catch up with us, at least in Terrestrial ships. By the time Sirenian designs are built, we must have an answer.

"That, then, is the nature of the problem we face. Our one hope— and it is a slim one—appears to be the discovery of the weapon by which the Dragbora overpowered the Sirenian hordes long ago. If we remain limited by the range of our own science, I am convinced the problem is hopeless, though I'm aware that happily there are those of you whose minds differ radically from mine and would not admit defeat even with such limitations.

"SOME of you had objections to our flight, arguing that we should remain and conduct an underground opposition movement. You were those who lacked a correct evaluation of our enemy. I want you to understand that such a movement would have been absolutely futile. A successful underground movement must be that of an oppressed majority against a minority of ruling numbers. Humanity wants Demarzule. Never forget it. That is why we are fleeing.

"But our battle is not with our fellow men; their faults are rooted in the dark processes of evolution and racial development. The appearance of Demarzule is an extraneous factor, however, one that evolution did not allow for. Without him, men would eventually attain maturity and balance out of the conflicts of their racial adolescence. With Demarzule as god and leader, generations of development may be wiped out.

"You must remember that we have committed ourselves to the only possible course—escape. We're nothing but children beside the racially old Demarzule. He's a superman from a super-race that outstripped ours long before our first cave ancestor discovered fire. Let us hope that we find the weapon of the Dragbora, so our kind may climb the long evolutionary ladder upon which they have stumbled so sorely."

After Dreyer's speech it was a solemn group of men that faced Underwood. The semanticist had conveyed for the first time to most of them the immensity of the threat that confronted them.

They proceeded then with the organizing of the large group into smaller units according to their specialties. Underwood found there was a preponderance of physicists and biologists. The thirty physicists were grouped under the leadership of Mason. To them went the task of investigating the possible weapons and defenses that could be employed against the attacks that would certainly come.

The men with strictly engineering qualifications were assigned to work with Mason's group.

The biological group included a dozen surgeons and four psychiatrists under Illia's leadership. Dreyer and his fellow semanticists were assigned with the archeologists to examine the records they had salvaged from the fire in the hopes of finding a clue to the Dragboran world and the weapon that might be there.

Most of the physical scientists had varying degrees of skill with machine tools and equipment and could assist in the fabrication of armaments for the ship.

The first task was to rig the ship with absorbing screens to prevent radar echoes and nullify this means of locating them from Earth. It was a relatively easy project and one that was completed by the end of their first twenty-four hours in space. That left only astronomical means by which they could be detected from Earth, and with each passing hour, this possibility became more remote. Underwood, however, could not put off the uneasiness that beset him in the face of the pursuit he knew must surely come.

Six days out and a hundred thousand light years from Earth, Phyfe uncovered the first evidence that fortune was with them.

He and Dreyer, along with Terry and Underwood and the other semanticists and archeologists were working in the single large chamber allotted to study of the records. Phyfe's sudden exclamation burst upon the silence of the room. He held up a small metal roll, fused on the outside, but unrolled in a spiral coil where he had broken the fused portions away.

"This looks as if it might have been the log of one of the refugee ships," he said. "Look at it."

Underwood bent over the small machine they had devised for supplying the correction radiation, which would render the characters visible. Normally, they stood out against their dull, metallic background like white fire, but these were dim almost to the point of obliteration. He read slowly, aloud.

"Meathes. 2192903. One *det-ela* since leaving Sirenia. Lookout reports Dragboran vessels within range. A thousand of them, which means we are out-numbered ten to one. Flight bearings 3827—"

UNDERWOOD looked up. He could read no further. "Those last figures—"

"Could they be the relationship between his own fleet and the home planet?" said Phyfe.

"More likely it would be the bearings of the Dragboran fleet in relation to the Sirenians. In any case, such figures would be a clue to the location of the worlds, because they would be related to their Galactic references. That's the catch, though, finding those references. To us, they would be entirely arbitrary. But if this is a log, it may give the location of the planets and their Galaxy that we can identify. If we can work out the changes in astronomical positions that take place in five hundred thousand years."

He took the roll from the machine and examined it more closely. "It's almost hopeless to get any more out of this. Is there any other specimen that was found in the same locality?"

Phyfe checked the records and shook his head. "This was found stuck to a completely fused mass of iron, apparently part of the ship in which it lay when the Dragbora struck. We may as well send it to the lab for restoration. If it becomes possible to read it, it may help."

IN four hours the duplicate record came back, restored as completely as possible, but there were long blanks which were unintelligible.

Underwood turned up the maximum radiation, which helped bring out the characters, but also burned them rapidly away if left on too long. Suddenly he caught his breath.

"Listen to this: 'Our bearings are now 6749367 Sirenia, having traveled 84 *tre-doma,* Sirenia. In two *te-ele* we land. Perhaps for the last time—'"

"That's it!" Phyfe exclaimed. "All but the key to their co-ordinate system," said Underwood. "Do you see any possibility of interpreting it, Dreyer?"

The semanticist shook his head. "It must be based upon entirely arbitrary reference points as ours is. I see no hope of interpretation with the figures we now have. Perhaps our astronomers could suggest something."

Masterson and Ebert, the two astronomers included in the group, were called in from their task of preparing star charts of the Universe of half a million years ago. They considered the facts Underwood presented.

Masterson said, "I'm afraid the bearings given by the Sirenians won't be much help. The distance is of value. That shows us that we have a shell at a radial distance of approximately ninety million light years from the Solar System. At best, then, we have this shell, which may be considered as several thousand light years thick, in which to search. If we could find even approximately the proper sector of this shell, we might soon isolate the possible planetary systems to which the Dragbora and Sirenians belonged, but without being able to narrow down the possible sectors of that shell, it becomes an impossible task. Just a single reference to some Island Universe that we might identify would do it, perhaps."

Underwood and Dreyer had to agree. They had gained something; if they could just obtain one more scrap of astronomical information, it might give them the key.

The search for that key went on among the records and artifacts. The repository itself was searched inch by inch—and still almost none of the artifacts found there could be identified or explained. Apart from the repository, most of the material they had was native to the planet on which the Sirenians landed.

By the eighth day Mason's crew had managed to construct equipment for throwing a force shell about the *Lavoisier,* and Underwood breathed considerably easier. They could travel indefinitely behind the protection of that impenetrable shield. Data for navigation was obtained through almost infinitesimal pilot units set outside the shell and connected through hair-fine leads running through equally small holes in it.

UNDERWOOD was proud of this accomplishment. With their limited facilities for manufacture, it was little short of a miracle that they had been able to turn out the mass of complex equipment in so short a time. Somehow, it seemed symbolic to him, as if there were definite laws favoring their success—the success of Earth.

And then on that same eighth day, when they were almost beyond the limit at which such small, dark objects could be identified, the lookout observer on duty sounded a warning to the control center.

"Fleet departing from Earth. Twenty warships. Corius type. Apparent course 169 46 12 and 48 19 06. Velocity—"

Underwood looked at Phyfe, who, was beside him at the time. "This is it," he said.

The warning went throughout the ship and the men looked up from their tasks a moment, then resumed with grimmer eyes and firmer mouths. Mason's group was working on the problem that had baffled armament men for generations, the problem of firing the Atom Stream through the force shell. Underwood had little confidence that they would solve the problem, but as it was they had no offense whatever.

As Underwood and Phyfe moved to the navigator's table to check their course and that of the pursuing fleet, he said, "I wonder how they spotted us. Our echo screen couldn't have broken down. It must have been sheer astronomical luck that put them on our trail."

Lieutenant Wilson, the navigator, frowned as he pointed to their course charts. "I don't believe that fleet is following us," he said. "If they are, they're going the long way around, because their course at present heading, is more than fourteen degrees from ours."

PHYFE and Underwood studied the trajectories, projecting them into space, estimating the rate at which the fleet would approach, considering its superior velocity and the divergent courses.

"It's easy enough to determine whether they're following or not," said Underwood. "We could simply change our own course by ninety degrees. Perhaps they haven't detected us after all, but are merely shooting blind in the general direction we might be, based only on the observations of the police as we took off. In that case, they may hope merely to approach near enough to obtain adequate radar echoes."

Dreyer had heard the news over the interphone and came into the navigation cell. He overheard Underwood's last statement.

"Demarzule would not send out a mere fishing expedition," he said flatly.

"Then what's the answer?" Underwood asked, but in his own mind he was evolving a wild theory. He wondered if Dreyer would confirm it.

"If we were merely going blindly into space to escape, Demarzule would have no concern with us, but if we were going to a destination where our arrival would be malevolent to him—then he would be concerned."

Underwood's eyes lighted. He read in Dreyer's face the same conclusions he had reached.

"And Demarzule would send his fleet not after us particularly, but to that destination to see that we didn't reach it. Therefore this fleet is headed for the Dragboran world!"

"Not so fast!" Phyfe objected. "Demarzule would be assuming that we know where it is. He has no basis for such an assumption."

Dreyer shook his head. "He doesn't know whether we know the way or not. He knows only that it must be guarded from any possible exploitation by us. If we don't go there, we are no menace to him. If we do, the fleet is there to take care of us."

Phyfe considered, then slowly nodded. "You're right."

"And Demarzule is going to show us the way to the Dragboran weapon!" said Underwood fiercely.

CHAPTER ELEVEN

THE course was changed so that the flight of the *Lavoisier* paralleled that of the Terrestrian fleet. The acceleration was increased to a twenty per cent overload of the inertia units, making it necessary for each man to use a small carrier unit against his own increased weight.

Still the fleet crept up, lessening the distance between them, but Underwood felt confident that the distance between their parallel courses was great enough to prevent detection by any means the fleet could mount.

There was new life in the ship as the working and sleeping periods passed rapidly. It was easier to concentrate on their work now that everyone felt he was heading toward a definite goal—they dared not doubt that that goal would yield what they hoped from it.

Under Phyfe's direction, daily classes in Sirenian culture were held. Every fact of existence they tried to view from the Sirenian viewpoint and anticipate its semantic significance to that ancient conquering race. The trip was estimated at approximately three months. A little impromptu party was held when the fleet passed them near the halfway mark. From then on it was a desperate race to see that the other ships didn't get out of range of the instruments of the *Lavoisier*.

IN the last week of the third month, a sudden, sharp deceleration was observed in the ships of the battle fleet. Underwood alerted his entire crew. If their deductions had been right, they were within a few hundred thousand light years of the Dragboran world.

As the *Lavoisier* braked some of its tremendous velocity by the opening of the entropy dissipators, the fleet appeared heading for a small galaxy with a group of yellow stars near its outer rim.

Underwood allowed their ship to close somewhat the enormous gap between them and the enemy but he wanted to maintain a reasonable distance, for the fleet would certainly begin to sweep—search the skies of the alien planet when they arrived and found the *Lavoisier* had not landed.

The fleet was finally observed to close in upon one of the yellow suns, which had a system of five planets. It was the fourth planet toward which the fleet drove. Underwood watched six of the twenty ships land upon it.

"Let's line up behind one of the other planets," he instructed Dawson. "The second appears closest. Then we can swing over and come in behind the moon of number four. We'll probably land on that moon and look the fleet over before deciding our next action."

The only disadvantage in the maneuver was that they could not keep a sufficiently close check on the fleet. They came out of the shadow of the planet for two hours and then were eclipsed by the moon of the fourth planet. During that interval they were in the light of the sun, and they saw no evidence of the fleet at all. The photographers busied themselves with taking pictures of the Dragboran world.

Like the second planet, the moon appeared to be a barren sphere at first glance, but as they approached and moved farther around its six-thousand-mile circumference, they found an area of lush vegetation occupying about an eighth of the surface.

It was the night side at the moment of their approach. No sign of habitation was apparent, though Underwood thought for an instant he glimpsed a smoke column spiraling upward in the night as they dropped to the surface. Then it was gone, and he was not sure that he had really seen anything.

The *Lavoisier* came to rest on the grassy floor of a clearing in the vegetated corner of the otherwise barren world.

At that instant Mason came into the control room. "I don't know what you expect to find on that planet down there," he said. He handed a batch of photos to Underwood. "We must have pulled a boner somewhere."

Underwood felt a sting of apprehension. "Why? What's the matter?"

"If there's any habitation there, it's under bottles. There isn't a speck of atmosphere on the whole planet."

"That makes it definitely an archeological problem, then," Phyfe said. "It was too much to hope that an advanced civilization like the Dragboran could have existed another half million years. But the photos—what do they show?"

He glanced over Underwood's arm. "There are cities! No question that the planet was once inhabited. But it looks as if it had only been yesterday that those cities had been occupied!"

"That would be explained by the absence of atmosphere," said Underwood. "The cities would not be buried under drifted mounds in an airless world. Some great cataclysm must have removed both atmosphere and life from the planet at the same time. Perhaps our problem is easier, rather than more difficult, because of this. If the destruction occurred reasonably soon after the Dragbora defeated the Sirenians, there may be ample evidence of their weapons among the ruins."

AS Dreyer, Terry and Illia drifted into the control room after the landing, an impromptu war council was held.

"We'll have to wait until the fleet gives up and goes back," said Terry. "We can't hope to go in and blast them out of the way."

"How do we know they'll give up?" asked Illia. "They may be a permanent guard."

"We don't know what they will do," said Underwood. "They might stay for months, anyway, and that is too long for us to wait. Even twenty ships are not a large force on a planet of that size. My plan is to make a night landing in some barren area, then advance slowly up to one of the larger cities and hide the ship. We can make explorations by means of scooter to determine if any of the fleet is in the city. If so, we can move on; if not, we can begin searching. It makes no difference where we begin until we get some kind of idea of the history and culture of the Dragbora."

"It's so hopeless!" Phyfe shook his head fiercely. "It would be a project for a thousand archeologists for a hundred years to examine and analyze such ruins as those down there yet a hundred of us propose to do it in weeks—hiding from a deadly enemy at the same time! It's utterly impossible."

"I don't think so," said Underwood. "We are searching only for one thing. We know it is a weapon. It is not unreasonable to believe there might be wide reference to it in the writings and history of the Dragbora, since it was the means of destroying their rival empire. The only real difficulty is with the fleet, but I think we can work under their noses for a long enough time."

"You're an incurable optimist," said Terry.

"So are the rest of you, or you'd never have come on this trip."

"I'm agreeable," said Illia. "There's only one thing I'd like to suggest. If this moon is at all habitable, I think we should take a day or two off and stretch our legs outside in some sunshine."

There was no objection to that.

DAWN on the moon of the Dragboran world almost corresponded with the end of their sleeping period. Analysis was made of conditions outside. The atmosphere proved suitable, though thin. The outside temperature appeared high, as was expected from their proximity to the sun.

Then, as Underwood ordered the force shell lifted and opened the port, he received a shock of surprise that made him exclaim aloud. Illia, not far behind, came running.

"What is it, Del?"

His finger was pointing down toward a group of figures at the base of the ship. They were quite human in appearance—in the same way that Demarzule had been. Taller than the Earthmen, and copper-skinned, they watched the opening of the port and bowed low before Underwood and Illia.

There were four of them standing, and they were grouped about a fifth figure lying on a litter.

"Maybe we ought to forget about leaving the ship," said Underwood doubtfully. "There's no use getting tangled up with superstitious natives. We haven't time for that."

"No, wait, Del. That one on the litter is hurt," said Illia. "I believe they've brought him here to see us. Maybe we can do something for him."

Underwood knew it was no use trying to oppose her desire to help. He said, "Let's get Dreyer. He may be able to talk with them."

Dreyer and Phyfe and Nichols were already coming toward the port together. They were excited by Underwood's report.

"This may be an offshoot of either the Dragboran or Sirenian civilization," said Phyfe. "In either case we may find something useful to us."

"They think we're gods. They want us to cure one of their injured," said Underwood. "We can't hope for anything useful in a society as primitive as that."

The semanticists looked out at the small group. Suddenly, Dreyer uttered sounds that resembled a series of grunts with changing inflections. One of the natives, a woman, rose and presented a long speech wholly meaningless to Underwood. But Dreyer stood with strained attention, as if comprehending with difficulty every meaning in that alien tongue.

THEN Underwood recalled hearing of Dreyer's statement that a true semanticist should be able to understand and converse in any alien language the first time he heard it. In all languages there are sounds and intonations that have fundamental and identical semantic content. These, Dreyer asserted, could be identified and used in reconstructing the language in a ready flow of conversation if one were skillful enough. Underwood had always believed it was nothing but a boast, but now he was seeing it in action.

The two women of the group and one of the men seemed utterly lost in their attitude of worship, but the other figure, standing a little apart, seemed almost rebellious in appearance. He spoke abruptly and at little length.

"That fellow is a healthy skeptic," said Dreyer. "He's willing to accept us as gods, but he wants proof that we are. He's liable to play tricks to find out."

"We can't bother with them," said Underwood. "There's nothing here for us."

"There may be," said Dreyer.

"We should let Illia see what she can do."

Underwood did not press his protests. He allowed Dreyer to direct the natives to bring their companion into the ship. There, in the surgery, Illia examined the injuries. The injured one appeared aged, but there was a quality of joyousness and exuberance in his countenance that Underwood found himself almost envying.

But Illia was shaking her head. "It's hopeless," she said. "There's nothing we can do for him."

She turned on the fluoroscope for Underwood to see. He moved it about, then exclaimed, "Illia! Those strange organs below the diaphragm—"

She caught her breath sharply. "The same as in Demarzule. These must be of the same race!"

Dreyer was speaking to the companions of the injured one, explaining that it was impossible to save the life of the aged man.

The response of the rebellious one was an almost savage growl in his throat. He spoke then more softly to the injured one, as if explaining. The serene countenance did not change, but the eyes closed quietly, and the Earthmen knew that he was dead.

Swiftly, the rebellious one drew a knife of glass from a sheath and slashed with careless skill at the corpse. He extracted one of the alien organs and placed it in a container, which he carried. With no other word, he left, and the two women followed sorrowfully and more slowly. They refused to speak further.

Underwood watched them go. "We seem to have gained a corpse," he said. "Get a couple of the men to take it out and bury it will you, Terry? I wonder what the whole thing means, anyway. Are these remnants of Sirenian culture?"

His speculations were suddenly interrupted by the blaring of the interphone. "Doctor Underwood, lookout reports entire Terrestrian fleet departing from the Dragboran planet!"

The group in surgery looked at each other in sudden silence.

"IT doesn't make sense," Terry said finally.

"It does," said Underwood slowly. "If they have found and destroyed what we hoped to find."

"Also if they wanted to draw us out of hiding," added Dreyer.

"We'd better wait a couple of days and see what they do. If they seem to be intent on continuing their flight, we can move to the planet with the sun behind us and they won't detect it. But I think that we should wait the two days at least, so if one wants to do any looking around on this moon, there's his chance."

Terry was enthusiastic about exploring the moon. It seemed that here might be a living fragment of a civilization thousands of years old, which should have been long dead in the normal course of events, but which had somehow survived the catastrophes that wiped out the parent civilizations.

Illia too, was anxious to get away from the ship. Together, they persuaded Underwood to join them in a scooter exploration of the surrounding territory. Phyfe and Dreyer were going, but it was necessary for Mason to remain in technical command at the ship.

Beyond the grassy plain lay a thickly forested section. The scooter party rose high into the air to clear the wooded area and were lost to the view of those aboard the *Lavoisier.*

For a long time they rode at treetop level, looking beyond toward the barren sand wastes that touched the far horizon.

Suddenly Terry pointed downward. "A road!"

A shimmering belt ran through the forest almost at right angles to their line of flight. They dropped into the sylvan canyon to examine it. Underwood halted just above the surface. Then he leaned over and touched it.

DREYER looked at his puzzled face without halting the column of cigar smoke. "Glass, eh?" glass highway—!"

"Looks and feels like it, but a limitation of materials," said Dreyer. "The moon obviously is lacking in mineral resources, being composed chiefly of nonmetallic silicates. The glass knife our friend used on the corpse indicates metal starvation; this highway clinches it because it shows they have a highly developed technology of glass working. Therefore, we are very definitely not in the presence of a primitive civilization as we supposed. We'd better watch our step because our friend seemed disillusioned about our failure to save his injured companion."

They chose a direction along the highway and pursued it a few feet above the surface. They traveled for twenty minutes or so with no break in the forest about them or the shining highway below.

Then abruptly a figure came into view in the distance. It was moving rapidly. Terry squinted and suddenly exclaimed, "We come how many light years to find a super-civilization, and we find bike riders!"

Phyfe said, "I don't see anything strange in it. Certainly the bicycle is an obvious mode of locomotion in a moderately mechanical culture. It may or maynot imply a lack of self-propelled mechanisms."

"Recognize that fellow?" asked Underwood.

They drifted forward as the rider approached rapidly. Finally they could see his features plainly and recognized him as the rebellious one of their morning encounter.

"I wonder if he is on his way back to see us again," said Terry.

"Our meeting is fortunate," said Dreyer. "I want to know what he did with that organ he removed from the corpse. I've never come across anything quite like that in all my ethnological studies. I suspect it may be some rite associated with the belief in that organ as the seat of life, just as the heart was once regarded among us."

They slowed as they came to the man—for so they had come to think of him in their own minds. He halted also and regarded them balefully. Then furious speech came to his lips. *"Shazer na jourli!"*

Dreyer frowned and muttered a few syllables slowly. The stranger repeated the furious assertion.

"HE says that we are not gods," said Dreyer.

"We could have told him that much," said Underwood dryly.

The conversation in the unknown tongue continued until Dreyer turned again to his companions. "The fellow calls himself Jandro, and the fact that we have metals still doesn't convince him that we are gods, an opinion which contradicts those of his fellows. Does that make sense to you?"

Phyfe exclaimed, "It makes wonderful sense! A planet devoid of metals, yet inhabited by a highly intelligent race. They make the best possible technological use of materials at their command, but they know somehow of the existence and properties of metals. What is more natural than for them to build a religion about the more fortunate metal-using gods?"

Dreyer said to Jandro, "We are not gods. We did not come to you as gods but as visitors. We are from a place called Earth."

The admission seemed a great shock to Jandro, for his expression changed markedly. "I am sorry," he said, "if I have accused you of a claim you have not made. But I do not understand what you say. If you come from the Heaven World, take me there and help me return with the secrets to lift my people."

"Heaven World?" Dreyer frowned.

Jandro pointed toward the horizon where the planet of the Dragbora hung like a silver disk.

"Why do you call it Heaven World?"

Jandro looked up with both longing and bitterness before, he spoke. "You did not come from there?"

"No."

"But you can go there in your metal?"

"Yes."

"Will you take me?"

"That is not for me to say, but perhaps I can influence the others. Tell me why you want to go and why you call it Heaven World."

"Long ago," said Jandro, "before men lived on Trear, they lived with the gods on Heaven World, but for rebellion and disobedience they were thrown down and exiled. Trear was a barren moon without life or materials. After many *dekara* man succeeded in expanding the tiny seeds of life he had brought and grew the great forests. That gave us wood, and the deserts gave us glass. So we have built a world on the barren Trear, and have looked to the time when the gods shall lift us again to Heaven World.

"That is the story the fathers have told, but I do not believe it," Jandro finished. "I do not know what to believe, except that I want the heritage of our home world to be restored to us."

Dreyer related the story to his companions. "It sounds very much as if Jandro's ancestors were some refugee group that fled the planet before the destruction that consumed the atmosphere."

"So he wants to go with us," Underwood said. "I wonder if he could be of any use to us in unraveling the secrets of the planet."

"I'd like to use the request to bargain with him," said Dreyer. "I very much want to know why he cut out that organ and what he did with it. That surgical skill he exhibited didn't come instinctively."

"It's all right with me," assented Underwood.

DREYER addressed Jandro again. "It is that you may go to the planet with us. There's only one thing we'd like in return—information as to why you opened the corpse and removed the organ."

"For the *discara*, of course. Oh! You mean you wish to present the apologetics?" Sudden expressions of understanding and of extreme puzzlement conflicted on his face.

Dreyer fumbled an instant. "The apologetics? Yes, of course! We wish to present the apologetics."

"Very well. You are guests of my house. My father will be pleased."

Jandro wheeled his bicycle about and sped down the road. Dreyer told the others what had happened and set his scooter in motion in the direction taken by the stranger.

Terry was explosive in comment. "What the devil are the apologetics?" he demanded. "We don't know how to offer them or who to offer them to. You're going to get us in a jam if we poke into the religious rites of these amateur surgeons!"

CHAPTER TWELVE

UNDERWOOD speculated about Dreyer. Behind the passive exterior of the man was a brain whose incessant activity often flowed in the most devious channels. What motivated this interest in the peculiarities of the alien culture? Underwood was sure there was more than appeared on the surface.

There was the fact that every organ presents a vulnerable point to the proper weapon. Was it Dreyer's idea to determine the properties of the unknown organs in the hope of finding weapons to which they would be vulnerable?

The forest gave way to green and they were in a clearing that shone in the sunlight like a pool of soap bubbles.

The houses, like the streets, were of multicolored glass that sparkled as if with light of their own. The Earthmen knew then for certain that they were not in the presence of any primitive people for the city was arranged with the artistry of a giant crown of jewels.

There were many of the tall, copper people in the streets and in the parkways. Seeing them together in their own setting, Underwood was impressed with their grace and simple beauty. Serenity and contentment were in their features and in the grace of their carriage.

THE Earthmen, astride the scooters, riding mysteriously above the surface of the road, soon attracted attention. Cries rose into the air, and scores of the people prostrated themselves in the road.

Jandro stopped and motioned the men to halt. Then he addressed his people in speech that was too rapid even for Dreyer's understanding. Dreyer managed to glean only that Jandro was saying the men had come to offer the apologetics to his father and that Jandro had been chosen to go to Heaven World for his people.

There were some who seemed to regard Jandro with astonished disbelief, and others who bowed before him as before the Earthmen. But when the group began moving forward again, the people rose and stood in silence and awe.

They stopped before a large, one-story cube of orange hue. Jandro dismounted and stood aside for them to enter.

"You do my house honor," he said.

Underwood strained to pick up some of the language, but he could only guess at it. Phyfe and Terry Bernard were getting much of it, but not with Dreyer's facility. The semanticist walked toward the building confidently, then stopped at the entrance and regarded his cigar doubtfully. It was impossible to toss it aside upon the immaculate gardens or walkways. He finally put it out against his shoe and stuffed the shredded remains in his pocket.

The interior of the house was fitted with simple luxury. Abundant light streamed from colored prisms, which brought in flooding beams of natural light from outside the decoratively translucent panels that formed the walls.

Almost at once, two others, women, entered from the opposite doorway into the room. One was elderly, but the other was younger than Jandro in appearance.

Then the Earthmen recognized them—the same who had been at the ship with Jandro that morning.

They gave involuntary cries at the sight of the Earthmen. Quickly, Jandro explained their presence and their denial of being gods. Gradually, the excitement of the two women abated and Jandro introduced them to Dreyer, who relayed the introductions.

"They will prepare our meal before we go," said Jandro, "but now you wish you view my father's *discara* and offer the apologetics. Come this way."

He led the way through the house to another room with a closed door. Even Dreyer's calm was deserting him as he wondered what would happen if he could not grasp instantly what was expected of him.

Jandro suddenly flung the door wide and ushered them in. "You will wish to be alone," he said. "I will await you."

He closed the door.

NONE of them had any preconceived idea of what they might see, nor could they have imagined the sight that met their eyes. The room was large and the walls were lined with shelves from floor to ceiling, like a fantastic library.

It was the objects on those shelves that held their attention. Square glass jars, completely identical, filled the spaces, and in each jar was a reddish-brown organ exactly like that taken from the corpse aboard their ship by Jandro. A clear, transparent preservative liquid surrounded the specimens, and the containers were sealed.

But in a small space before them a table stood, and on it rested a single jar with a fresh-looking specimen. Instinctively, they knew it was the one they had seen excised that morning.

Terry expelled a lung full of air. "Well, this *is* something. A morgue for extinct livers, kept by an amateur surgeon who rides a bike to work. What the devil do you make of it?"

Illia was examining the specimens closely. "All of them weren't as good surgeons as Jandro. Most of these look as if they'd been out with a meat axe. Some of them look as if they've been here since the beginning of time."

"Some sort of ancestor worship," said Underwood. "The apologetics must be some form of social rite offered to the ancestors of a friend, all of it interesting but quite useless for our purposes at the moment."

"It's not that simple," said the semanticist. "Consider the fact that even though Jandro understands we are from another world; he believes us familiar with all of this. He therefore believes these things familiar to all humanoid beings. There could be a scientifically valid reason behind it."

"What?" said Underwood.

"I don't know, but I'm going to find out."

Jandro was waiting for them when they emerged. He showed them to the table where a meal was prepared and waiting.

For Underwood and Illia it was a strange meal, for they could not communicate with their hosts in the slightest degree. Phyfe and Terry were entering gradually into the interchange.

There was awkwardness due to the oversize furniture and eating equipment, but tolerant allowances were made on both sides. The two women had difficulty in dropping their stiff reserve, but by the end of the meal they seemed to have forgotten that the men were anything but old acquaintances in for a visit.

It was then that Jandro said, "I suppose you would like to see our *resa* and the installation of the *abasa?*"

Without a sign of incomprehension, Dreyer repeated the question.

"I'm willing to see anything there is to see," said Underwood. Though he was restless, he knew they must give more time for the Terrestrian fleet to get away.

They left the house and crossed the city afoot, Jandro leading the way toward one of the major jewels in that sparkling city. It was a large building of blood-red glass standing apart from other structures.

"I should have explained," said Jandro. "This is where my duties are performed. I am an installer. Today I am not working, but operations are being performed, so that you will be able to witness our methods as well as the mother-flesh of the *abasa.*"

He led them through the winding corridors of the magnificent structure of glass. By some means, Underwood observed, the glistening floors had a high friction coefficient without losing any of their sheen. Abruptly, they came into a chamber that formed a small amphitheater, similar in some respects to the operating amphitheaters of Terrestrian hospitals. With something of a shock, they discovered that was exactly what it was.

They took seats by the protective railing. Below them, on a table where a pair of surgeons worked, an infant lay with a large abdominal incision. One of the surgeons lifted a small, fleshy object from a nearby bath and skillfully inserted it through the incision. They watched in spellbound amazement as the organ was sutured into place, tiny blood vessels were spliced and nerves from adjacent organs were slit and led into the new mass.

ILLIA clutched Underwood's arm. She whispered, "They're *grafting* in those strange organs we haven't identified. They aren't born with them at all!"

"But where do they get them?" Terry muttered. "Maybe that's why they take them out after death—to use them over again. But that couldn't be because they pickle them. I give up. This is too much for me."

Illia's eyes were only for the skilled hands below that were working such miracles with living tissue. Once she looked aside at the calm features of Jandro and recalled his passing remark that he was an "installer." If this was the sort of thing he did, he could stand with the greatest of Earth's surgeons.

The operation was a long one. When the two surgeons finally closed the incision, they began a similar operation at the base of the brain, grafting in a fragment of shapeless flesh there.

The Earthmen could not comprehend how the infant could stand the shock of such radical surgery, yet if they were to believe the evidence, this was performed on every child born on the moon.

Jandro said, "You have seen our technique. How does it compare with yours?"

Dreyer nodded, noncommittally. "Very similar, except that we have found it advisable to delay the brain operation. It relieves shock and appears to help recovery."

"The *tri-abasa*, you mean? So that is the explanation. I will be frank. I've been attempting to detect your *epthalia* since your arrival. I have wondered about your reasons for concealment, but of course that is your own concern. It seemed impossible, however, that you should prevent me from detecting."

"Yes," Dreyer replied sagely.

He reported the double talk to his companions. "I don't think we can keep this up much longer, and I don't believe it would be a good idea to disclose our lack of these organs. Jandro assumes all humanoid life requires it. He would be likely to consider us sub-human if he knew."

UNDERWOOD nodded. "Tell him we'll be on our way, then." It had been, fruitless, he thought. He didn't know what Dreyer had expected of their diversionary visit among these people, but as far as Underwood could see it had accomplished nothing. He had become rather attracted to Jandro, however, in their few hours together, recognizing in him something of the same rebellion against the conventions of his world that Underwood felt on Earth. Perhaps, on the trip to the Dragboran planet, they could become acquainted.

Jandro led them from the chamber. "You must see the mother-flesh. It will only take a few moments. It has never once died and now is far older than our historical records."

The Earthmen followed through the winding corridors again to a door that opened only after a complicated code system, and then by being drawn wholly inward. As they walked through the opening, they observed the walls were nearly four feet thick, of solid glass of a lead-gray hue.

"The protection is necessary to guard the mother-flesh against natural disturbances and the occasional unfortunates among us whose will is to destroy. No force of which we are aware could penetrate the barrier."

Underwood's interest was aroused concerning the nature of this mysterious mother-flesh. He suspected the meaning of the name, but the nature of the substance was impossible to guess at.

The room into which they came was very large and equipped as a laboratory, with wooden and glass instruments on every side.

The central feature of the room, however, was a large, dome covered container about twenty feet in diameter. Inside it, rising about halfway to the top, was a shapeless mass of flesh, grayish for the most part, but shot through with livid streaks of red. It pulsed as if some quiescent, sleeping life possessed it.

"This is our mother-flesh," said Jandro.

Illia shuddered faintly at the sight. "It looks almost like an enormous cancer," she said.

They peered into the vat, the base of the mound of flesh being hidden by a thick, soupy liquid.

A technician approached as they neared the dome. He carried a long-handled instrument, which he had just removed from a sterilizer. As they watched, he opened a port in the dome and thrust the instrument quickly into the mound of flesh and turned it. The mass quivered and recoiled, but the instrument withdrew, holding a core from deep within the mass. Slowly, the wound closed and the thick, dark blood ceased flowing.

THE technician dropped the core into a container and carried it across the room to one of several hundred cage-like units about a foot square.

"There you see it," said Jandro. "The primeval flesh is cut out and placed within its forming box where surgical manipulation and radiation will cause the formation of the specialized cells that will turn it into one of the three *abasa*."

"I'd swear that is cancerous tissue," said Illia. "Whatever the purpose of these strange organs developed from it, it may be that these people have succeeded in perfecting the mutation that nature has been struggling with on Earth for thousands of generations."

"But what could be the purpose of it?" Underwood demanded. "What abilities do these organs give that we do not already possess? I don't see any evidence in Jandro nor did I see any in Demarzule, showing the results of these organs."

"Who knows?" said Dreyer. "But I believe Illia may be right. Among us, cancerous formation has all the appearance of a mutation gone wild, yet it seems to be one that nature insists on. Perhaps with Jandro aboard the ship we can find out what these organs do."

They returned to Jandro's house. There Jandro bade goodbye to his mother and his sister. They seemed curiously unmoved by what must be an event of tremendous significance in their history, Underwood thought.

Jandro mounted behind Underwood on the scooter. They rose high in the air and set a straight course for the spot where the *Lavoisier* lay. Jandro gave no outward sign that such flight was unusual for him.

Within a few minutes they spotted the ship, and groups of the crew gathered outside, some at a distance of a mile or two. They circled and landed, returned the scooters to the locks.

Mason came up as if greatly relieved to see them. "The men are anxious to be on the way," he said. "The fleet of Demarzule is definitely returning to Earth, even more rapidly than they came here. There appears to be no more reason for delay."

Underwood went to the control room to check the observations. Before his eyes the mighty fleet was melting into the depths of space toward Earth. He checked their velocity, and frowned. What purpose was there in this sudden retreat? Did it signify a trap that had been prepared for the scientists on the Dragboran planet?

There was no way of knowing—and no way of combating the unknown.

Underwood stood up from the viewing plates and nodded. "Let's go."

CHAPTER THIRTEEN

AS IF awaiting the completion of the final step of his long journey to destiny, Jandro watched the stars swing past the field of his vision as the *Lavoisier* turned sharply to get into the shadow of the planet to prevent observation by the fleet.

Underwood watched the alien individual trying to fathom the mystery of Jandro and his people. What was the truth about their myth of a fall from Heaven World, which Jandro admitted he did not believe? How had the strange mass of flesh originated, from which they perpetuated the unknown organs within their own bodies? Underwood wondered if Illia were right, if it were the harnessing of some cancerous mutation that had occurred long ago in some forgotten individual and perfected for the whole race.

Most important of all, could Jandro and his people have any bearing on the problem that had brought the scientists across the vastness of space?

To Underwood it seemed unlikely. They had come in search of a strange and deadly weapon, hinted at only in scant records half a million years old. Jandro's people knew nothing of the vast techniques of producing metallic instruments and equipment. They were wizards in glass technology, and in surgery, but it was doubtful if they even knew of the existence of electricity.

The journey was only a matter of hours from the moon to the planet, but it seemed the longest part of the trip to the scientists who crowded about the scanning plates turned up to their highest sensitivity.

FROM a quarter of a million miles away, the faint details of the ancient cities began to be recognizable on the large screens. The sharpness with which they were revealed was awe-inspiring, for the airless world permitted perfect clarity of vision, and there had been none of the ceaseless winds that were quick to hide the works of man on other planets beneath dunes of sand. Here it looked as if the inhabitants had made a quick, orderly exodus only yesterday, leaving the vast cities for whoever might want them.

Phyfe was ecstatic at the sight. "The archeologists' dream," he said. "The perfect preservation of an ancient civilization."

"I can't see how the atmosphere was destroyed without considerable effect all over the planet," said Underwood. "It doesn't seem possible. Wait—there it is!"

On the horizon of the world appeared a vast scar that looked as if it encompassed at least an eighth of the planet's surface. It looked relatively shallow, though they knew it must be miles deep at the center, as if a searing torch had been touched at that one spot in a great blaze that consumed all the gases in the planet's atmosphere. For hundreds of miles around, the cities and plains showed evidence now of the destruction. It was only on the opposite side of the planet that the works of the ancient inhabitants had escaped.

"That's what did it," said Underwood. "I've got an idea that we'll find actually few cities without considerable damage, but this is more than I hoped for. If there is evidence of the weapon here, we may be able to find it yet."

They circled the planet out of sight of the departing fleet, taking scores of pictures of the remains below for future study. At a point farthest removed from the center of destruction lay one of the largest of the undamaged cities. It was nearly five hundred square miles in area, and almost in the center of it was an area that looked as if it had been a landing for ships. There, Underwood ordered the *Lavoisier* brought down upon the surface of the Dragboran world.

Under their predetermined plan, Phyfe was now given charge of their archeological activities. He had already outlined the method of procedure. They would move outward in small groups, mapping the city as they went. Their initial goals would be libraries and laboratories, for their first task was to obtain command of the Dragboran language.

As Jandro looked out upon the barren planet, his face displayed its first sign of emotion. He stared at the deserted ruins and his lips moved.

"Heaven World!" he murmured.

Dreyer came up behind him. "It was just a world where men lived," he said. "Something happened a long time ago that made it unfit for your people to live here. Some few of them apparently escaped to the moon and carried on your civilization. That is what is behind your legends of Heaven World."

Jandro nodded slowly. "And it means that we can never possess our world again. I had thought that I would lead my people back here, be the first to reclaim my heritage—and there is nothing to reclaim. Forever, we shall remain in our barren moon of glass while only the ghosts of the gods possess our metal Heaven World!"

"You don't believe in the gods, and less in their ghosts," Dreyer reminded him bluntly.

JANDRO remained facing the port without speaking. Dreyer continued, "Your people would never have followed you here even if the planet had been all that you dreamed. You know that, don't you?"

Jandro whirled, startled, as if Dreyer had been reading his mind. Dreyer pretended not to notice.

"In every civilization there are those who dream of better things for themselves and their world. Would it help if I told you that of all the worlds and peoples that men have found in their wanderings in the void, there are none as highly civilized as yours?"

"A world of bits of glass?"

"A world where the perfection of the individual is the most urgent community enterprise. But you know all of that. Let's go out and see what your Heaven World was like when your people lived here."

Clad in spacesuits, the Earthmen began to pour out of the ship. Phyfe and Underwood directed the dispersal of the small exploring groups who were to move radially in all directions. Though few were trained in the methods of archeology, they understood their objectives well enough to assist in the preliminary identification of specialized centers and in gathering information.

One by one, the groups left the scooters soaring into the sky like bees swarming from a hive. Underwood chose to remain near the landing area with Phyfe and Terry and Dreyer. Illia and Jandro also were part of this group, which were to explore the buildings in the immediate vicinity of the landing area.

Underwood was curious about the thoughts passing through the mind of the stranger as he viewed for the first time the long-dead remains of Heaven World. Here, where there should have been sunlight and gardens and life, there was only the mad contrast of blindingly bright planes and shadows of terrifying darkness, out of which the ghosts of the half-million-year-old dead might suddenly rise.

But since stepping out of the ship in the hastily modified suit that hardly accommodated his bulk, Jandro's face had taken on a look of inquiry and expression of expectancy, as if waiting for the Earthmen to do something, yet not quite understanding their delay.

Underwood was impressed by this curious expectancy but there were too many other things to be concerned with at the moment. He drew the attention of the others toward an edifice that reared at least two thousand feet into the sky a mile beyond the landing area, but which was connected with it by a long road or ramp.

"Let's have a look at that," he suggested.

JANDRO opened his lips hesitantly as if to speak, then suddenly closed them tightly and a new and dreadful expression came upon his face. Underwood was mystified, but dismissed the puzzle from his mind.

His eyes were upon the great structure that loomed just ahead. He soared up around it. Nowhere were there windows or other openings in the heights of the vast, featureless walls.

He dropped back to ground level and found his companions at the edge of the enormous ramp leading down into the depths beneath the building.

He noticed there were only four of them. "Where did Jandro go?"

Terry glanced quickly about. "I thought he was with you."

"No. He probably went after something that looked familiar to him. I guess he can't get lost. The ship is obvious enough out there in the center of the field. Shall we see what's down here?"

Dreyer pointed toward a track leading from the depths. "It's possible this is an underground hangar for their vessels, perhaps an embarkation station, from which the ships were towed to the takeoff area."

UNDERWOOD touched the controls of his scooter and led the way down the decline, a scant few feet above its surface. In the field illuminated by the spotlight of the scooter, he could see that the opening at the bottom was close to a hundred and fifty feet in diameter.

The others followed cautiously down the long slope. At the bottom they paused, glancing back, estimating their distance under the great building above. Then Underwood led the way slowly forward into the darkness of the ancient terminal.

Suddenly, in the glare of his light, distant metallic facets reflected the gleam. He went forward swiftly, swinging the light about. Then he realized they were already in the center of a double row of metallic walls.

He focused the light more sharply. "Ships!" he exclaimed. "You were right, Dreyer. They couldn't be anything else."

The hangar was filled with row on row of the monstrous vessels, towering ellipsoidal shapes whose crowns were lost in the gloom that was more desolate than the absolute darkness. But the long shining hulls looked as if ready for flight on an instant's notice.

The Earthmen dismounted from the scooters and headed for the nearest ship, eyes searching for a port.

"These are wonderful finds from an archeological standpoint," said Terry, "but they're not likely to contain our weapon because they seem to be strictly commercial vessels rather than warships."

"We can't know," said Underwood. "If there was such a state of Galactic unrest as the conflict between the Sirenians and the Dragbora indicates, it might have been that all commercial ships were armed."

"Is that a hatchway?" said Phyfe, pointing suddenly upward.

Underwood stared in the direction of the beam from the archeologist's flashlight. As he did so, a score of beams flashed upon them from all parts of the terminal. Running figures could be seen dimly in the side reflections.

The Earthmen whirled about in astonishment and sudden fear. They started for the scooters on a run, then stopped short.

A voice rang harshly in their ears. "Halt and disarm in the name of Demarzule, the Great One!"

The enormity of their blunder broke upon them simultaneously with all its mind-crushing force. They had imagined every possible contingency—except that of a garrison left upon the planet by the Terrestrian fleet.

Once again they had underestimated Demarzule!

Underwood called suddenly into his microphone, turning up the power to reach the other groups of explorers and those yet at the ship. "It's Underwood calling. We have been attacked by Demarzule's garrison. Defend—"

A laugh cut him off. "They would like to defend, no doubt, but the rest of them are as helpless as you are. Do you suppose that you could outwit the all-knowing mind of the Great One? He will be pleased to see those who dared match wits with him. He will be even more pleased with his servants for returning you."

Underwood could not see the speaker because the ring of lights blinded them, but now one of the space-suited figures stepped forward into the light of the other lamps and gestured imperiously.

"Back to your ship!" he commanded. "We will return to Earth at once, as soon as all of you are rounded up. Don't think of escape. We outnumber you ten to one in this city, and those of us who stood guard in other places will join us. Our fleet has been notified already of our success and they will return immediately to escort us back."

There was no identifying the voice of the speaker as other than Terrestrian, but there was something in it that none of their semantically trained minds had ever heard before, something that chilled and terrified the sensitive Dreyer.

Underwood sensed it, and his mind struggled to evaluate its implications. The voice was that of one who has seen a great and mighty destiny for himself and his race, all the more shining because unrestricted by reality. And in that great and illusory dream, all creatures other than himself and his chosen god sank into insignificance.

IT was the voice and the dream of a madman.

None of the others spoke, but they remained like diligent herdsmen as the scientists were forced to walk back up the long incline, leaving the scooters behind.

Out on the surface again, they saw that there were at least two dozen of the Great One's Disciples, indistinguishable in space garb. They had planned with obvious care, doubtless with maps provided by Demarzule, placing units of their garrison at strategic points where the scientists would be most likely to explore first. Underwood hoped that perhaps some of the other groups had had better luck than his, but it was unlikely, for the scientists had been totally unprepared for attack. When the fleet had been seen retreating into space, they had assumed that the threat from that quarter had vanished with it.

They marched slowly between the black and shining planes of the city's walls toward the *Lavoisier*, and as they moved they saw other groups of the scientists being led back from the opposite side of the landing area.

The ship had already been taken over. That hadn't been difficult, Underwood supposed. Any approaching figures would have been taken for some of the scientists returning. Inside the ship, when the invaders burst from the airlocks, weapons ready, the scientists would have had little chance.

Underwood and his group were led into the lock and followed by four of their captors with readied weapons. The scientists were ordered out of the spacesuits. When the lock was opened, they were turned over to others who were waiting for them inside the ship. Their original captors returned to the outside.

Underwood's eyes searched the faces of those who had taken over the ship, as if for some sign of the superiority by which the scientists had been trapped, but there was nothing in those faces, only the light of fanaticism shining dimly in the eyes.

Underwood felt sick as he watched Illia led away to be imprisoned in her own stateroom. The men were herded together into another room, and the sound of the locking door was like the final blow to all their hopes.

FOR moments they looked at each other in silence. At last Terry grinned bleakly. "It looks as if we missed the boat this time, doesn't it? Even if we could find the way out of this rat trap, there are the battleships of the fleet on their way here."

Sound came dimly from other parts of the ship, but the men could identify none of them. They supposed that the other groups were being rounded up and imprisoned. The whole thing had been worked out as if with foreknowledge of their movements. Underwood wondered if Demarzule didn't almost possess such powers.

He crossed to a chair in the corner of the room and sat down to try to think. His thoughts only went around in circles that seemed to grow smaller and smaller until he could concentrate on only the one inescapable fact of their imprisonment.

He wondered what was passing through the minds of the others, Phyfe, slumped upon a bunk, seemed to have been abandoned by the fierce, bright spirit that had carried him along this far in the face of their obstacles. Terry was squirming restlessly. Dreyer sat heavily in the opposite corner from Underwood, a cloud from his cigar almost obscuring him from view.

BUT there were deep lines in Dreyer's forehead and his face bore a fierce desolation that Underwood had never seen there before—as though all Dreyer's own personal gods had fled at once.

Underwood knew that Dreyer's mind must be wrestling more with the problem of responsibility for their failure rather than with the problem of escape. To the semanticist it would be important to determine whether the men or their science had failed. He had probably eliminated the problem of their escape by evaluating it as impossible.

While his thoughts revolved in endless procession, Underwood's senses became more acutely aware of the scores of sounds carried by the metallic walls and framework of the ship. He found himself straining to identify and separate the sounds.

There was one that persisted above all the others, but it was not the scrape of feet against steel floors, nor the bumping of closing and opening ports. Rather, it was the sound of a voice, so distant as to be scarcely audible.

It tapped at the threshold of his consciousness for minutes before he admitted it was more than imagination. He turned his eyes toward one after the other of his companions, wondering if they had heard it. Then for the first time he distinguished words.

"Men of Earth," the faint voice called.

Underwood stood up suddenly, Terry jerked his head about. "You heard it, too?" he asked.

Underwood nodded. "I could have sworn someone was in this room talking. Listen, now—it's getting louder."

While they stared at each other questioningly, there came a sudden wavering of light in the center of the room. They glanced at the illumination panel but nothing was wrong there. Still the distortion of light in their midst took on vague shape. It wavered and writhed, as if it were an image on a sheet being tossed in the wind. Then it assumed questionable solidity.

It was human in form, taller than a man and copper-skinned.

"Jandro!" Underwood exclaimed.

The image faded and wavered again.

"How can it be?" murmured Phyfe.

The image was not a thing of reality, Underwood knew. It was no more than conjuration within their own brains, yet the experience appeared identical to all of them. That Jandro was in some strange manner communicating with them, Underwood had no doubt, but the means were utterly beyond comprehension.

"I do not know whether you can hear me or not," the voice of Jandro spoke in their minds. "Listen to me if you can. I see and hear you, and your actions indicate you are aware of my presence. I am communicating by means of the *abasic* senses. I know now that you neither possess nor understand the *abasic* organs. It had puzzled me that you did not use them.

"What you are or who you are, I cannot guess. You are not men, of course, for men cannot live without the *abasa*. Proof that you did not possess it was provided when you allowed yourselves to be trapped and captured. I could not understand it, for I perceived your enemies the instant your ship touched the surface of the planet.

"Our ancient myths and legends speak of creatures such as you animals who could survive without the *abasa*, but never were they spoken of as having the intelligence you display. Whatever you have done, you have dispelled our one great legend—not only is metal not reserved for the non-existent gods, it is also permitted to such creatures as you.

"Therefore, I will bargain with you. I will teach my people to know and value the ancient science and the metal culture that they have been denied. You will help me in exchange for my help in overpowering your enemies. Are you willing to do that?"

"Where are you? How can you do this?" Underwood demanded.

"YOU can understand the thoughts that I speak, but I cannot understand your language." Jandro said.

"There's only one answer," Dreyer said to his companions. "Is it agreeable to all of us?"

The others nodded, and Dreyer spoke quickly in Jandro's tongue. "We will do whatever is in our power."

"I feel that you are sufficiently intelligent to keep your word," said Jandro. "When one of your enemies next enters the room, I will overpower him and you will be free to seize his weapon and to leave. I will be with you later, though you do not see me. I will visit the others now."

The image and the voice were suddenly gone, and the four men looked at each other as if awakening from a dream that they had miraculously shared.

"So the organs they graft in give them telepathic powers," said Terry. "It's funny he didn't get wise to us from the very first when we used spoken language all the time. Or was he reading our minds?"

"No, he wasn't, and can't," said Phyfe. "Recall his words that he had to have us speak in his own language in order for him to receive communication from us here. It would suggest that one faculty was used in impressing our minds with his message, and another was used in detecting our speech. As for our using spoken language at first, he probably allowed for it because we were strangers and gave us the prerogative of selecting our own medium of communication. Do you agree, Dreyer?"

THE semanticist nodded. "I think we have witnessed at least two separate functions of the organs grafted into Jandro. And I would suggest that we are about to witness still another if he is able to keep his promise of overpowering the next Disciple to enter our room. Also, do not forget the semantic implications of the *abasa* to Jandro. He is a man and we are lower animals to his way of thinking. It may not ever be possible to alter that view. We should act accordingly."

There was a moment of silence, then they grew tense with expectancy as the sound of the door lock clicked in the silence and one of the Disciples entered the room.

He stood in the doorway surveying them, a middle-aged man, erect of bearing, obviously a professional militarist. He said stiffly, "In the name of the Great One you are ordered to appear before the Commander for questioning. You will come at—"

A sudden glassy stare crept into his eyes, and a look of intolerable agony flashed across his face. His stiffened, arrogant form stood in utter lifelessness. Then, slowly, it crashed to the floor.

CHAPTER FOURTEEN

UNDERWOOD swept up the gun that fell from the loosened fingers before it hit the floor. He jerked it into firing position and approached the open iris of the doorway cautiously. The corridor was clear for the moment.

"You and Dreyer remain here," he said to Phyfe. "Terry and I will try to make it to the control room or wherever this so-called Commander is keeping headquarters. If we can capture him and gain control of the ship, you should hear from us within an hour. If not, you'll know we have failed, and then it will be up to you to make a try."

The older men nodded. Silently, he and Terry slipped through the doorway.

The rest of the iris doors on the corridor were all closed. Underwood pressed the release lock on the one adjacent to his own recent prison. The opening flared wide, revealing Roberts, one of the surgeons, and the three men who had formed his party.

"Underwood!" Roberts exclaimed. "What happened?"

Underwood cautioned him to quiet and explained briefly. "Locate some weapons if you can. There should be some in the corridor lockers. Make your way down and release them. Try to hold the locks against the entry of any more of the Disciples until we can gain control inside the ship. We have no idea how many are here."

The men nodded, exuberant at the opportunity for action against the enemy. There should be weapons in a corridor compartment only a short distance toward the rear, Underwood knew. Ahead, there was an additional compartment from which he and Terry could reinforce their own armament.

The next room they tried was empty. They thought at first that the one adjacent to it was also empty, but as they started to move away, Terry exclaimed, "Look! There on the floor!"

One of their men was lying sprawled, the back of his shirt covered with blood and burned tissue.

Underwood and Terry stepped in and shut the iris door. The man looked up and smiled feebly as they looked down at him.

"Hi, Doc," he said.

It was Armstrong, one of the ship's engineers.

"What happened?" asked Terry. "Did you try to buck them?"

The engineer answered painfully. "No. It was a sort of object lesson. I think. The Commander—Rennies, they call him—gave me his personal attention. But have you got the ship back?"

Underwood shook his head. "We've just broken out and managed to free a few of the others. Can you hang on a while until we can get help?"

"Yeah, sure. Don't worry about me."

"DO you know how many of them there are aboard?"

"About twenty took us over in the beginning. We were puzzled when we thought so many of you were coming back at once. Sessions and Treadwell down in the engine room were killed outright and a couple more of the boys were pretty badly shot up when they tried to resist. They're the only ones I know of, besides me. Rennies and his gang took up headquarters in the control room the last I heard. That's about all the dope I can give you."

"It helps," said Underwood. "We can take care of twenty of them, if we can get organized. Take it easy, old man, and we'll be back with help."

The engineer smiled and his eyes closed.

Underwood and Terry hurried out, closing the iris door behind them. They came to the storage closets and found to their relief that the invaders had not removed the weapons stored there. Underwood selected another gun; Terry took a pair.

"I wish we'd hear again from Jandro," said Terry.

"He may be helping the group down at the locks. We're on our own here, it appears."

They came to the end of the corridor and the passage split, forming a U around the control room because the navigational machinery had to be located on the axis of the ship.

"Let's separate," Underwood said. "It'll give us a chance to attack from two directions. They may not have a guard that's too alert, since we couldn't be expected to need much guarding."

"Good idea," said Terry. He checked his watch with Underwood's. "Begin firing in exactly sixty seconds!"

They separated and went swiftly in opposite directions.

As Underwood came to the abrupt turn that would put him in a direct line with the door to the control room, he halted and listened for sounds from beyond. Footsteps were moving carelessly and hurriedly. Only one person, Underwood thought; therefore, it must be one of the Disciples. There was the unlikely possibility that one of his own men had escaped independently and had already been to the control room. He'd have to risk that.

He stepped around the corner and fired.

The shot caught the man—a Disciple, luckily—full in the chest. An instant's surprised agony did not prevent a wild cry from issuing from his throat. Underwood leaped over the fallen body before the Disciple ceased struggling.

From inside the control room there were sudden confused shouts and orders. Underwood saw two figures running toward the iris. He fired twice, then dropped to the floor. The first man collapsed in the path of the second, but the latter was only slightly wounded. He raised his weapon toward Underwood even as he fell.

FROM his prone position, Underwood fired again. The blast missed and reddened the metal of the far wall of the room for a moment.

Underwood did not dare move. He could find little shelter in the small corner where the circled doorway did not fully meet the rectangular corridor, but there was no other to be had.

Shots from within the control room were coming close now. He could feel the heat they generated in the metal floor. While he tried to edge closer into the corner, somebody else came into his view. It was an impressive, militaristic figure, undoubtedly Commander Rennies, for his harsh, arrogant voice was ordering one of the men to call for assistance from the other end of the ship.

Then, suddenly, the Commander stiffened. Even Underwood could glimpse the stare that glazed his eyes like polished glass. Jandro?

The others in the room saw it also and heard the crash as the heavy body fell to the floor.

The disaster to the Disciples disrupted their attack for an instant. It was long enough for Underwood to get his gun up and fire straight at his opponent. The man started and whirled with a look of surprise on his face for an instant before he died.

And then another shot came from the opposite side of the room and caught one of the remaining defenders unaware. Terry was there at last!

UNDERWOOD breathed heavily in relief. He had been afraid Terry had been caught. Apparently the archeologist had met opposition of his own and had eventually succeeded in overcoming it.

Terry and Underwood rushed the control room simultaneously. Only a single member of the Disciples was able to offer resistance. Beams from the two guns crossed the room and caught him in a lethal blaze.

Cautiously, Underwood advanced not quite inside the doorway.

"Terry, you there?" he called.

"Check. I ran into one of them in the corridor."

"Keep out of the way. I'm going to come in blasting in your direction in case any more of these fanatics are hiding."

"Right. If I don't get your okay in five or so, I'll come in the same way."

Underwood set the beam to a low but deadly intensity and fanned it up and down, bringing the plane of motion ever nearer the wall that could be hiding an attacker. Without exposing himself, he extended his hand and brought the gun about until he knew the room was cleared or that anyone hiding there had been hit.

He entered then and called to Terry. The redhead entered grinning, but a smear of blood covered his left arm from the shoulder down.

"Terry! You're hurt!"

"I didn't get him good enough with my first shot. I'll be all right. What do we do now?"

"We can clear the ship by throwing some chloryl triptanate into the air system. But even after that, we can't even go back to the moon to return Jandro to his own people—that would bring the whole fleet down on them."

"We'll figure something out," said Terry optimistically. "We didn't expect to get this far. I wonder what happened to that guy Jandro. Have you found out where he actually is yet?"

"No. He apparently killed Rennies, but I've heard nothing from him."

"I'll get the triptanate, and some mesarpin for antidote. If I'm not back in half an hour, it'll be your baby."

"You guard here," said Underwood. "You'd better take it easy with that arm of yours."

"You're more important around here than I am. I'll be back in five minutes." Terry disappeared in the direction of surgery.

Underwood sat down wearily and suddenly became aware of the fixed dead stare of the eyes of Commander Rennies, who lay on the floor.

His name had been vaguely familiar to Underwood and now he knew why. Rennies had attained considerable renown in the interstellar military field. He had been an able leader, highly trained, widely read, intelligent, and a clever tactician—yet his mind had been as vulnerable to Demarzule as the most illiterate of the Disciples.

Then Underwood became aware of a slow stirring upon the floor. The last Disciple he had shot was not dead. The lips twisted in a snarl of hate.

"Fools!" The Disciple spat out. Blood poured from between his lips. "Do you suppose you can block the Great One? The human race waited ten thousand years for this savior. Man shall become the greatest in all the Universe with him as leader. Pay homage to the Great One as all the Galaxies shall pay homage to us!"

Underwood said, "Why?"

"Because we are the greatest!"

He looked at the man curiously. It was as if the knowledge of semantics did not exist, yet for twelve hundred years semanticists had slowly been prying loose the ancient false extensions that cluttered men's thinking and dwarfed their concepts.

Demarzule had wiped out all of that merely by his presence. Underwood found himself wondering why he should be at all concerned with the matter.

HE knew, however, that as a member of the human race he had to keep on hoping that the course of evolution would lead it to something greater than constant strife and insecurity. He had been blind when he had tried to escape. There was no escape; he saw that very clearly now.

A sudden sound in the corridor alerted his senses. His gun moved slightly to cover the entrances.

Then Terry burst into view with the containers of chemicals from the surgical lab.

"MADE it," he said. "Any trouble here?"

"No, just one revived for a little while to gab. He's dead now." The man was quiet in a pool of his own blood. "How do things look out there?"

"A lot of racket in the direction of the lock area. Must be fighting going on down there. I didn't see anyone at all near this end."

While he spoke, Terry bent over and moistened a strip of his clothing with one of the liquids. He held it to his nostrils for a moment and passed it to Underwood. Then he opened the return air vent and poured the contents of the other bottle into it. The highly volatile liquid quickly vaporized and passed to the fans of the central ventilating blowers, from which it passed into every chamber of the ship. Within ten minutes it had anesthetized every person aboard the ship except the two whom had inhaled the antidote.

While they waited, Underwood stared thoughtfully at the dead Rennies. "I wonder how Jandro kills," he said. "Can there be any defense against such silent power? Have you thought of what that implies with relation to Jandro's people and the society they live in?"

Terry nodded. "I haven't thought much of anything else since I first saw him kill that guard in our state-room. A civilization in which every member holds a silent secret weapon over the head of his neighbor. It's incredible that it could exist."

"But it *has* existed and continues to exist, and I'll bet that Jandro is the first of his kind to use this power for generations."

"It certainly implies a stability and individual recognition of responsibility that has never existed among us. I doubt that it ever will."

"Someday it *might.*"

"We won't be around."

"There's something else, too," Underwood said. "This may be the way out for us. It could be."

"What do you mean?"

"Suppose just one of us had the power Jandro has. That would be the weapon against Demarzule that we need!"

Terry hesitated. "We're not likely to get that power—and if we did, we could never get near enough to Demarzule to use it."

"No?" Suppose we let the fleet capture us and take us back. It's my guess that Demarzule wants us alive. His pleasure in our downfall should come from personally witnessing our defeat. It would fit his character. So we'll be brought back as prisoners. Then all that would be necessary would be to dispose of him just as Jandro did with Rennies."

"You're forgetting that Demarzule has the same organs and the same powers. You don't know what kind of defense could be offered against them—perhaps they are immune to such attacks themselves. That would explain this mystery of Dragboran civilization. Maybe Demarzule could detect it if any of us possessed the organs. Lastly, there is absolutely no possibility of our getting them, anyway."

UNDERWOOD'S face darkened. "That's the one thing I haven't figured out yet, but there's got to be a way. It looks as if this is the only hope left us to destroy the alien. We'd have to defeat the whole fleet to continue searching for the Dragboran weapon, and there's no chance of that."

"I hope you're right. Well, the anesthetic has had time to act. Let's revive our men and set to work on it."

They made sure of their weapons, and left the control room. Within the whole ship there was no sound except their footsteps in the corridor. One by one, they opened the stateroom doors as they went down toward the locks. They held the cloths moistened with the restoring vapors to the nostrils of each of their own men.

181

The first were Dreyer and Phyfe. Mason and his crew were found in the next room toward the stern. Quick explanations were made and those revived went to the task of restoring still others.

In Illia's stateroom, they found her lying composed upon her bunk. For a moment, as he looked down upon her serene features, Underwood forgot the intense urgency of his tasks. He tried to recall just why he had been willing to sacrifice the life that Illia and he had hoped to share—sacrifice, because she had believed in man, while Underwood had wanted only escape from the pressure of an erratic and chaotic society. Surely that life together would not have been postponed if he could have seen the choices earlier as he saw them now. Was it too late to hope now for reprieve from the destruction that hovered over them? He dared not answer.

Gently, he restored her to consciousness.

"I had the nicest dream," she said. "I knew you were in control as soon as the first whiff of triptanate came through."

"We're not in control yet. The main fleet will arrive within a few hours and have us cornered. Most of us are revived with the exception of a large group down by the locks. Will you go up and help Armstrong, the engineer? He's in B 05 and badly hurt. We haven't been able to do a thing for him yet."

Illia nodded. "I'll take care of him. Any others?"

"Terry here." He motioned at Terry's blood-caked arm. "You'd have to tie him down to work on him, though. Maybe he can go until we get organized."

They separated in the corridor and Underwood hurried on toward the stern locks. As he came up he could see a large group of the men gathered around. Apprehension drove him to a run along the narrow passageway. The group turned as they heard his footsteps and made a path for him.

A scene of death lay before him. Bodies of scientists and Disciples lay side by side on the floor. There were Roberts, the surgeon, and Parker and Muth, two of the chemists. Three others were not recognizable. Six of his own men had died and five of the Disciples before the gas had brought an instant and bloodless end to the battle.

He turned away. He wished there might have been some other way than sacrificing those men, but if the scientists had not held the lock, the Disciples might have remained in permanent control of the ship.

HE beckoned to Terry, who was checking the roster with Mason. "Have you accounted for everyone yet?"

"Peters, Atchison, and Markham appear to be the three we couldn't identify," said Terry. "And, of course, Jandro. No one has heard or seen anything of him since he killed Rennies."

"Jandro!" Underwood was suddenly and fearfully aware of Jandro's absence. "We've got to find him. There's no use of any of us leaving unless we do."

"I couldn't be sure, but I think I saw him from the lock viewplates a minute ago," Captain Dawson said. "There's no way of telling except by that oversize spacesuit—but he may be lying on the ground out there."

"If he's been killed—" Underwood raced toward the nearest viewing station.

He switched it on and scanned the area about the ship. Disciples were milling about, hesitant about using their Atom Stream weapons to force entrance without orders from their Commander.

Dawson pointed. "Toward the stern—there!"

It was unmistakably Jandro, though a blast had blackened the upper right portion of the spacesuit and a gap showed in it.

"If the self-sealers worked, he may not have been out there too long," Underwood said urgently. "Dawson, drive the mob back with the big Atom Stream, then throw a force shell over to Jandro so we can go out and get him."

DAWSON hurried away, calling for his mates and engineers on his way to the control room. Underwood remained watching the exterior from the plate. Abruptly, the Disciples turned and fled in panic. The blue radiance of the Atom Stream played about the ship, clearing a space beyond Jandro. Then the view of all the ancient city and the fleeing Disciples was cut off as the impenetrable force shell went out. Mason and two of the crew were already in suits and in the lock. They opened it the instant the force shell stabilized.

Jandro had been lying in the sunlight. That might have saved him. Underwood thought, for the suit absorbed the radiant heat.

The three men reached the Dragboran and lifted him carefully. They did not know whether he was dead or alive as they gently rolled him onto a stretcher and carried him to the ship.

Underwood located Akers, the surgeon next in skill to Illia, who ordered the surgery prepared. Underwood left his post and sought Illia, Jandro would need all her skill if he still lived. But he wondered if the engineer, Armstrong, did too.

Underwood found her still in the room where Armstrong lay. She was rising from her knees as he entered.

"There was nothing to be done for him," said Illia. "I stayed until he died. Do you need me anywhere else?"

"Yes. Jandro was shot outside. Akers is making ready, but I want you to take over. Jandro is the key to our whole success here. If he's alive, he's got to be kept alive."

Illia looked at him questioningly.

"I'll do my best," she cried.

Akers was quite willing for Illia to take over when he saw Jandro. The wound was ghastly to see, slashing across the full width of the chest.

While Jandro was in surgery, Underwood called a general meeting. They gathered rapidly in the conference room, but their worn and strained faces were little short of tragic.

"We've lost our chance for any Dragboran super-weapon we might have found in the ruins here," said Underwood without, preamble. "We're defenseless—except for the shell—and outnumbered. We can't run because the fleet can run faster, and we can't stay bottled up here forever. I can think of only one thing possible that we can do."

The others did not need to be reminded of the hopelessness of their situation, but their eyes lighted with interest at the last sentence. Then he outlined briefly his idea of obtaining the organs and powers that Jandro possessed and allowing themselves to be captured and taken to Demarzule.

"It sounds good for a last-ditch stand," said Mason. "But you haven't explained how we are going to get back to the moon so that we can obtain these things from the Dragbora."

"That is the one missing element of the plan," said Underwood. Then he added fiercely, "And it's got to be solved! That's why I called you here. I haven't the answer, but together we've got to find it. It's our last chance to stop Demarzule."

Mason jumped to his feet. "There ought to be several hours yet before the fleet arrives. We might have time to rig up a field generator and set up a dummy here to make the Disciples believe we're hiding under it, while we actually take off for the moon."

"That's it!" Underwood exclaimed. "Only we'll have to move around the planet to avoid detection by the local garrison. But that will do it!"

The interphone sounded. Illia said, "We're finished, Del. Jandro is alive, but he'll be dead within an hour. If you want to see him, you'd better come now."

CHAPTER FIFTEEN

UNDERWOOD started for the door without hesitation. "We'll try your plan, Mason. Take Over. Dreyer, Phyfe—please come along with me."

They hurried to the room next to surgery where Jandro lay in bed, motionless and unseeing. Only Illia and Akers were with him.

At the sight of that unmoving figure, Underwood experienced a depth of sorrow and pity that wiped out all other thoughts for a moment. He felt that he alone of all the Earthmen could understand the deep rebellion, the dreams and the hopes that had been the driving force in Jandro's life. And this was a mean end too such bright dreams—death at the hands of crazed fanatics on a Heaven World that had proved to be anything but that.

Underwood thought of the green, shining moon of the refugee Dragbora where men lived in peace with one another. The moon that Jandro would never see again.

Jandro's eyes fluttered open slowly and gradual recognition came into them. Dreyer said softly, "We're sorry. If there were anything within our power to get you back to your own world and your own people, we would do it. I hope you know that."

"Of course," said Jandro slowly. "I would like my *seea-abasa* to be with those of my ancestors for the day when life will return. But I think perhaps it never will. It is like our dream of the gods, only a delusion. As for death, that is certain for every man. How or when it comes is not important. It is strange for me to observe the grief of animals for a man. Strange—"

"Doesn't he suppose there was a time when the Dragbora never had the mother-flesh and the secret of the *abasa*?" asked Underwood, and Dreyer translated for him.

"Naturally," Jandro replied. "We were merely animals then, as you are now. When you came in your ships of metal, all of us thought surely the gods had come to return us to Heaven World again. You did us a great favor in showing us how wrong we were in our legends and our dreams. But until we arrived on this planet, I still thought you were superior beings because I could not detect your *epthalia*. None of us have the ability to hide it from each other."

"But you knew it when we were attacked?" said Dreyer.

"I could not understand why you did not act to forestall your enemies who were so apparent to me. Then I realized that it was because you did

185

not possess the *abasa* at all. I was frightened because I did not know what to do. I had never dreamed in all my life that I would meet with creatures that might be gods because they possessed the metals, and yet were lower than men because they did not have the *abasa*. I did not understand."

"WE do not understand many things about each other," said Underwood, "but perhaps you understand us well enough now to know that we need your help against these enemies of ours and of yours.

"Many hundreds of thousands of years ago, there was a race, called the Sirenians, and they were deadly enemies of your race, the Dragbora. Like you, they possessed the *abasa*, but instead of living peacefully they set out to conquer all the worlds and the Galaxies. In the end they were defeated by your people who had some mysterious weapon that penetrated every defense of the Sirenians. We came to your ancient world to find a clue to that weapon because one of the Sirenians succeeded in surviving and is now at large upon our own world. He has seized control over our people and is setting out to sweep the Galaxies with conquest and blood. In time he will find even your little world. The civilizations of many Galaxies will suffer centuries of retrogression.

"We didn't find the weapon we came for, and now our chance is gone, for the fleet of Demarzule, the Sirenian, is almost upon us. There is just one hope left to us.

"We believe that his men will capture us alive and take us to him if we permit it. If we could be taken into his presence bearing the power of destruction that lies in the *abasa*, we might be able to destroy him.

"Can you—will you—make it possible for us to gain that power by grafting the *abasa* in some of us upon your world?"

Dreyer translated as rapidly as possible the swift spoken words of Underwood while Jandro lay with closed eyes, as if sleeping a dreamless sleep. It was a long time after Dreyer finished that Jandro slowly opened his eyes again.

HIS voice was so low that Dreyer had to lean forward to catch his words.

"It is a strange story you tell," he said, "but I am impressed that what you say is true. As to your request—no. It would be utterly impossible for you to be given fresh *abasa* as are the young of our race. Not that I wouldn't make it possible for some of you—a very few—to receive them, if I could, but the *abasa* can be installed in only the very young.

"The use of the *abasa* is similar to that of the organs of walking or speaking. The organs must develop from their rudimentary forms through long years of usage, and skill with them comes much more slowly than any of the other common skills. Though they are installed in us in infancy, most of us are well matured before we gain great skill. For this reason alone it would be impossible for you to have the organs."

Across the bed, Underwood's eyes met Illia's and held for an endless moment. In her he sought strength to endure the crushing disappointment. Illia's eyes gave him blind assurance that there would yet be a way.

"Your race will, in time, develop and learn the use of the *abasa*," Jandro went on, "but not for many hundreds of generations. From what I have seen of your people, I wonder what your world would be like if everyone possessed the power to kill at will, silently, and without detection. I do not know the answer to that, but I ask you to answer it for yourselves. The mere fact that you have not yet developed the *abasa* is proof that you are not ready for it.

"The Dragbora live in peace not because they have such terrible power; they can live with such power because they have first learned how men must live with one another. You cannot understand why the power of death is inherent in the *abasa*. It is merely one of the inevitable functions that accompany the other greater and more useful powers, most of which you shall, of course, never know. I wonder if you would want the *abasa*, even if it were possible for you to possess it," Jandro finished.

FOR our race? No! Underwood shuddered at the thought of every man of Earth possessing instant, undetectable powers of death over his neighbor. "You are right in that, Jandro. Whatever the other powers of the *abasa* may be, we could not live with it. But Demarzule is a totally extraneous factor not considered in our own evolution. We have no defense against him. If the power of death in the *abasa* could be used to destroy him, it would give our race its one chance of staving off this threat.

"Yet you say it is impossible. It means for us no hope against the barbarism that will destroy our civilization and brutalize our people, not to mention what it means to the other civilizations of the Galaxy—including your own."

There was scarcely the sound of their breathing within the room as the Earthmen avoided each other's eyes now, staring down at the closed ones of Jandro.

"Your people hardly deserve the scourge of Demarzule and the Sirenian demand for supremacy," said Jandro slowly. "And what you say of the rest of the Universe is true. In a way, the Dragbora are responsible.

Demarzule is a product of the Sirenian-Dragboran culture. My ancestors should have made more sure of the total extinction of the Sirenian branch. Perhaps there is one way in which we could yet help."

"You *can* help?" Underwood asked eagerly and incredulously.

"I have little longer to live. It would be worthwhile if, in that hour left to me, I could complete the task of extinction—or at least enable you to do so. If one of you is willing to take the risk, I will do what I can."

"No risk is too great! But what can be done?"

"As far as I know, it has never been attempted, but perhaps my own *abasa* could be transferred to you."

Dreyer translated the offer, his glance going from Illia to Underwood. Something of hope seemed to come again into his eyes.

Underwood caught his breath sharply. "A set of fully developed *abasa* transferred to my own body! There would be one of us to meet Demarzule on his own level. Illia—"

Her face was suddenly white. "It's impossible, Del! I couldn't perform such an operation without any previous study with their anatomy. I can't do it!"

"It's got to be done, Illia. I'll take a chance on your skill."

"That's an utterly ridiculous statement. I have no skill in a case like this. Tell him, Dr. Dreyer. He can't expect that much of me."

"I don't know, Illia," said the semanticist. "It seems to me that you are confusing your analysis by your own personal emotions. You cannot be evaluating properly under such conditions."

She bit her lips to hold back a further outburst. Then, at last she said, "Don't ask the impossible of me, Del. I saw the way they split the nerves in the operation we watched. It couldn't be done without long practice. Most of all, I couldn't do it to you."

As if sensing the meaning of their argument, Jandro spoke suddenly. "You will have great difficulty in making a successful installation because you are unfamiliar with the anatomy of the *abasa*, true, but I can help. I can guide and direct your hands up to the very point of cutting the nerves to the *tri-abasa*. You shall succeed if you allow me to guide you."

UNDERWOOD kept his eyes upon Illia. Her face was as pale as her shining hair.

"I'll try, Del," she said.

News of the projected experiment sped swiftly through the ship, and its significance was greeted with awed incomprehension as if Underwood has suddenly stepped from their midst into a misty realm beyond their reach. And their awe was magnified by the knowledge that it could very well mean death.

Within minutes of the decision, assistants were rolling the tables bearing the white sheeted forms of Underwood and Jandro into the surgery.

A strange peace, a sort of ecstasy, seemed to have come over Jandro. Underwood had seen and heard of resignation in the face of death, but never such serenity as possessed Jandro. It had a calming effect upon Underwood and he shed the thoughts of his own possible death or maiming as a result of the strange operation. He thought only of the mission that would be his once he owned the powers of the Dragbora.

Whatever turmoil possessed Illia had vanished as she faced Underwood. The sterile white of her surgeon's garb masked her personality and her feelings, and left only a nameless agent possessed of science and skill.

Underwood grinned up at her as the anesthetic was injected. "When I wake up I'll let you know how it feels to be a Dragboran."

AT the adjacent operating table, Akers was preparing Jandro for the preliminary work of exposing the *abasic* organs.

Then, to each of them came the unspoken command to abandon their minds by Jandro. It was an incredible, unearthly experience, but they released their senses and gradually the guiding impulses from the Dragboran brain surged into their own.

For just the barest fraction of an instant, Illia's hand trembled as she touched the electronic scalpel to the flesh at the base of Underwood's shaven skull. The skin severed, and her nerves were threads of steel.

With increasing speed, Akers and Illia made the incisions in the bodies before them. Their hands moved surely, as if Jandro were seeing with their eyes and using their hands.

The deep incision was made in Underwood's skull. The pulsing brain lay exposed. Illia concentrated for an instant as waves of instruction flowed from Jandro. Then, swiftly, the scalpel cut a bloodless path through a section of unused tissue.

She moved to the adjacent table and peered into the wound that Akers had made in Jandro's head. She paused as his words came to her.

"This is the final step. I can go no further with you. Attend to my instructions now and you shall succeed."

Flashing, incomprehensible things flooded into her mind, imperishable photographs of the remainder of this operation and the one to follow, in which the two abdominal organs would be transferred. Illia knew that every picture would return in its own time to guide her hands in unfamiliar paths.

"Proceed!" Jandro suddenly commanded. "I retire to the *seea-abasa*. Farewell!"

The flowing pictures ceased and Illia felt suddenly alone, like a child lost amid a blinding storm. There was nothing to depend on now but her own skill and the telepathic instructions.

She faltered for an instant and breathed a name, "Del–Dell!"

Akers was watching her sharply as she stood staring at the strange, unearthly organ lying in the brain pan of the dead Dragboran.

But it was not strange. She knew its constitution and anatomy and the complex nerve hookup that connected it with the brain. They were as clear as if she had studied them for many years.

A surge of gladness and confidence filled her. She was alone in this yes, but that did not matter any more. She alone possessed the ability to perform the operation, and a world awaited the results.

Her scalpel entered the incision and touched the flesh with a pinpoint of destruction that sheared away the tissue from the delicate white nerve channels serving the *abasic* organ.

For a full hour, and then another, Akers watched in unbelieving fascination as Illia freed the twelve separate nerve filaments serving it, then cut the artery and filled the vessels with the chemical solution that would feed the cells until Underwood's blood could be sent pouring through it.

At last all that remained was the severing of the connecting tissues that held the organ in place. Illia cut them and plunged her hands into the sterilizing, protecting compound that had been prepared at Jandro's instructions. She salved the organ and lifted it out, then thrust it quickly into the corresponding cavity in Underwood's brain pan.

This phase of the operation was less than half over. Blood vessels had to be prepared to serve the new organ in Underwood's body, and the twelve nerves had to connected into the Great Sympathetic where no such nerves had ever been connected before.

ANOTHER two hours passed before the final sutures closed the wound in Underwood's head.

When at last she laid the needle down, Illia's hand suddenly trembled and she quivered throughout her body.

"Can't we postpone the others for a time?" asked Akers. "You surely can't go on with two more like that."

"I'm afraid the tissues will degenerate too much if we delay. If I were only as fast as those Dragboran surgeons. What men they must be! Get me a shot of neostrene and better have one yourself. We'll go on."

Akers was willing, but he didn't believe that Illia could stand more hours of exacting surgery. After a moment's rest however, and a shot of the stimulant drug, she stepped back to the operating tables to perform the abdominal operation. Once again, Akers made the preliminary incisions.

In the control room the group leaders waited for news in nerve-racking inactivity. Terry Bernard paced about, his flaming disheveled hair like a signal flare swinging through the room. Phyfe stood at one of the observation panels watching the inexorable approach of Demarzule's fleet. Dawson sat at his Captain's position fingering the inactive switches on the panel before him. Most placid of all, Dreyer simply sat in the navigation chair and smoked cigars so unrelentingly that it taxed the ventilating system of the ship.

TERRY glanced at the clock anxiously and stopped his pacing. "It's been over thirteen hours since Underwood went in there. Don't you think we ought to ask Illia—"

"There are only two alternatives," said Dreyer. "Success or failure. Our questioning will not assure success. We had best keep out of the way."

Mason kept anxious watch of the progress of the fleet. No one knew what would happen when the battleships arrived and surrounded the *Lavoisier*, but they had not long to wait. The ships were hardly more than minutes away from the planet.

As if guided by a single mind, the ships turned slowly in the black sky as their navigators and lookouts spotted and set a course for the luminous bubble that marked the force shell hiding the *Lavoisier*.

To the crewmen watching from within, it was a fearful sight to witness the sudden plunging flight of those twenty mighty ships. Simultaneously, a score of fearful Atom Streams were turned upon the bubble, apparently not in the futile hope of burning through the protection, but to destroy the minute sensory probes and prevent the ship from navigating away from the planet.

In spatial combat, where the ship was free to wheel and turn and defend itself, it would not have been so easy to destroy the probes. But with the ship motionless upon the surface of the planet, the streams of incomprehensible fire washed over every square millimeter of the surface of the shell, probing, destroying and setting off the multitude of relays within the *Lavoisier*, closing the hair-like openings in the shell as the probes were burned away.

Mason moved away as one after another of the segments on his plates went dead until there was no vision whatever of the outside world.

He turned to the others and motioned toward the dead plates. "This is it."

The spell that fell upon them was broken minutes later by Illia's abrupt voice on the interphone.

"The operation is finished."

CHAPTER SIXTEEN

CONSCIOUSNESS came to Underwood as if he were responding to the persistent voice of some unseen speaker. It called him out of the depths of eternal existence into the realm of conflict and reality. Curiously, it sounded like Jandro.

He opened his eyes. Illia was there, her face white and strained. But as he looked at her, her blue eyes glistened and she bent down.

"Del! Oh, Del—!"

Terry, Phyfe, Mason and Akers were standing near the bed, watching with anxious faces.

Pain was beginning to show itself in burning streamers, but he managed a quick smile to those about him. "Looks like we made it all right," he said. "I wonder what I can do with these gadgets now. Think they'll work, Illia?"

She raised up, brisk and business-like once more. "You aren't going to find out for a while. I intend to knock you out for a good, cold twenty-four hours. Give me your arm."

She reached for a hypo needle on the table beside the bed.

It was like stumbling around in the dark at first, trying to run from an unseen pursuer. But all at once, Underwood knew he didn't need to run at all. The hypo was blocking the sensory equipment in other parts of his body, but it couldn't affect the *abasic* organs if he didn't want it to. He stopped running and watched the ordinary faculties of his body give way while he stood aside in complete immunity. It was as if he could step outside and look at himself.

And, suddenly, that was what he was doing!

HE could see the room, the watching scientists, and Illia carefully checking his heartbeat and respiration. He could see himself lying still with eyes closed. Curiously, he could not identify the point of view. He thought for a moment that he was up near the ceiling somewhere looking down, but that wasn't right, either, because he could see the ceiling just as well as the floor or the four walls. The scene was like a picture taken with a lens having a solid angle of perception of three hundred and sixty degrees.

He wondered if he could go beyond the limits of the room, tried it and found it quite easy to do. There was some clumsiness due to inexperience and conditioning that stopped him at the walls, where he had a moment's claustrophobic fright of being trapped between the metal panels, but it was over in an instant and he was through. He went toward the control room and found it occupied only by Dreyer, who remained placidly smoking a cigar in the navigator's chair.

Underwood wanted to communicate with the semanticist, only he wasn't sure how to go about it. It was like trying to talk with a mouth full of dry crackers.

But Dreyer stared around with a sudden start. He removed the cigar from his mouth and looked agape for an unseen speaker.

"Dreyer, can you hear me?"

"Underwood! You succeeded!"

"After a fashion. So far it's like walking around in deep mud, but I'm getting used to it gradually."

"This is wonderful—*wonderful!*" Dreyer breathed. "I hadn't dared hope that I would ever hear your voice again. Where are you?"

"That's a tough question. Theoretically, I'm unconscious back in sick bay with a shot of neo-morph that will keep me out for twenty-four hours. Illia and the others are back there watching me. The *abasic* senses aren't at all affected by the drug. I seem to be able to wander anywhere I wish about the ship. The funny part is that I can't pin down a point of view. I don't seem to be anywhere. Nevertheless, my senses perceive distant sounds and objects—including my own corpus."

"Can you detect my thoughts when I don't speak? Jandro didn't seem able to do that."

Underwood laughed. "I don't know whether I can or not. I try, but all I get is a fuzzy static. I'm sure that these organs have dozens of functions that we haven't even dreamed of yet. I hope that I can learn to use them all."

"What do you plan now? Do you need a period of exercise and study?"

"Some, but not nearly as much as I would have needed if it hadn't been Jandro's mature organs that were grafted into me. There is something that we never thought of before, though."

"What is that?"

"We can still search for the Dragboran weapon we came here for. I can go outside the ship with these new senses. I don't know whether I can cover the whole planet or not, but if not, we can move to keep in range of my powers. It will be slow because I am the only one who can do it, but it may be faster in the end because I can get around more quickly."

"I wonder if it will be possible in the presence of the fleet—or didn't you know that they had arrived?" Dreyer pointed toward the blank viewplates.

"I didn't know. What are they doing there?"

Underwood realized immediately the absurdity of the question. Dreyer could know no more about it than he, since all communication with the outside was destroyed.

With all the strength he could gather, he hurled his new powers beyond the scope of the ship, out into the contrasting heat and cold of the barren planet. It was as if he had hurled himself high into space, for he was viewing the broad expanse of the Dragboran world and the busy fleet of Demarzule.

Underwood's senses revolted at what he saw. Completely surrounding the ship was utter, flaming destruction. The great city of the Dragbora had been turned into molten ruin by the twenty ships, which spiraled slowly; their powerful beams of the Atom Stream turned upon the buildings below. Even as Underwood watched, they completed their work upon that city and traveled toward another great city less than a hundred miles away.

What purpose was behind the wanton ruin, Underwood could not comprehend. Perhaps now that the scientists had been cornered, the Terrestrians hoped to destroy the super-weapon that could unseat Demarzule.

Within hours, the major cities of the planet would be shapeless mounds of frozen lava.

He debated trying to enter those vessels and overpowering members of their crews. At once his reason told him no, for he was still a toddler in the use of the new faculties he possessed. But there was a greater reason, too. If he should expose himself by such attacks, the ships would send word to Earth, and Demarzule would easily identify the methods used against his men and be prepared. Underwood knew how this destruction of archeological treasures would affect Phyfe and Terry, but more important was the loss of any chance to search for the weapon.

HE turned his senses toward the bubble of the shell that hid the *Lavoisier.* Its shining surface was the only thing in all that broad city that did not reek of destruction.

As Underwood regarded it, a shock of comprehension hit him. In the impetuousness of his flight above the planet, he had overlooked the most significant point of all.

He—his senses, at least—*had passed through the impenetrable force shell.*

Sudden fear mingled with that devastating realization. Could he get back through it? How had he passed the barrier in the first place? It was mathematically impossible for matter or energy to be transferred across it.

Did his senses represent neither one?

He impelled himself toward it, waited for the impact—and felt none. Then he was through, looking at the interior of the shell and the ship within it.

His mind was afire with the significance of his discovery as he burst into the control room. The others had rejoined Dreyer there. Mason and some of his men were struggling to replace some of the probes now that the attack upon the ship had ceased for the moment.

"We've found it!" Underwood shouted. "We've got the weapon that Dragbor turned upon Sirenia!"

Illia screamed at the sudden impact upon her worn nerve cells.

Mason whirled around in horror and cried, "Underwood! Where are you?"

"We can hit them wherever they try to hide," said Underwood. "No matter where Demarzule tries to flee, I'll find him. There's no place in the Universe he can hide from me!"

CHAPTER SEVENTEEN

UNDERWOOD'S physical body recovered slowly from the severe shock of the operation. He was immune to the pain of it, however, for having the *abasic* senses was like possessing another body. He could close all the normal channels of perception and exist with his consciousness operating only through the *abasic* senses.

While the fleet sped about the planet on its path of useless destruction, Underwood spent his hours practicing the use of his new powers.

Gradually, he obtained an understanding of their properties and some of their functions. The *tri-abasa* was the sensory organ, located at the base of his brain, which could pick up distant, focusable sensations, which any of his normal five senses could detect. They were controllable in their subjective effects, however, as he had found when going beyond the limits of the ship. Though he had been unaware of the interstellar cold, it had no subjective effect upon his body or his sensory apparatus.

The *dor-abasa* was the organ of communication, but it worked in combination with the *tri-abasa* in order to transmit and receive sensory effects. So it was that the two of them in combination could transmit not only ordinary communication, but could convey the actual sensations of heat, cold, light, sound.

And these same two organs were capable of dispensing swift and silent death.

How this happened was the greatest mystery Underwood had to solve. He experimented by hurling the powers upon an artificial nervous system rigged up from a network of wires. A strong electric field was definitely measured within the wires, but it had properties that were not within the physicists' prior experience. Regardless, Underwood continued with his practicing and found that he could increase the strength of that field more each time. If necessary, a full understanding of how it destroyed nerve tissue could wait until they reach their objectives upon Earth.

The third organ, the *seea-abasa,* was the strangest of all. Interconnected intimately with the other two through nerve channels, it nevertheless had no obvious functions. Jandro had referred to it as the receptacle of life. It appeared to be the belief of the Dragbora that everything representing the individual could be drawn into the *seea-abasa* when death approached.

Eons ago, the art of artificially reconstructing new bodies into which the organ could be placed, a process constituting literal resurrection, had been lost, but the Dragbora lived in hope of recovering the forgotten knowledge. This was their explanation of the preservation of the *seea-abasa*, each family possessing the vast collection of its ancestral organs back to the time of the expulsion from their parent world.

What basis in fact there was to this theory, the scientists did not know. Apparently, such resurrection had never been accomplished, yet with each death, the *seea-abasa* was religiously removed and preserved.

UNDERWOOD felt like some ancient gladiator training for an arena battle, but never had any gladiator fought for such a prize. No one knew better than he that at the moment he faced Demarzule and challenged the Sirenian, he might face equal and perhaps superior powers of destruction, for Demarzule was old in experience.

There was a defense against it, and to this Underwood turned his attention, for it was difficult in function. The *dor-abasa* had the power to absorb and store the destructive energies. Underwood discovered it almost by accident when Mason's technicians set up equipment for duplicating the destructive force as nearly as possible. It was weak and wholly ineffective, but it acted upon the *dor-abasa,* and the organ absorbed it involuntarily.

He was absolutely confident that they had succeeded in finding the great weapon for which they had come. The ancient Dragboran-Sirenian culture had obviously possessed the force shell as a protection. Toshmere's words made that plain, but they had misunderstood the implications when he had said, "They have found a way through the barrier. Our men are falling one by one."

TRAINED in physical ways of thinking, they had overlooked any such possibility as the superior powers of the Dragboran *abasa.*

There was one other thing that worried Underwood, however, and that was the possibility of producing the effects of the *abasic* weapon by electronic means. Though the scientists were failing almost completely in their attempts to do that, he wondered if perhaps the Terrestrians under Demarzule might not succeed.

In the scientists' favor, however, was the fact that though he possessed a vast reservoir of scientific knowledge, Demarzule was still only the dictator, the politician. He was no scientist.

On the third day following the operation, Underwood was able to be up about the ship for a few moments though by means of the *abasic* senses he had been actively supervising the work in the laboratory during the entire time.

He felt his powers growing almost hourly, and the vista of the new world of physical and mental powers into which he was coming was almost overwhelming. He sensed other new and untried properties of the organs, which he dared not experiment with yet. There would be time enough when they reached Earth.

An accurate watch had been kept on the battle fleet from Earth. Its wanton firing of the ancient cities was completed by the time Underwood was able to rise physically from his bed. The observer reported the ships were turning about and returning in the direction of the *Lavoisier.*

"We'd better get into space," said Underwood. "There's no reason for staying here longer, and I don't want them to burn away all our probes again if we can help it. They may try to send a surrender demand or something of the sort, but let's be in space where we can maneuver when they do it."

The *Lavoisier* lifted from the surface of the planet, its course set for Earth, more than ninety million light years away.

The force shell about it glistened in space like a new star, and through the probes the observers aboard saw the fleet swiftly shift its course in pursuit.

Underwood left the ship and let his senses rove through the space about the vessel. He remained like some omnipotent observer in space, while the shining bubble sped through the heavens. Behind it came the twenty mighty battleships, their acceleration high enough to overtake the *Lavoisier.* Impulsively, Underwood drifted toward the nearest and entered through the hull.

It was the giant flagship, *Creagor.* The Disciples who formed the fighting forces were like men reborn. There was none of the blasé, disillusioned attitude that had been prevalent upon Earth before the coming of Demarzule. Instead, there was a zealous, inspired attitude that frightened Underwood. It was a fanatic, desperate, unhealthy thing.

He tried to picture the nations of the Earth filled with such men driven by the same kind of unholy inspiration. It sickened him, for even if Demarzule were destroyed, the Earth would be no place where a sane man could find peace for decades to come. In death, Demarzule might become a martyr and live more strongly than ever in the minds of his followers.

AS Underwood moved so strangely among his enemies, he heard occasional remarks concerning the *Lavoisier* and its scientists. Blasphemer and infidel were the mildest terms applied to them.

He came to the control room, where the Admiral was in conference with the Captain of the flagship.

"We have our orders, Captain Montrose," the Admiral was saying. "Destruction of the ship and all it's occupants is to be complete."

"That supersedes the command to take prisoners, then?"

The Admiral nodded. "Orders will be dispatched to all vessels at once. We will make a combined attack with the new force shell disrupter."

Underwood froze at the words. Had Demarzule brought back with him some terrible means of penetrating the force shell and rendering it useless? That was absolutely the only defense the *Lavoisier* had. Her own Atom Stream projectors would be ineffective against the twenty encircling ships.

Underwood heard the orders given. Throughout the flagship an electric tension filled the air. It was the first time the weapon had been tried against an enemy, Underwood supposed. The crewmen were eager with a sickening lust to kill.

Underwood went swiftly through the ship, searching to locate the machines that would be turned upon the helpless laboratory ship. He still didn't quite believe that anything could break down the force shell. But when he saw the weapons, he knew that defeat had come for a civilization, which had learned to depend upon the force shell for its protection.

HE watched the crewmen at the complicated boards that controlled the input of power and the focusing of the radiators upon the distant target.

Underwood sped away to the distant *Lavoisier* to see what effect the onslaught was having. The force shell about the ship glowed with the faint, pinkish aura of the twenty beams that converged upon it.

As he came up there was no apparent effect, but all at once the glistening shell grew red in a spot as the force field weakened.

Then Underwood comprehended the means by which the disrupter worked. It did not penetrate the shell. That was an impossibility. But it unbalanced the forces that held the field in a shell and caused it to rotate. This, in turn, created a tremendous flow of energy through the generators aboard the *Lavoisier* and shortly would burn them out, leaving the ship the defenseless prey of the Atom Streams.

There was no time to enter the *Lavoisier* to warn them. Underwood returned with bodiless velocity to the *Creagor.*

There in the depths of the ship he found the Chief Operator who was directing those beams toward the *Lavoisier*. With all the power of his *abasic* organs, he hurled a devastating wave of energy into the man's nerve channels.

The result was shocking to one unaccustomed to killing. The man jerked upright before his panel, staggered uncertainly, and fell across the maze of switches.

There was no time for reaction within Underwood at his merciless first slaying. The complex machinery of the disrupter sputtered to a halt amid the clatter of relays.

Underwood moved into the next sector of the ship where the powerful Atom Stream projectors awaited their prey. He carefully extended the powers of the *dor-abasa*. It was almost as if he could feel his way along the nerve channels of the operator's mind into the depths of the brain. There he sent forth a sudden, wild command.

The operator unquestioningly spun the wheels that shifted the radiators. They came to rest upon the nearest ship of the fleet.

"Fire!" Underwood commanded.

The operator's fingers closed upon the switches. The Atom Stream lashed into space, tore open the vitals of the sister ship and flung the fragments out into space. Some crashed into other ships, battering them, throwing them off course.

For a moment after the catastrophe, the commanders of the fleet were stunned to inactivity, while confusion swept the ranks. The hysterical cries of the operator who had pulled the switches filled the room.

"I didn't do it!" he screamed. "Something made me—"

Some of the ships were still attacking the *Lavoisier*. Underwood didn't know how long they could hold out. He sped to the nearest ship where there was milder but no less disrupting confusion as news of the unexplained disaster filtered down to the lowest astro-man.

Underwood sought out the fire control chamber. He fingered his way along the nerve channels of the operator and swung the projectors around. This time the target was the mighty flagship.

The operator gasped with horror as the titanic hull came into view in his sights, yet with unerring accuracy his hands moved the radiators to center exactly on the target.

His fingers pressed the switches.

Soundlessly, the blossom of flame sprang into being where once had been the leviathan of space. Viewplates throughout the fleet suddenly blacked out in protection against that terrible overload. When they came on again, they showed the drifting, helpless hulk of the rear third of the ship.

The immediate objective had been accomplished. The disrupter beams vanished as the eighteen ships converged upon the black hulks to take off any possible survivors.

Underwood seized the moment and diffused his powers until he encompassed the fleet. He spoke and his voice found hearing in every man of those mighty ships.

"Men of Earth!" You have sworn allegiance to Demarzule, the Sirenian, because of his might. Now you will swear allegiance to might that is great enough to wipe Demarzule from the face of civilization. I have killed your fellows right in your midst, and destroyed two of your mightiest ships—yet none of you have seen me. You know not how I come into your midst, nor how it is that every man of every ship can hear my voice at once.

"You have betrayed your kind to an alien who has destroyed worlds and ruined Galaxies. You are guilty of the highest treason to mankind. What is there that you can do to wipe out such infamy?

"You can join the forces that will wipe out the monster Demarzule! You can accept the leadership of greater might—or be destroyed. Choose!"

THERE was a moment of stunned quiet within the ships, then a bedlam that would not die for many minutes.

Underwood withdrew from the fleet and returned to the control room of the *Lavoisier*. There he found a chaos of despair. Mason had properly diagnosed the weapons the fleet had turned upon the ship.

Though his physical self lay in the sick bay yet, the members of the crew were becoming accustomed to his unexpected voice in their minds. Quickly he told them what he had done. When he finished, he said, "What damage did you suffer, if any, Mason?"

"Only two very doubtful generators left. We couldn't stand another blast like that. Where did they get such machines?"

"I don't know. It's possibly something Toshmere was on the edge of developing. Perhaps some of our own men have worked it out with clues given by Demarzule. There's no telling. The important thing now is that we've got a bear by the tail. For a moment we have the upper hand, but I'm not sure just what will happen when they pull themselves together again. If they don't accept my ultimatum, we may be in a spot."

"And if they do—what are we going to do with a whole fleet of fanatics and dupes?"

"We'll need every ally that we can get now. Undoubtedly word was flashed back to Earth of this disaster before I talked to them. Demarzule knows we're coming and is aware of the power I have. He'll undoubtedly send powerful interceptors to wipe us out. If we can gain control of these ships, we can throw them against his interceptors, and maybe sneak through the Terrestrian defenses. It doesn't matter what happens to every one of us—just so I can get close enough to Demarzule to tangle with him."

At that moment, Captain Dawson approached Mason. "Message from the fleet. They offer to surrender unconditionally."

CHAPTER EIGHTEEN

AUXILIARY engines were removed from the hulk of the destroyed flagship. Installed in the *Lavoisier*, they could easily bring her speed up to that of the fastest ship in the fleet.

So with the small laboratory ship, *Lavoisier*, as flagship, the ravaged and reorganized fleet turned once again toward Earth. As the long days in space passed while they sped Earthward at incredible velocities, the physicists and engineers turned the *Lavoisier* into a deadly warship, the equal of any in their fleet. New and more powerful Atom Stream projectors were installed, and massive disrupter units were built into previous areas of more peaceful uses.

And while they hurled through the vault of space, Underwood moved from ship to ship by means of his *abasic* senses, testing, examining and filtering out the men of the battle crews.

If he could have afforded pity, all he possessed would have been expended upon them, for they were a pitiable lot. He knew that their standards of values had been shattered again by their defeat at his hands. If their belief in the invincibility of Demarzule, and themselves because they were the Disciples of Demarzule, had not been so great, their defeat would have been less easy. Underwood was thankful for the conceit that rendered them vulnerable when defeat hove in sight.

Their allegiance to him was no stable thing, he knew. But most of them were willing to throw their loyalties with the scientists because they hungered for leadership with a neurotic longing, and the power that could silently and unseen wipe out two of the Great One's warships was surely a power to command their respect. So they reasoned in their bewildered minds.

Underwood removed from the key places those who were doubtful and rebellious, and he spoke to them daily throughout the long voyage, sometimes reasoning, sometimes commanding, but always with a display of power that they had to respect. In the end he felt he had a set of crews as trustworthy as Earthmen could be made in this culture of doubt and universal disregard of trust and honesty.

He practiced constantly in perfecting the powers of the *abasa*, and as his facility grew, so did his regard for the little offshoot of Dragboran culture that had flourished upon the barren little moon. Such powers as he possessed would have meant suicide to his own race. Sometimes he wondered if he could himself endure their temptations long enough to accomplish his goal. Certainly, with that completed, he would have the organs removed. Their call to power, wealth, and the misappropriation were almost more than any human mind in this stage of evolution could endure.

ALMOST in Earth's own front yard, at the orbit of Mars, the first signs of the coming struggle appeared. The lookout called his warning. A score of fast interceptors were leaving Earth, headed in their direction.

Underwood wished that he'd paid more attention to the military arts. He dared trust none of the warriors, who were his by conquest, for he could not appear to be less than they in any respect. But neither he nor any of the other scientists were competent to lead a complex military unit, such as his fleet represented, into the vortex of battle.

Yet he must do what had to be done. He formed the fleet into a massive tactical cylinder with the *Lavoisier* at the center and the remainder of the ships at the periphery. There would be no fancy maneuvering, only blunt, smashing force, every erg of it that could be generated within the hulls of those warships.

The entropy dissipators were already at work absorbing a fraction of the momentum that had carried the fleet across the reaches of space, but as it drove into the heart of the Solar System, its velocity was still immeasurable by Solarian standards.

The interceptors were powerless to match that speed in so short a time, but one wave approached on a near collision course with the fury of all its disrupters and Atom Streams bearing upon the fleet.

The effect was negligible, however, as the fleet smashed by, its own weapons flaming.

But that passage meant nothing. If the *Lavoisier* were to attempt a landing, it couldn't continue to hurl by at such velocities, for already it was passing Earth.

UNDERWOOD, though, was satisfied as he opened his physical eyes in the control room and abandoned the *abasic* senses for a return to his normal self.

"I'm sure my useful range with these powers is at least eighty thousand miles. Jandro ought to have been able to examine the Dragboran planet by means of the *abasa*, but maybe he didn't realize it. I know that my own range is increasing constantly."

"What do you intend to do?" asked Terry. "Are you going to try a landing or attack Demarzule without going down?"

"I believe we'll be safer to remain in space. If we can maneuver into an orbit of fifty thousand miles or so from Earth, and can hold off the attacks long enough for me to find Demarzule, that ought to be our greatest chance of success. If we landed we'd be sitting ducks."

There was general agreement with Underwood's estimate, though no one aboard the ship felt very much confidence in their ability to hold off the attacks they knew were coming. They kept reminding themselves that it was not important to save themselves or their ships. What mattered to give Underwood an adequate opportunity to hurl the powers of the *abasic* weapons at Demarzule. After that, chance would have to take care of the rest.

The hurtling projectile turned long after it had passed Earth. The entropy dissipaters absorbed the flaming energy of the ships' flight and dispersed it into space to recreate the infinitesimal particles that had been broken down to obtain that energy.

So, as the fleet braked its momentum and turned into an ever-tightening spiral, the interceptors swept down once more.

The thundering mass that was the fleet held its course now. Torrents of energy, slashed from the hearts of incalculable numbers of atoms, washed into space from the throats of the great radiators aboard the battleships. Three of the interceptors went down in that barrage before their own force shields went up.

It became a fantastic battle between almost irresistible forces. Both the Atom Stream and the disrupter beams could be fired only through a hiatus in the force shell, but such an opening was itself vulnerable to the enemy fire of Atom Streams. Therefore, the technique of warfare between similarly armed forces consisted of rapidly shifting the attack from radiator to radiator in a given vessel, so that no single opening would exist long enough for the enemy to concentrate fire upon that spot.

The interceptors were too small to mount the equipment for such defense tactics. Their only value lay in maneuverability. Slashing across the lanes of the battleships, their beams could cross the radiator pattern in unpredictable courses. The laws of chance were sometimes with them and their Atom Streams struck an opening directly. Regardless of the speed of closing the hiatus, such a coincidence was sufficient to destroy the ship. And so Underwood and his companions, watching, saw one of their great battleships explode in a nova of atomic fire as such a hit was scored upon it.

THE interceptor itself was fired an instant later by the concentrated fire of the two adjacent battleships, but its loss was negligible to the enemy. The interceptors were expendable, expendable for now another score were seen leaving the rim of Earth and taking up the pursuit of the fleet.

But it was not their approach that caused the hearts of the men aboard the *Lavoisier* to quail. Behind them, slowly and ponderously, rose a terrible fleet of fifty dreadnoughts with vast firepower.

"What's our orbital radius at present?" Underwood demanded abruptly of the navigator.

"Sixty thousand."

"Take it, Mason," Underwood said. "I'm going down."

The impact of that moment hit them all, though they had been trying to anticipate it since they had first known that it would come. It was not their regard and friendship for Underwood, who might presently die before their eyes. It was not their own almost extinction before the fire of the invincible fleet rising to do battle.

It was that this moment would decide the course of man's history.

Everything depended upon a single strange weapon snatched from the hands of a forgotten people in a little eddy of civilization, whose sole purpose in existence might have been to carry this weapon through time to this moment.

And only one of them could wield that weapon, while the others stood by, neither knowing the progress of that conflict nor able to assist.

UNDERWOOD sat down in the deep chair that would hold his body restfully while his *abasic* senses swept Earthward to envelop and crush the anachronism that he had turned upon civilization.

It was more than just, more than ironic, he thought. It was his high privilege to wipe out some of the guilt that he knew he could never smother or rationalize out of his mind, the guilt of having been the one to bring Demarzule back to life.

Of them all in that control room, only Illia uttered a sound, and hers was a half audible cry choked back before it was fully spoken.

He lay apparently relaxed with eyes closed in the huge chair in the control room of the *Lavoisier*, but the essence, the force that was Delmar Underwood, was sixty thousand miles away, hovering over the force shell dome that hid the Carlson Museum.

Simultaneously with Illia's cry there came a smashing alarm that rang through the room with its insistent, murderous message.

"We're hit! Number three and four shell generators have gone out!"

As Underwood held to the point of view of the advancing wave front of perception, he had the sensation of diving headlong toward the throng that was gathering as if by magic about the white, shining columns of the building. As if knowing of the battle that was to be fought between the titans, the waiting thousands had gathered when the force shell went over the Carlson and the battle fleets took to space. They watched, waiting for the unknown, the unexpected, somehow sensing their destiny was being decided.

Sight of the milling thousands was lost to Underwood as he plunged deep below the protecting shell over the building as if it did not exist. The lightlessness inside the shell was broken by the blaze of lights that showered their radiance everywhere upon the grounds and museum that had become a monstrous palace.

Waiting, hesitant guards and servants moved about the grounds, gathering in knots to ask one another what the appearance of the battleships and the sudden use of the shell meant. It was inconceivable that anyone should be challenging the Great One, but the very improbability of it filled them with fearful dismay.

Underwood entered the building. The vast assemblage of instruments and machines that had filled the main hall when he last saw it was gone now, replaced with rich paintings and fabulous tapestries that had been ransacked from the treasuries of the Earth.

There was no one in sight. Underwood continued on until he came to the series of large exhibition rooms toward the rear. Here, apparently, were set up administrative offices to maintain whatever personal contact was necessary between Demarzule and the Disciples he ruled.

THEN Underwood came to the central room at the rear of the center section of the building. Demarzule was there.

It was with an involuntary shock that Underwood saw again the alien creature he had restored to life. As he sat in the throne-like chair in the center of one wall of the room, the Great One seemed like some sculpture of an ancient god of evil executed in weathered bronze. Only the startling white of his eyes gave evidence of life in that enormous bulk.

Underwood hadn't expected the twenty Earthmen who sat near Demarzule, forming a semicircle with the Great One in the center, as if in council. They sat in brooding silence. Not a word seemed to be passing between them, and Underwood watched in wonderment.

Then, slowly, Demarzule stirred. His white staring eyes moved, as though searching the room. His words came to Underwood.

"So you have come at last," he said. "You challenge Demarzule the Great One with your feeble powers. I know you, Delmar Underwood. They tell me it was you who found and restored me. I owe you much, and I would have offered you a high place in my realm, which shall encompass the Universe. Yet you set yourself against me.

"I am merciful. You may still have your place if you choose. I need one such as you, just as I needed the brain and hands of Toshmere, who was so foolish as to think he could be the one to conquer the eons in my place. You know of his fate; I am sure."

Demarzule's speech was a paralyzing shock. Underwood had made no revelation of himself, yet the alien had detected his presence. Through the *abasa*, he sensed the might and power of Demarzule, the full potentialities that lay in the three organs that the ancient race had developed, potentialities that he had scarcely touched in the short weeks of experimentation.

It made him sick for an instant with the fear of almost certain defeat. Then he struck, furiously, and with all the power that was in him.

Never before had he hurled such a bolt of devastation. With satisfaction he sensed Demarzule's powers sway and wither before its blast, but the Great One absorbed it and recovered after an instant.

"YOU are a worthy opponent," said Demarzule. "You have accomplished much in so short a time, but not enough, I fear. Once more I extend my offer to join me. As my lieutenant, you might become governor of many Galaxies."

Underwood remained silent, conserving his forces for another blast, which Demarzule could surely not endure. He hurled it and felt the energies flowing from him in a life-destroying stream. Demarzule's bronze face was only smiling sardonically as he met that attack—and absorbed it.

"When you have exhausted yourself thoroughly," he said, "I shall demonstrate my own powers—but slowly, so that death will not be too quick for you."

The use of such waves of force was exhausting to Underwood, but he knew that Demarzule's absorptive organ should soon reach maximum capacity, if it were not allowed to drain away in the meantime.

A third time he blasted. Then sudden, terrible realization came that Demarzule was not absorbing the energy. It was being diverted, drawn aside before it even approached the Sirenian.

In something approaching panic, Underwood directed his senses to locate the source of the diversion, and found it in the twenty Earthmen sitting motionlessly about Demarzule.

Demarzule seemed to know the instant that Underwood became aware of the fact. "Yes," he said, "we have duplicated the *abasa*. *Cancer* is plentiful among you. In five thousand more years you would have stopped fighting it and learned how to use it. There are twenty of us. You would not have come had you known you would have that many to fight single-handed would you? Now it is too late!"

With that word, a wave of paralyzing, destroying force swept over Underwood. How it was affecting him, what senses it was attacking; he did not know. He only knew that a flaming agony was burning out life, as if reluctant to give him a speedy, merciful death.

He must withdraw to the ship to recover his forces. He could never withstand the attack of twenty-one *abasas*.

Underwood relaxed and threw his powers back toward the ship—and failed!

Abruptly, the metallic glint of Demarzule's lips parted in a roar of laughter without merriment, but of triumph.

"No, my brave Earthling, you cannot retreat. You did not know that. For those who would challenge the Great One there is no retreat. Your decision is made, and you will fail and you will die—but only when I wish, and your fellow Earthmen will find amusement in toying with you as a cat with a mouse before I give the final blow that will destroy your rash, impatient ego."

The flaming fire of Demarzule's attack continued while Underwood fought savagely and vainly to retreat. How was he being held there against his efforts to retreat? He did not know that the *abasa* held such powers and he would not have known how to exert them himself if he had been aware of them.

He gave up and turned back, letting the power flow into the absorptive cells of the *dor-abasa*, but it could not be for long, for the organ would disrupt under such stress.

Then, as if in keeping with his promise to prolong the agony, the attack ceased, and Demarzule allowed him to rest.

"You were brash, were you not?" he taunted. "How could you dare come against the mightiest power of the Universe, the greatest mind ever created, and attack with your puny powers? You blaspheme the Great One by your presumption!"

"Once, long ago," said Underwood, "the Sirenian forces were defeated by the Dragbora. Again it is the Dragbora you face, Demarzule. Remember that, and defend yourself!"

UNDERWOOD was startled. Incredibly, it seemed that he had not spoken those words, but rather that the dead Jandro was with him, silently backing him, teaching, advising—

He lashed out, but not at Demarzule. He struck swiftly at the nearest Earthman. Almost instantly, the unfortunate shuddered and fell to the floor, dead. In quick succession Underwood struck at the nerve cells of the next five and they died without sound.

In snarling fury and retaliation, Demarzule retaliated. Underwood absorbed the blow—and incredibly hurled it back.

It was as if he had suddenly become aware of techniques that he had never dreamed of. He had not known it was possible to absorb the nerve-destroying force with his own *dor-abasa* and whip it back upon the attacker, like a ball caught and thrown.

It hardly seemed as if he were acting through his own volition, yet he acted. He felt the surprise of Demarzule, and in that moment he knew the secret. The Earthmen apparently possessed only a single primitive organ, hardly identifiable as one of the *abasa*, for they had the capacity for defense, but not for attack. Four more of them toppled, and then Underwood was forced to face the attack of Demarzule again.

Something like terror had entered the mind of the alien now. Underwood sensed the thoughts of possible defeat that flooded Demarzule's mind.

"REMEMBER that day on *Vorga?*" Underwood asked. "Remember how the Dragboran powers pierced the great force shell you flung about the planet? Remember how your men fell one by one, and their weapons went cold and the force shell dropped for lack of control? Remember, Demarzule, it was the Dragbora you fought that day, and it is the Dragbora you fight now. I have not come to challenge as a puny Earthmen. I come as a Dragboran—to complete the unfinished task of my ancestors!"

The Sirenian was silent and new confidence filled Underwood. He felt that he was not fighting alone, that all of the ancient Dragboran civilization was behind him, battling its age-old enemies to extinction. He felt as if Jandro himself were there.

The energy he absorbed from Demarzule he turned upon the cohorts, who sat as if frozen with fear as they watched their fellows slump and fall to the floor in soundless death.

In near-madness, Demarzule increased his attacks. He adopted a shifting, feinting attack that shocked Underwood's *abasa* with each surging wave of force. But Underwood learned how to control those surges, to pass them on to his own attacks, which still were directed upon the Earthmen within the chamber.

Within moments of each other, the last two on either side of Demarzule fell. The Sirenian seemed not to have noticed, for all his energies and concentration now were directed at Underwood.

Underwood was tiring swiftly. The energies draining out of him seemed as if they were sapping every cell of his being, and back on board the *Lavoisier*, every spasm of torture was reflected involuntarily on his physical face. Those who watched suffered for him.

Illia sat in a corner of the room opposite him and her fists pressed white spots into her cheeks. Dreyer's nervous reaction was expressed in the incessant puffs and chewing on his normally steady cigar. The others merely watched with taut faces and teeth sinking into their lips.

In the chamber of the great museum palace, the tempo of the battle was slowly building up. Though he felt exhausted almost to the point of defeat, Underwood strained for more energy and found that it was at his command. His *dor-abasa* fed upon the attacking force of Demarzule and returned it with added energy potential.

In each of them, the same process was going on, and the outcome would be determined by the final resultant flow of destroying power.

He could retreat now, Underwood realized. He doubted that Demarzule could exert a holding force upon him, but nothing would be gained by abandoning the battle now. He drove on with increasing surges.

Suddenly there was a faltering and Underwood exulted within himself. Demarzule's force wavered for the barest fraction of an instant, and it was not a feint.

"You are old and weak," said Underwood. "Half a million years ago, civilization rejected you. *We reject you!*"

He smashed on almost without hindrance now. Demarzule's great form writhed in pain upon the throne—and fought with one desperate surge of energy.

Underwood caught and hurled it back mercilessly. He felt his way into the innermost recesses of the Sirenian mind, groped along the nerve ways of the Great One. And as he went, he burned and destroyed the vital synapses.

Demarzule was dying—slowly, because of his resistance—and in endless pain because there was no other way. He screamed aloud in ultimate agony, and then the giant figure of Demarzule, the Sirenian—the Great One—crashed to the floor.

THE relief that came to Underwood was near agony. The wild forces of the Dragbora tore relentlessly from him and filled the room with their lethal energy before they died.

Then, in greater calm, he regarded what he had done. It was finished, almost unbelievably finished.

Yet there were a few things to do. He left the building and sought out the guards and the caretakers and whispered into their minds, "Demarzule is dead! The Great One has died and you are men once more."

He sought out the controls of the force shell and caused the operator to drop the shield. Then he whispered, "The Great One is dead," and like the wind, his voice encompassed the vast thousands who had gathered.

The message sank unspoken into their minds and each man looked at his neighbor as if to ask how it had come. They pressed forward, a battling, maddened mob who had for an hour lived in a childish, primitive world where men were not required to think but only to obey. They pushed forward and flowed into the building, battering, clawing one another. But they managed to view the body of the fallen Sirenian, so that the message was confirmed and spread, soon to circle the Earth.

UNDERWOOD studied the writhing, bewildered mass. Could Dreyer possibly be right? Would it ever end—men's unthinking grasping for leadership, their mindless search for kings and gods, while within them their own powers withered? Always it had been the same; leaders arose holding before men the illusion of vast, glorious promises while they carefully led them into hells of lost dreams and broken promises.

Yes, it would be different, Underwood told himself. The Dragbora had proved that it could be different. Their origin could have been no less lowly than man's. They must have trodden the same tortuous stairway to dreams that man was now on, and they had learned how to live with one another.

Man was already nearer that goal—far nearer now that Demarzule was dead. Underwood formed a silent prayer that fate would be merciful to man and not send another like Demarzule.

And he allowed himself a moment's pride, an instant of pleasure in the thought that he had been able to take part in the crisis.

With a final pity for the scene below, he fled back into space. What he saw there turned him sick with fear. The great fleet was broken and burned with atomic fires. Only two of the battleships remained to challenge the attackers. But they were no longer challenging. They signaled abject surrender and were fallen upon by ravenous interceptors.

The *Lavoisier* herself was darkened and drifting, her force shell feeble and waning, while the flaming disrupters of a trio, of dreadnoughts concentrated upon her.

Underwood hurled himself toward the nearest of the enemy ships. In its depths he sought out the gunners and cut off life in them before they were aware of his bodiless presence. Swiftly he turned their beams upon each other and watched them wallow and disappear in sudden flame.

Others rushed forward now. Still more than a score of them to defeat the single crippled laboratory ship, more than he could hope to conquer in time.

BUT they did not fire. Their shields remained intact; then slowly their courses changed and they drifted away. Without comprehension, Underwood peered into those hulls and knew the answer.

The news had come to them of Demarzule's death. Like men in pursuit of a mirage, they could not endure the reality that came with the vanishing of their dream. Their defeat was utter and complete. Throughout the Earth Demarzule's defeat was the defeat of all men who had not yet become strong enough to walk in the sun of their own decisions, but clung to the shadow of illusory leadership.

Underwood swept back toward the darkened *Lavoisier*. He moved like a ghost through its bleak halls and vacant corridors. Down in the generator rooms, he found the cause of the disaster in the blasted remains of overburdened force shell generators. Four of them must have given way at once, ripping the ship throughout its length with concussion and lethal waves.

The control room was dark, like the rest of the ship, and the forms of his companions were strewn upon the floor. But there was life yet and he dared to hope as he spoke to their minds, insistent, commanding, forcing life and consciousness back into their nerve cells. He seemed to become aware of unknown powers of resurrection that dwelt within his own being.

His mission was complete. He returned to his own physical form and abandoned the *abasic* senses. He sat there in the huge chair in the control room, while those about him revived and life gradually returned to the dying ship. Of the enemy fleet there was no more, for it was descending to an Earth shorn of the hope of Galaxy-wide conquest.

They did not know yet where they would go or where they could find refuge, but when the wreckage was cleared and the ship lived again, Underwood and Illia stood alone in a darkened observation pit, watching the stars slip across the massive arc of the screens.

As Underwood watched, he thought he sensed something of the drive that might have whipped Demarzule's brain, the goad that made vast superior powers intolerable in the possession of even a beneficent man, for he would no longer remain beneficent.

By the might that was in him he had vanquished the Great One! He could stand in the place of the Great One if he chose! He did not know if his powers were becoming greater than those of Jandro, like a strengthened plant in new soil, but surely they were growing. The secrets of the Universe seemed to be appearing before him, one by one.

A mere glance at a slab of inert matter, and his senses could delve into the composition of its atoms and sort out and predict its properties and reactions. One look into the far spaces beyond the Solar System and he could sense himself soaring in eternity. Yes, he was growing in power and perception, and where it might lead, he dared not look.

But there were other things to be had, other, simpler ambitions in which common men had found fulfillment throughout the ages.

Illia was warm against him, soft in his arms.

"I want you to operate again, as quickly as possible," he said.

SHE looked up at him with a start. "What do you mean?"

"You must take out the *abasic* organs. They've served their purpose. I don't want to live with them. I could become another Demarzule with the power I have."

Her eyes were faintly blue in the light that came from the panel and they were intent upon him. In them he read something that made him afraid.

"There is always a need for men with greater powers and greater knowledge than the average man," she said. "The race has need of its mutants. They are dealt so sparingly to us that we cannot afford not to utilize them."

"Mutants?"

"You are a true mutant, whether artificial or not, possessing organs and abilities that are unique. The race needs them. You cannot ask me to destroy them."

He had never thought of himself as a mutant, yet she was right for all practical purposes. His powers and perceptions would perhaps not have been produced naturally in any man of his race for thousands of years to come. Perhaps he *could* use them to assist man's slow rise. A new wealth of science, a new strength of leadership and guidance if necessary—

"I could become the world's greatest criminal," he said. "There's no secret, no property that's safe from my grasp. I have only to reach out for possessions, for power."

"You worry too much about that," she said lightly. "You could no more become a villain than I could."

"Why are you so sure of that?"

"Don't you remember the properties of the *seea-abasa?* But then you didn't hear the last words that Jandro ever spoke, did you? He said, 'I retire to the *abasa.*' Do you know what that means?"

Suddenly, Underwood felt cold. A score of whisperings came thundering into his mind. The moment when he had first awakened from the operation, when it seemed as if death would have him and only the power of a demanding will had helped him cling to life. The voice that seemed to penetrate and call him back. The voice of Jandro. And then the final conflict in the chambers of Demarzule.

New skills and new strength had suddenly come to him as if out of nowhere. He had been conceited to call it his increased experience and ability. Yet could it have come from outside himself? He sought frantically and urgently within his own nerve channels in the cells of his own being, and in the pathways of the alien organs that lent him those unearthly senses. There seemed nothing but an echo, as if within a great empty hall. There was no answer, yet it seemed as if down those channels of perception there was the dim shadow of a wary prey who could never be caught, who could never be found in those endless pathways, but who would never be far away.

Underwood knew then that if it was Jandro, he would never make himself known for reasons of his own, perhaps. But there was a sudden peace as if he had found some secret purification, as if he had been taken to a high place and looked about the world and had been able to turn his back upon it. Whether he would ever find Jandro or not, he was sure that the guardian was there.

Illia was saying, "I can't operate, Del. Even if you hate me for the rest of our lives, I won't do it. And there is no one else in the world who would know how. You would be killed if you let anyone else attempt to cut those nerves. Tell me that you believe I'm right."

"I do," he said in cheerful resignation. "But don't forget it's half your funeral as well. It means that you're going to have to spend the rest of your life with a mutant."

She turned her face up to his. "I can think of worse fates."

THE END

If you've enjoyed this book, you will not want to miss these terrific titles…

ARMCHAIR SCI-FI & HORROR DOUBLE NOVELS, $12.95 each

D-11 **PERIL OF THE STARMEN** by Kris Neville
THE STRANGE INVASION by Murray Leinster

D-12 **THE STAR LORD** by Boyd Ellanby
CAPTIVES OF THE FLAME by Samuel R. Delaney

D-13 **MEN OF THE MORNING STAR** by Edmund Hamilton
PLANET FOR PLUNDER by Hal Clement and Sam Merwin, Jr.

D-14 **ICE CITY OF THE GORGON** by Chester S. Geier and Richard Shaver
WHEN THE WORLD TOTTERED by Lester Del Rey

D-15 **WORLDS WITHOUT END** by Clifford D. Simak
THE LAVENDER VINE OF DEATH by Don Wilcox

D-16 **SHADOW ON THE MOON** by Joe Gibson
ARMAGEDDON EARTH by Geoff St. Reynard

D-17 **THE GIRL WHO LOVED DEATH** by Paul W. Fairman
SLAVE PLANET by Laurence M. Janifer

D-18 **SECOND CHANCE** by J. F. Bone
MISSION TO A DISTANT STAR by Frank Belknap Long

D-19 **THE SYNDIC** by C. M. Kornbluth
FLIGHT TO FOREVER by Poul Anderson

D-20 **SOMEWHERE I'LL FIND YOU** by Milton Lesser
THE TIME ARMADA by Fox B. Holden

ARMCHAIR SCIENCE FICTION CLASSICS, $12.95 each

C-4 **CORPUS EARTHLING**
by Louis Charbonneau

C-5 **THE TIME DISSOLVER**
by Jerry Sohl

C-6 **WEST OF THE SUN**
by Edgar Pangborn

ARMCHAIR SCIENCE FICTION & HORROR GEMS SERIES, $12.95 each

G-1 **SCIENCE FICTION GEMS, Vol. One**
Isaac Asimov and others

G-2 **HORROR GEMS, Vol. One**
Carl Jacobi and others

If you've enjoyed this book, you will not want to miss these terrific titles...

ARMCHAIR SCI-FI, FANTASY, & HORROR DOUBLE NOVELS, $12.95 each

D-21   **EMPIRE OF EVIL** by Robert Arnette
       THE SIGN OF THE TIGER by Alan E. Nourse & J. A. Meyer

D-22   **OPERATION SQUARE PEG** by Frank Belknap Long
       ENCHANTRESS OF VENUS by Leigh Brackett

D-23   **THE LIFE WATCH** by Lester Del Rey
       CREATURES OF THE ABYSS by Murray Leinster

D-24   **LEGION OF LAZARUS** by Edmond Hamilton
       STAR HUNTER by Andre Norton

D-25   **EMPIRE OF WOMEN** by John Fletcher
       ONE OF OUR CITIES IS MISSING by Irving Cox

D-26   **THE WRONG SIDE OF PARADISE** by Raymond F. Jones
       THE INVOLUNTARY IMMORTALS by Rog Phillips

D-27   **EARTH QUARTER** by Damon Knight
       ENVOY TO NEW WORLDS by Keith Laumer

D-28   **SLAVES TO THE METAL HORDE** by Milton Lesser
       HUNTERS OUT OF TIME by Joseph E. Kelleam

D-29   **RX JUPITER SAVE US** by Ward Moore
       BEWARE THE USURPERS by Geoff St. Reynard

D-30   **SECRET OF THE SERPENT** by Don Wilcox
       CRUSADE ACROSS THE VOID by Dwight V. Swain

ARMCHAIR SCIENCE FICTION CLASSICS, $12.95 each

C-7   **THE SHAVER MYSTERY, pt. 1**
       by Richard S. Shaver

C-8   **THE SHAVER MYSTERY, pt. 2**
       by Richard S. Shaver

C-9   **MURDER IN SPACE** by David V. Reed
       by David V. Reed

ARMCHAIR MASTERS OF SCIENCE FICTION SERIES, $16.95 each

M-3   **MASTERS OF SCIENCE FICTION, Vol. Three**
       Robert Sheckley, "The Perfect Woman" and other tales

M-4   **MASTERS OF SCIENCE FICTION, Vol. Four**
       Mack Reynolds, "Stowaway" and other tales